Margo Maguire

The Highlander's Desire

AVON

An Imprint of HarperCollinsPublishers

AVON BOOKS
An Imprint of HarperCollins*Publishers*
10 East 53rd Street
New York, New York 10022-5299

Copyright © 2013 by Margo Wider
ISBN 978-0-06-212290-2
www.avonromance.com

First Avon Books mass market printing: August 2013

Avon Trademark Reg. U.S. Pat. Off. and in Other Countries, Marca Registrada, Hecho en U.S.A.
HarperCollins® is a registered trademark of HarperCollins Publishers.

Printed in the U.S.A.

10 9 8 7 6 5 4 3 2 1

A Taste of Temptation

"I very much enjoyed the berries you left me on my arrival," he said quietly in an attempt to put her at ease.

"I am glad to know it." Her voice was hardly more than a reserved murmur now.

Lachann stepped closer as he lowered his head and tipped hers up. He closed the inches between their mouths, brushing his against the soft, sweet warmth of her lips.

Lachann felt her sharp intake of breath, but she did not pull away. Her eyes drifted closed, and so did his an instant later. He slid his hand 'round to the back of her head to capture her lips more fully.

She made a slight moan when he wrapped his fingers 'round the thick plait of her hair and pulled her deeper into the kiss. Ach, but she was as sweet as the berries she'd given him.

Her body was soft and warm, and molded perfectly to his. And though Lachann knew this fruit was forbidden, he had no desire to stop.

Romances by Margo Maguire

*This book is dedicated to my
husband, Mike—always there with a
great suggestion, or a plotting session.*

*And to my editor, Amanda Bergeron,
whose vision for this book was often
clearer than my own. Thanks, Amanda!*

The Highlander's Desire

Prologue

Braemore, Scotland. Late Spring, 1714.

Lachann MacMillan had been pacing the battlements of Braemore Keep since dusk, his nerves on edge, his muscles taut. His grandfather was sure the Macauleys would come raiding soon, for their last foray into Mac-Millan lands had been profitable.

Next time, they would attempt to take Braemore itself. All of it.

When the Macauleys had last attacked, there'd been illness at Braemore, making the MacMillan clan vulnerable. This time, there was no such weakness. And the MacMillans were damned if they'd subject their people to the mercy of Laird Cathal Macauley. He was an old barbarian, brutal with his own clan and even worse with captives.

His nephews were just as bad.

There were three of them, and only one would become the Macauley laird after their uncle. Old Cathal intended to wrest lands for the other ones, and the sport of warfare to achieve this end seemed to suit him well.

Lachann and his brothers had been expecting a raid for days, so they'd taken turns manning the signal fires and keeping watch. Lachann's hands itched to wield his sword in battle against the savages who had not only stolen cattle during their last raid but carried away two unwilling MacMillan maidens as well.

Robert and Dugan had gotten them back, but neither had returned unscathed.

Lachann saw the signal fires from the distant hillocks and knew the raiding had begun. He clipped down the steps of the keep and shoved open his brother's bedchamber door as he ran past. "Take up your sword, Dugan! The Macauleys have come!"

Dugan was out of bed in an instant and catching up to Lachann as he ran down the narrow wing of the huge stone keep. They were going to best the damned Macauleys and bring home Cathal Macauley's head on a pike.

'Twas the least of what he and his vile clan deserved.

Lachann clambered down the narrow hall, nearly tripping over his grandfather, Laird Hamish MacMillan, as he ran. "Come on, old man!" Lachann shouted, hearing the eagerness in his own voice. He was very much looking forward to this battle, as were his brothers and their grandfather.

The Macauleys were a wealthier clan but always looked for ways to improve their lot, even at the cost of their neighbors. Not that Braemore bordered their properties. The Macauleys had crossed MacNeil lands to get to Braemore. They'd met no resistance as they'd driven their stolen MacMillan cattle through the high valley to the west of MacMillan land and on to Glendreggen.

Lachann and his brothers fairly flew from the keep, where their horses were saddled and ready. They joined another score of Braemore warriors who had been alerted by the signal fires and the shouted alarms from the watchmen. The men mounted their horses and galloped through the village toward the hilly lands to the west, where they would meet the rest of MacMillan's armed men, intent upon routing the Macauleys before they could get any closer to the village or the keep.

'Twas dark, with only a sliver of moonlight to see by, but the MacMillans knew their territory well. Lachann and Robert saw the raiders at the same time. The two brothers drew their swords in unison and spurred their horses into the crowd of Macauleys, targeting the leaders, Cathal and his grown nephews, Cullen, Archie, and Ewan.

"You dare trespass on my lands?" Hamish roared. He clashed swords with the first Macauley warrior he met and quickly dispatched him. He'd always been a fierce defender of his beloved clan, and the Macauleys offended his basic sensibilities.

Lachann joined battle, backing up his grandfather and furiously defending his clan and their lands, following the strategy he and Robert had laid out after the last attack.

They pushed back against the Macauleys, flanking them on the left and right as they battled sword to sword. Lachann heard the clank of metal on metal. Horses reared and men grunted with the strain of battle.

Suddenly, Hamish was flanked on two sides by Ewan and Archie, and he struggled to fend them off simultaneously.

"Here, Macauley!" Lachann bellowed, spurring his horse toward his grandfather. "Over here!"

Archie screeched a battle call as he turned to charge Lachann. Lachann wanted the wee bastard's blood, but Hamish had warned against killing the laird or his heirs. The Macauleys' retaliation would be savage. Far better to outwit them in battle and take one of the nephews as hostage.

Or rout the army so thoroughly they would never return.

Hamish unseated Ewan, who ducked and ran, while Lachann engaged Archie. They thrust and parried, and Archie got in a lucky jab, slicing Lachann's arm. The wound enraged Lachann, who charged Archie and the rest of the Macauleys. All the MacMillans joined the offensive, driving the Macauleys back and trapping them beneath a deep crag at the western edge of the valley.

Lachann raised his sword just as someone pulled him from his saddle onto the ground. 'Twas Cullen Macauley, and he thrust his sword at Lachann. He would have skewered him had Lachann not rolled quickly to the side and risen to his feet.

"'Tis all you're good for, eh, Macauley? An attack from behind?" Lachann raised his claymore and brought it down with enough force to cleave Macauley in two, but his enemy brought up his shield and averted the blow.

Lachann was undeterred. Regardless of Hamish's orders, he wanted to see Cullen Macauley's blood. He wanted to wipe the superior smirk from the bastard's face with it and then watch it soak the ground beneath him.

"You cannot defeat us, MacMillan!" Macauley growled as he jabbed his broadsword at Lachann. "Your miserable clan has not the strength to withstand the Macauleys!"

Lachann and the rest of his clan intended to prove him wrong. They'd been building a fighting force to rival any in the highlands, though the Macauleys had caught them shorthanded only a few weeks before. That was not true this time. The MacMillans were healthy now, and they outnumbered Macauley's forces nearly two to one. Their training had been unsurpassed in all the highlands.

This time, the MacMillans were going to trounce their enemy so well the bastards would think twice and again before they attempted to raid MacMillan lands.

Lachann's sword clashed with Macauley's, and just as he would have delivered a killing strike, the miserable stoat's cousin came to his defense and the battle changed its course. At the same time, several MacMillans joined the fight and kept Lachann from killing Cullen or Ewan.

They drove their foes back, deeper and deeper into the lee of the crags until there was nowhere else for the Macauleys to retreat.

Hamish cornered Laird Cathal and pulled the man from his saddle, putting his knife to the old tyrant's throat. "Yield!"

The Macauleys halted.

Lachann took advantage of the moment and seized Ewan, taking him hostage. One of the MacMillans tied the young man's hands behind his back while Lachann held his sword ready.

"The lad is ours, Macauley! Do you yield!"

"Nay! Never!"

"Lachann," Hamish called to him, keeping his hold on the Macauley laird. "Run him through."

Lachann pulled back his sword, but before he delivered the killing blow, Cullen shouted, "Yield, Uncle! You cannot—"

"Hold, MacMillan!" Laird Macauley shouted against the blade at his throat. "Aye. I'll yield."

"'Tis glad I am to hear it, Macauley," Hamish said. "Mount your horse."

As soon as the laird was up, they lashed his hands together behind his back and disarmed every one of the marauding Macauleys. The MacMillans drove them from Braemore lands, and some of the men went to round up the cattle that had been taken.

They kept Ewan as hostage to ensure against further assaults against the MacMillan clan.

By the time Ewan died of fever more than a year later, the Macauleys were no longer a threat—at least not to the MacMillans. Old Cathal was dead, and Archie became laird in his place. The Macauleys made it a point to avoid MacMillan lands after the sound defeat that had resulted in Ewan's capture, but they continued raiding other clans and making themselves wealthy in the process.

When Archie became laird of the Macauleys, Cullen found himself a new clan. He traveled to Skye and offered Laird MacDonald a princely bride price for his daughter, Fiona, only a few days before she was to marry.

The groom was to have been Lachann MacMillan.

There was no doubt Macauley was aware that

Lachann and Fiona had already made a love match. Cullen's interference was an underhanded means of exacting revenge upon the MacMillans—specifically Lachann. And it worked.

Lachann's heart shattered. When Fiona came to him in tears, he roared his fury, ready to commit violence against every Macauley who came to witness Cullen's marriage to the MacDonald chieftain's daughter.

Only old Hamish had the power to keep him from going after Cullen Macauley and butchering him in cold blood. Lachann's grandfather refused to allow Lachann to escalate the feud between their clans, for 'twould isolate them from their allies and deplete their resources if they went to war.

Lachann spent the night before Fiona's wedding getting thoroughly jaked on some potent island whiskey, and he made his decision never to lose his heart over a beautiful lass again.

Chapter 1

The Minch, just outside Loch Ewe. Summer, 1720.

The sea was calm, but there was enough wind to carry Lachann MacMillan's ship, the *Glencoe Lass*, northward toward the Minch, the sea that lay between Scotland and the western isles. Lachann's destination was Kilgorra, a fertile island at the edge of the Minch that guarded the entrance to Loch Ewe, and hence the passage to Braemore.

Lachann and two of his kinsmen stood at the bow of the ship and watched as they approached their destination.

The isle was broad and hilly. The northwestern side consisted of a wall of black rock on a promontory that rose straight up from the sea. Kilgorra's massive castle was situated at its peak, the windows of the keep still dark without the afternoon sun. The castle's walls and towers were perfect for posting lookouts to alert the Kilgorran army and sailors to encroachers.

But Kilgorra had no army, no sailors trained to fight.

Lachann's cousin and good friend, Kieran Cameron, looked askance at the land ahead. "Are you sure this is what you want, Lachann? To wed Laird MacDuffie's daughter, sight unseen? 'Tis said she is as plain as an oatcake."

"Of course he does," Duncan MacMillan answered for Lachann. "Once he weds Catrìona, the old laird will make him his heir, and then there will be no more chance for pirates to attack Braemore lands."

"Aye, but there is more to taking a wife than coveting her father's lands."

"Oh, aye?" Duncan challenged. "Name one thing."

"Well you certainly wouldn't know. You are the—"

"And you have been wed how many times, Kieran?"

"Enough," Lachann said, ending the argument before it could gain any momentum. "Braemore needs Kilgorra. Even if the laird's daughter is a mud hen, if I must wed her to assure the protection of Braemore, so be it."

He did not care who Catrìona was, nor had he any interest in her appearance. He'd learned not to trust his eyes when it came to women. He'd loved his fair Fiona fiercely, but when Cullen Macauley had arrived on

Skye and paid her father so handsomely he'd not been able to refuse . . .

Lachann's grandfather might have forbidden him to murder the damned bleeter, but Lachann had come up with another solution. He and Fiona could have left Skye, could have left their clans to strike out on their own.

But Fiona would not run away with him. She might have wept while professing her love for him, but she'd cited her duty to her clan, and she'd chosen her father's will over anything she'd felt for Lachann.

That had been the last time Lachann had allowed his heart to rule his choices.

"Tell me again, Lachann," Kieran said. "Are you committed to this marriage? Is there a way out if you . . . Well, if she is too . . ."

Lachann and his brothers had been corresponding with Bruce MacDuffie all summer. All they needed now was Catrìona's consent, and, once given, they would wed as soon as possible.

Lachann had no doubt he could convince the lass to marry him.

"I'm not entirely committed," Lachann said. "Catrìona must agree."

"You'll have no trouble, Lachann," Duncan said.

Kieran laughed. "Nay. I've yet to see you fail with a lass you've chosen to bed."

Aye, because he was careful, choosing only the most

carefree, the most willing of lasses. Never again would he choose the kind of woman who could damage his heart as Fiona had done.

"Enough," Lachann said. "We need Kilgorra. We'll create a fighting force that can defend the isle as well as the channels 'round it. No ships will sail past without our knowledge and consent."

"And Braemore will be safe from a sea attack," Duncan said.

"Aye." That was all Lachann cared about.

On the Isle of Kilgorra.

The massive brigantine sailed into Kilgorra's harbor and tied up at Kilgorra's pier just as Anna MacIver rowed her curragh to the far end of the pier. She could see that this was no trading vessel.

As its crew lowered the plank, Anna could only gape in awe at the first man to disembark. With his regal bearing and aura of command, the highlander could only be Lachann MacMillan.

And he'd arrived a full day too early.

Anna did not think she'd ever seen a finer specimen of highland might. Tall and dark-haired, his shoulders were broad and muscular, his legs as sturdy as tree trunks. The angle of his jaw was entirely uncompromising, but his lips were full and . . . interesting.

Unlike the rest of him, they were not the least bit rigid.

Anna's heart thrilled at the sight of him, but she quickly tamped down any excitement she might feel. For what business did she have, gaping at the young man from Braemore? He had certainly not come to meet her.

Which was just as well. The last thing Anna needed was a man . . . a husband. Her mother, Sigrid, had had two of them, and where had her marriages gotten her?

To a home far away from her family and everything she'd known in the Norse country, married to a Scottish husband who'd died, leaving her with naught but a wee daughter to care for. And then a second husband, the laird of Kilgorra, whom she'd met and fallen in love with when he'd visited Kearvaig soon after Anna's father's death.

Sigrid had returned to Kilgorra with Laird MacDuffie and had soon gotten with child. But when both Sigrid and the bairn had died, MacDuffie had forgotten all about his stepdaughter. For the past fifteen years, Anna had been left to her own devices on Laird MacDuffie's island home, serving her mother's widower and stepdaughter according to their whims.

Anna made do, for what choice did she have? She did her work and escaped whenever she could to her own wee isle across the narrow straits off the Kilgorra coast. Luckily, 'twas a mountainous, forbidding place that no one cared to visit—especially not when Gudrun, the Norse maid who'd come to Scotland with Anna's mother—had let it be known the place was beset by a fearful *sluagh dubh,* a dangerous, malevolent spirit.

To Anna's knowledge, there was no *sluagh dubh* on Spirit Isle, but the wary Kilgorrans believed it. And they all believed Anna and Gudrun had some method to keep the terrible spirit at bay.

True or not, the tale suited her well.

Anna tied her curragh to a post on the pier and stepped out of the small boat. She would have stayed on Spirit Isle longer on this bonny morn but for Mac-Millan's visit. He had not been expected to arrive until the morrow, and Anna knew there would be hell to pay when her stepsister Catrìona realized he was already there and Kilgorra Keep was not fully prepared.

At least she and the other servants had already cleaned the bedchambers that were to be used by the men from Braemore, sweeping out the old rushes, washing the floors, putting fresh linens on the beds, and laying fires in the grates. She had directed Alex and Graeme to prepare the barracks where the laird's warriors would reside, so there could be no complaint there.

Anna reached for the basket of berries she'd picked on the isle, but the familiar sharp wail of a wee bairn caused her to turn and look for the infant's mother, her very dearest friend. Kyla Ramsay staggered toward Anna, her face and arms bruised and bloody. It looked as though she was about to faint.

Anna quickly took the child from Kyla's arms. She was about to ease her friend down to the curragh when there was a rush of footsteps, and then a pair of brawny arms caught Kyla and cradled her against his chest with ease.

"Where's the best place to take her?" the highlander asked, his voice deep and rich. "The public house?"

"No!" Anna cried. For Birk might well be there, drunk and mean and ready to do further damage to his wife. "Ah, no, sir . . . ," she said more calmly. "If you would carry her just there . . ."

Holding Kyla's bairn, she led Lachann MacMillan to Janet Carnegie's cottage, some distance from both the public house and the lane where the stone croft Kyla shared with her husband was located.

Janet came out as they approached her cottage, and led the way inside to a simple pallet near the fire. "Put her there," she said. "'Tis good that ye brought her here, Anna."

The highlander laid her down, then stood back, his arms crossed over his broad chest.

"Ach, the clarty bastard has beat her again," Janet remarked with a frown, as though 'twas every day that a stranger brought a broken and bleeding young woman to her cottage.

Anna could not help but take note of MacMillan's kindness toward her poor friend. He must have seen Kyla's wobbly approach on the dock and recognized her distress, else he wouldn't have known to move so swiftly. If not for his quick actions, Kyla might have crashed to the wooden decking at the harbor, causing even more injury to herself than Birk had done.

"You are called Anna?" he asked, and Anna nodded. "You know who did this to her?" His tone was gruff and incredulous.

"Her husband," Anna replied. His deep blue eyes captured Anna's full attention. They were rimmed with the blackest, thickest lashes—far too beautiful for a man. But Anna sensed a wariness in those eyes, as though he trusted no one and nothing.

Good, she thought. Then he would not be taken unawares by the leeches up at the keep. Anna's stepfather was a useless drunkard, and Catrìona was the vilest woman on the isle.

Anna could not understand what the appeal of Kilgorra could possibly be to a braw fellow like this warrior from the mainland. Who would ever *choose* to stay here?

"Lachann." One of MacMillan's men stepped into Janet's cottage and placed Anna's basket of forgotten berries on a table. "I'm sure they took note of our approach into the harbor up at the castle. Laird MacDuffie will be expecting us."

"Aye," MacMillan replied. He wasted no further time in Janet's cottage but turned quickly and made his exit.

And somehow, Anna found her breath again.

There was little that Catrìona MacDuffie liked better than a man's intimate touch. Some of her earliest memories were of the impossible yearnings she'd felt while watching the young men in the fields and the fishermen hauling in their nets. She'd always loved the hard, heavy lines of their bodies—their square jaws and thick whiskers, their solid muscles bunching and flexing as they'd worked.

She'd grown into a plain face and body, and she knew she would never receive much male attention. She'd seen the other lasses, some much younger—Kyla and Anna, for instance—who never failed to capture the wandering gazes of every man they passed, both married and bachelor.

'Twas one more reason to despise Anna MacIver.

To make matters worse for Catrìona, she was the laird's daughter. What man would look at her with the same kind of admiring eyes that followed Anna MacIver, knowing he would have to answer to her father, the laird?

None of the island men were suitable candidates for marriage, and the one time her father had actually sought a proper husband for her had been a disaster. Catrìona would rather have had no husband at all than the waster from the Isle of Lewis he'd invited to court her.

The man had been as ugly as he'd been useless, and had seemed to think he deserved better than Catrìona.

Aye, well, she'd found a strapping young lad to her liking, a sailor from the ship that had brought her would-be suitor from Lewis. She'd had her way with the fellow, and he'd discovered that she might not have had the comeliest face or form, but she'd been entirely female.

And Catrìona had discovered everything that had been missing in her life, but her pleasure had been short-lived. When her lover had set eyes upon Anna MacIver, he'd forgotten all about Catrìona MacDuffie.

Lachann and his men returned to the pier, where several long, low boats were docked. They were fishing birlinns with their sails down and heavy nets stowed tightly in their hulls.

The birlinns were not fighting vessels, and Lachann didn't intend to use them as such. His own brigantine was outfitted with four guns and would likely be able to ward off a sea attack, unless she happened to be outnumbered. Then Kilgorra would need land fighters—an army of well-trained, well-armed men to defend against a raid on land.

Lachann thought it unconscionable for such a rich isle to be without defenses. Word was that MacDuffie had grown old and feeble, even as Kilgorra's distillery had become increasingly productive and known far and wide for its fine whiskey. Traders came to the isle specifically for it, and Lachann suspected that if any powerful chieftain decided to invade and take control, Laird MacDuffie would have no choice but to yield.

The old laird had welcomed Lachann's proposal for developing a defense for the isle, and if Catrìona accepted him as her husband, Lachann would eventually become laird in MacDuffie's place. 'Twas yet another very good reason for coming to Kilgorra. The chance for Lachann to become laird of his own realm.

A few years ago, his brother Dugan's gamble had made his family and his clan wealthy. Aye, Lachann had been part of that venture and had shared in the treasure they'd found. But Lachann intended to distinguish himself in his own right. As laird of Kilgorra, he would do exactly that, even though leaving Braemore, leaving his kin and clan, was the most difficult thing he had ever done.

Lachann's men were at work unloading their horses and all the equipment they'd brought—weapons and gunpowder—from the *Glencoe Lass*. Lachann mounted his horse, and while he waited for Duncan and Kieran to do the same, he looked up toward the castle where his fate awaited him.

He hoped Catrìona was at least beddable. He had no need of a great beauty to bear his children—only an honest wife who understood the requirements of their clan. 'Twould not be amiss if his future wife had a deep concern for her people—the way the fair young woman at the healer's cottage had cared for her injured friend.

'Twas a most attractive trait, mayhap even more than her comely features or the pale golden hair she'd tied into a thick plait down her back. Lachann chose to ignore the pull of attraction at the thought of her blue-green eyes and her clear, sun-kissed skin. He'd sworn off beautiful women after Fiona. He'd learned the hard way they were more trouble than they were worth, and he knew only a handful of them who could be trusted—his brothers' wives and his sister.

"There were no guards at the pier," Lachann said.

"Mayhap they were not at the pier because we arrived a day earlier than expected," Duncan remarked.

"What good are such guards then, eh?" Kieran said. "A warrior should be ready at any time."

Both Lachann's men were right. There should have been an armed contingent of men to meet them when their ship put into the harbor and when the *Glencoe Lass* approached the pier. If there had been any lookouts at the top of the castle walls, they'd have seen Lachann's ship coming from a long way off. But Laird MacDuffie would have had no assurance that it was friendly. He should not have assumed it would be the MacMillan brig, or even a benign trader.

"Their defenses are exceedingly poor, Lachann."

"All the better for me," Lachann said.

"Aye," Duncan agreed. "MacDuffie cannot fail to see the value you bring him."

They started for the road up to the castle, but Lachann was distracted by the sight of a tall, burly Kilgorran staggering drunkenly in the opposite direction. The man made his way into the village, alternating between muttering and shouting a string of curses so vile that Lachann's ears burned.

Lachann rode on for a moment, then halted, realizing what the drunkard's destination was. The healer's cottage. "Wait for me here!" He turned and took to the lane that led to the cottage.

"Do you think this is wise, Lachann?" Duncan shouted after him.

Chapter 2

Lachann did not stop to think about wisdom. The drunk had to be on his way to the healer's cottage, and he was not so jaked that he could not do more damage if he wished. And from the sound of his words, that was his intent. He was likely to kill someone.

Lachann was only a minute or two behind the drunk, but when he came to the cottage, the man had already managed to pin the fair-haired lass up against a wall and was shouting his vile abuse directly in her face. The injured woman was trying to get up from her pallet—to help, Lachann supposed.

The lass struggled to get free, but the bastard's hands were at her throat, and her face was turning a livid shade of red. Lachann wasted no time, but yanked the bloody fool off the woman, whirled him around, and landed a punch that dropped him to the ground.

The woman's attacker lay insensible on the floor.

"Weel now," said Janet, "ye're a bonny fetcher, are ye no', lad?"

Lachann paid no heed to the woman but knelt beside the lass, who'd slid down the wall to the ground, looking stunned. "Are you all right?" he asked.

She swallowed tightly and gave a wee nod, but there was a look of shock about her lovely eyes, and she seemed to be in no small amount of pain. Lachann tipped her chin up with two fingers and saw that a bruise was already forming 'round her throat.

He resisted the urge to caress the injury, to try and give her more comfort than he ought, considering his purpose here on Kilgorra. "'Twill be sore for a few days."

He heard Duncan's voice behind him. "Lachann."

Both his men stood at the open door, peering into the croft. Their expressions reminded him he should not allow himself to become distracted by an altercation taking place in the village. "Aye. I'm coming."

Even so, he bent down and picked up the drunkard. Tossing the blighter over his shoulder, Lachann stalked out of the cottage and down the path. He heard his men mount their horses behind him and follow as he headed down to the pier once again. When he arrived at the water's edge, he realized he had an audience of fishermen, arriving in their fishing boats with their catch. He ignored them and threw the fellow into the drink.

"*Gesu*, Lachann," Duncan said. "What if he drowns?"

"No great loss to Kilgorra, then," Lachann replied.

The drunkard came up sputtering, and Lachann leaned forward to address him. "If I hear of one more bruise on either of those women, you sorry excuse for a man, you'll answer to me. And I will not be so gentle next time!"

Lachann strode back to his horse and mounted up as though naught had happened to deter him from his destination. He glanced 'round and took in the faces of the people who stepped out of the shops and cottages and were walking down the various paths from the village to the pier to see what the disturbance was.

Kieran laughed aloud as they started up the road that led to the castle. " 'Twill be an arrival they will not soon forget, Lachann!"

Lachann forced away his feelings of concern for the lass at the cottage and her injured throat. She was with the healer. He had done all he could for her.

Truly, he wanted to do no more. Such a woman could be poison to his purpose here.

"Did you see the look on that bawbag's face when he surfaced?" Kieran added with a laugh.

"Aye," Lachann replied. "A tyrant never expects any ill treatment in return, does he?"

"Lachann, what if MacDuffie hears of this?" Duncan asked, his tone serious. Worried.

"You can be assured he will, Duncan," Lachann replied. "As will every other man on the isle—men whose laird I intend to become. They'll do well to understand I'll brook no unwarranted bullying on this isle."

"Aye, but—"

"'Twill be known that I am not a man to be trifled with. Aye?"

Kilgorra's only village lay just beyond the pier, a hilly little town tucked beneath a wall of craggy cliffs above it. The distillery was at the rear of the village, standing beside the bank of a wide river that flowed from a waterfall dropping impressively from the crags.

Behind the distillery was a large wooden granary for storing the barley before it was used in the distilling process. As the *Glencoe Lass* had sailed into Kilgorra waters, Lachann had seen cottages amid well-tended fields up in the hills. Everything he had seen of the isle had so far pleased him, except for the beaten woman.

Lachann and his two cousins rode up the path to MacDuffie's castle. No one could attack the stronghold from the sea, and there was only the one road that led to it from lower ground. It seemed a perfect location.

The MacMillans entered through the outer gate into a wide bailey, where numerous buildings stood, from the armory that sat empty and dormant, to a smithy, and a large, stone building that had the look of a barracks. Clearly, Kilgorra had once been a mighty force in the Minch.

As matters stood now, there was no one to stop a raiding ship from sailing freely through Loch Ewe and on down to Loch Maree, where Braemore lands lay.

Braemore had met one such attack in spring, when pirates had sailed down to Loch Maree from the Minch, right past Kilgorra. The battle had cost Lachann's clan dearly. Their treasure had been preserved, but they'd lost too many men to the marauding pirates.

'Twould never happen again if Lachann had his say, and Kilgorra was strategic to his plan. The isle guarded the seaway to Braemore, and since Lachann's clan had recently become wealthy beyond imagining, it needed the protection Kilgorra could provide. He knew rumors were spreading of the French gold he and his brother had discovered three years earlier. He intended to do everything in his power to protect against rival clans and raiders who would use any means to take their gold.

They rode through the inner courtyard and saw the huge stone Kilgorra Keep beyond, with its tall towers and a parapet rising from its roof.

Duncan tipped his head toward the massive wooden door of the keep, where a stoop-shouldered, bald-pated man stood waiting beside a younger fellow. "That must be Laird MacDuffie," Duncan said. "But there was never any mention of a son."

The second man had a thick head of dark red hair and was far taller than the other. Lachann looked closer. *Gesu, no.*

"Lachann . . . ," Kieran said warily. "That man . . .

standing beside MacDuffie. Is that . . . Could that be . . . ?"

"Aye. I think it is," Duncan said, giving voice to Lachann's worst nightmare. "'Tis Cullen Macauley."

"Ach, do you think he brought his wife with him?" Kieran asked. Both cousins knew what Fiona had meant to Lachann. They knew he'd loved the lass to distraction and her father had halted their wedding in favor of the wealthier Macauley.

Lachann put his hand on the hilt of his sword.

"Lachann, you cannot," Duncan said.

"Aye. I most certainly can." He would rid himself of his most hated enemy and make Fiona a widow all in one slash of his sword.

"Not if you want Laird MacDuffie's goodwill."

"It sickens me to say it, Lachann, but he's right," Kieran said. "We do not know what Macauley is doing here."

Lachann did not care. All he knew was this was a Macauley. Worse, this was Cullen Macauley—the bastard who'd stolen his woman.

Lachann's hand tightened on his sword. He narrowed his vision as his mouth dried and his heart sped up. But some part of his brain took in Duncan's words, and he knew his cousin was right. He hated the thought of backing down now, while he had the bastard within reach.

But knew he must.

Chapter 3

"Let me up, Eòsaph," Catrìona demanded when her lover pinned her to the shabby bed that lay in a small room at the back of the deserted chapel. He was nipping at her neck and breasts, and 'twas all becoming too tiresome for words.

Cullen Macauley was far more interesting. Unlike Eòsaph Drummond, Macauley had come from the Isle of Skye, where the wealthy MacDonalds ruled.

And he was intent upon courting her as his wife.

Macauley pleased her well. He was handsome and refined, a far cry from the lovers Catrìona was accustomed to. And after all these years, she was going to have two candidates to choose from. 'Twas as though fate had decided to play some strange jest upon her.

Mayhap 'twas to balance the scales after bringing beautiful Anna to Kilgorra with her mother years ago. How could Catrìona ever have hoped to compete with her father's new family? And when Sigrid had gotten with child, her father had seemed to forget his "wee wren," as he'd liked to call his one true daughter.

He'd called Anna his golden lass and had showered his attentions upon his new young wife's comely daughter.

She pushed away from Eòsaph and pulled on her clothes. "I must go. We have much to do up at the—"

"Will you meet me on the morrow, Catrìona?"

Her hands stilled for a moment, and she gazed down at him. "Do you never tire of . . . of"—she gestured toward the unkempt bed—"this?"

"Are ye daft? Ach, no." He took her hand and put it on his swollen erection. "Even now . . ."

Catrìona laughed, retrieving her hand to finish dressing. She was anxious to meet the young man from Braemore who would arrive on the morrow, though no one knew quite when his ship would put into the harbor. So she'd made plans to meet Cullen at the distillery, which had become her favorite trysting place, by far.

She went to the creaky old door and opened it. "I cannot meet you tomorrow, Eòsaph. I'll send word to you when it suits me."

He reached for her. "When?"

She pushed him away, irritated now. "You know I can make you no promises. We have guests arriving, and I'll have duties to attend to."

Catrìona followed the narrow path back to the keep, her thoughts on Cullen Macauley and his reaction to the news that Lachann MacMillan was coming to marry her.

'Twas almost as though he'd known.

But how could he?

Ach, what did it matter? She'd taken him to her bed, well aware that her father had made a tentative pact with the MacMillans stipulating that Lachann would become her husband.

But only if she agreed to it after they met.

'Twas so very amusing to see Macauley taking more notice of her than of her impossibly innocent stepsister, Anna MacIver. For the first time in her life, Catrìona was the one coveted—*desired*—by an incredibly interesting, sophisticated man.

It wasn't until she reached the door of her father's keep that she realized something was amiss. There was far more activity inside than she expected.

The MacMillans had arrived early.

Anna sat against the wall of the healer's cottage with her hand at her throat.

"Come on up, lass," Janet said, reaching a hand down to help her. Kyla was weeping quietly on her pallet.

"Where is he?" Anna asked. "Where did MacMillan take Birk?"

Janet shrugged and shook her head.

Anna rose to her feet and started for the door, but three familiar young boys came running up the hill toward the cottage, laughing. Angus MacLaren called to her. "Anna! Ye should've seen it! He threw Birk into th' drink, he did!"

"Who, Angus? Who threw—"

"The stranger," the boy quipped before running off with his friends. "He dropped him into the sea and threatened him about puttin' bruises on any more women."

Anna leaned back against the door.

"You do'na believe the Braemore man will take any further interest in Birk, do ye?" Janet asked, rocking Kyla's bairn, Douglas, in her arms. "His business is with them up at the keep, and no' wi' the likes of Birk Ramsay."

"Aye," Anna rasped. But the man had come to Kyla's aid, and then Anna's—all within minutes of his arrival.

But mayhap Janet was right. He happened to have been standing on the dock when Kyla had nearly collapsed, and he'd later recognized Birk as Kyla's husband—or a threat, at least—on his way up to Janet's cottage.

Lachann MacMillan had not needed to go out of his way to assist them. Still, it had been a glorious rescue, like the ones recounted in tales of old.

"If ye're all right, Anna, ye should hasten up to the

keep," Janet said. "Ye know they'll be wanting ye with MacMillan arrivin' early. Wait until Catrìona sees the braw lads that sailed in this time!"

Anna ignored Janet's reference to Catrìona's inordinate lusting after the men of the isle and the seamen who came in to trade. It had naught to do with anything now, for Catrìona would marry Lachann MacMillan, and 'twould be his responsibility to deal with the wife he'd chosen.

Anna knelt down beside her friend. The cuts and bruises on Kyla's face should not have shocked her, for she'd seen the results of Birk's beatings before. But the man's brutality was never easy to witness. She hoped MacMillan had put the fear of God into him.

Anna swallowed and winced at the pain in her throat. 'Twas uncomfortable, but she'd survived injuries at the hands of her stepsister, who'd treated her with malice from the day she'd come to Kilgorra with her mother. Anna did all in her power to avoid the nasty-tempered witch.

But Ky could not evade her own husband for long. There wasn't a hiding place anywhere on the isle where he would not find her if he was of a mind to search.

Anna delayed her return to the castle, quite willing to endure Catrìona's wrath for Kyla's sake. She wrung out the cloth in the bowl Janet had filled with water and dabbed at the cuts on Kyla's forehead and lip. The lass was trembling fair to shake the pallet beneath her.

"Ah, Kyla–you're all right now. We've got you, Janet and me."

But Kyla shook her head, and the tears streaming down her face tugged at Anna's heart. She'd been horribly betrayed by the man she loved. Nor was Kyla the first woman to suffer at the hands of her husband. Anna had long ago resolved never to let it happen to her.

She gazed down at her friend, wishing she could say something of substance that would comfort her. Kyla was more a sister to her than the one who was connected to her by her mother's second marriage. Both Kyla and Anna had been orphaned young, and when loneliness and fear had darkened the days of their childhood, they'd clung to each other for comfort.

"No," Kyla whispered. "No one's got me but Birk."

"Aye," Janet railed. "And the lad's turned into a right wee bawbag." She put Douglas on the pallet beside his mother and got busy mixing a potion that would help ease the worst of Kyla's pain.

"He has," Anna whispered, her temper flaring. "I hope he drowns."

"Anna, no," Kyla whimpered.

"And why wouldn't I hope such a thing?" Anna demanded, unable to contain her anger. "The damned dolt is likely so jaked he can't even swim—"

"Because he is my husband. He drinks to quell his headaches." She said the words, but her voice was tremulous.

"Oh, aye. And a fair bit of good that's done him," Anna said acerbically.

"Ye'd best finish here, lass," Janet said to Anna. "Ye know how Catrìona will behave when the MacMillans arrive up at the keep and you are not there to serve them."

Anna blinked back her tears of anger, aware that Janet was right. 'Twas likely Catrìona had already gotten herself into a state with the early arrival of Lachann MacMillan.

"Kyla, you know I must go, but I want you to stay here until I get back."

"No, Anna," Kyla whispered. "I must take my son and go home."

"Are you daft? You can do no such thing," Anna cried, causing the pain in her throat to flare. "You're in no decent condition. I'll come back for you and we'll find somewhere—"

"No use delayin' it, Anna," Janet said. "Birk won't be back. At least, not for a while. He knows MacMillan will wed Catrìona and become laird. He will'na care to risk the man's ire."

"Aye," Kyla added. "Go now. Before your sister gives you a beating like mine."

Leaving Kyla this way was the last thing Anna wanted to do, but she gritted her teeth and went for the door. "I'll be back as soon as I can, then we'll find a place for you to stay where Birk won't find you."

Kyla turned her face to the wall in resignation.

Anna hesitated a moment, but she knew she could not stay. "I *will* come back for you, Kyla," she said before picking up her basket of berries and leaving Janet's cottage.

She hurried down the path to the pier and searched for signs of Birk floundering about in the water.

Young Angus and his two friends skipped onto the pier. "He climbed out and went away," the lad said with a great belly laugh. "Ye should've seen him, Anna! Sputterin' and cursin' to beat all!"

"Angus! Does your father know you're wandering about the village?" Anna asked. Donald usually kept a close watch on his mischievous son. Ever since his wife's death, he'd kept the lad inside the castle walls and under the watchful eye of his brother, Alex, to minimize the amount of trouble the boy could get into.

"Only if ye tell him, Anna!" he shouted as the three young lads ran up the path to the castle walls.

Without further delay, Anna followed the lads up the steep road. She wished she'd been able to see Birk brought low by the man in the red plaid. If anyone ever deserved it, 'twas Birk Ramsay.

He'd been a braw young fisherman two years ago when he'd courted and wed Kyla. But soon after he'd gotten her with child, taken a bad fall, then he'd started with the drink, and he had not been a pleasant drunkard. 'Twas as though someone other than Birk lived inside his body. He'd beaten Kyla so viciously that she'd nearly lost Douglas when the bairn was barely started in her belly. A few months later, he'd burned his own boat in a fit of temper, and now he had to work on his father's birlinn as he'd done as a lad.

Everything seemed to set him off, from the crying of his own son to the paltry state of his larder. And it seemed Kyla was to blame for it all.

Anna arrived inside her stepfather's fortress. She circled 'round the bailey and past the huge Bruce Tree in a small close, and on to the back of the keep, where the kitchens and scullery were located. Taking an apron from a hook, Anna joined Flora, the castle cook, who was working at a frantic pace along with Nighean and Meg, the two scullery maids, to produce a suitable meal for the newly arrived men from Braemore.

Already, someone had summoned the fiddlers, and they were upstairs near the great hall, tuning their instruments, making ready to entertain.

Flora stopped what she was doing and looked at Anna. "What happened to yer neck, Anna? Ach, no! 'Twas the *sluagh dubh*!"

"Nay, Flora, 'twas—"

"I've always said that nasty boggle on the isle would do ye harm one day. Years ago, I told Gudrun—"

"'Twas Birk. Not the *sluagh dubh*."

Flora narrowed her eyes, muttering something entirely unholy under her breath. She did not care for Birk any more than she liked the *sluagh dubh*. "How did this come to be, lass?"

"Well, after he beat Kyla nearly to death, he came up to Janet's cottage, grabbed me by the throat, and pinned me to a wall."

"No." Flora covered her mouth in horror.

Anna tied a cloth 'round her neck to hide the bruise Birk had given her. There was naught she could do about her raspy voice. "But then Lachann MacMillan dumped him in the sea for it."

"What? MacMillan did *what*?"

Anna grinned. "At least, that's what Angus Mac-Laren told me."

"Serves him right, and more. Did he drown?"

"I wish. But Angus said no," Anna retorted.

"Ye ought to take Kyla and the bairn into that wee curragh of yours and sail as far from Kilgorra as you can go," Flora said, taking hold of Anna's arms.

"You know she will not leave her husband."

"If anyone can convince her, 'tis you, lass."

"Where would we go, Flora?"

"To your father's people."

"The MacIvers?" Anna retorted. "Gudrun said that when my father died, the new laird of Kearvaig drove my mother out."

Flora furrowed her brow. "Ye could go to your mother's people, then."

Of course Anna had thought about that. Often. But

to sail across the open seas to the Norse country? The mere thought of it terrified her. She could contain her fear of deep waters long enough to row her curragh across the narrow straits to Spirit Isle, but not all the way 'round the north of Scotland and across the North Sea.

Besides, she did not know her mother's people, except by reputation. 'Twas said Sigrid had come from a prestigious family in Norway. But all connections had been lost. Anna had no idea if her mother's family still lived. Or where she might look for them.

"Flora, I have no money for passage either by land or by sea," Anna said sadly. "How would I manage it?"

Flora pressed her mouth into a tight line of resignation.

Anna put her hand on the older woman's arm. "Tell me what I can do to help you here."

"Ach, well." Flora sighed heavily and returned to her work. "The mistress has been clamoring fer the meal. So if ye'd carry this tray up to the hall, 'twould be a great help."

Anna made a derisive sound. "MacMillan did not seem the type of man to demand any special treatment. He arrived unexpectedly early. Surely he does not expect a lavish meal."

Flora's eyes widened. "Ye met him?"

"Aye, at the pier, before he threw Birk into the sea," Anna replied. "I'll tell you later."

"Ach, and what will that radgy wench upstairs say when she hears of it?"

"I hope that never happens," Anna said. "And you ought not to use such raw words when you speak of— You know." Anna leveled a pointed glance toward the youngest maid, Glenna, a wee lass of eight years who'd been orphaned and taken into service at the castle, much the same as Anna and Kyla, years ago.

"Ach," Flora said, "that wench is what she is. And she'll lay claim to the MacMillan lad faster than he can climb the stairs to his bedchamber."

"Where will that leave Cullen Macauley?" Anna asked, for Catrìona had put her hooks into the man from Skye the minute he'd come to the isle more than a fortnight ago.

"Where does it leave Eòsaph Drummond?" Flora asked.

'Twas thought that Catrìona knew every secret trysting spot on the isle and had used them all, most recently with Eòsaph, who had a wife and children.

Anna shrugged. What Catrìona did was her own concern and had naught to do with her, though it pained her every time she saw Eòsaph's wife in the village. She liked Ilisa Drummond very much, and her heart clenched in her chest every time she saw the poor woman with her eyes cast down, assuming everyone knew of her husband's infidelity. Catrìona had been man-hungry ever since adolescence, though most of the island men had known well enough to stay clear of her. Anna suspected her stepsister had had her earliest assignation with a sailor who'd come on a trading ship from the Isle of Lewis, but that had been years ago.

"Eòsaph would do well to turn his attentions to his own family," Flora fumed as she placed bowls and platters on a large wooden tray.

Anna nodded in agreement but went back to the original question. "Don't worry about Catrìona hearing about what MacMillan did for Kyla and me, Flora. The talk will be all about Birk. Not us."

Besides, Catrìona had little interest in what went on in the village. She only cared about making as favorable a first impression with Lachann MacMillan as she'd done when Macauley had arrived a few weeks earlier. Both men seemed to believe that marriage to Anna's sister would be a conduit to the lairdship of Kilgorra.

The talk in the village indicated they were likely right. But only one of them could be laird.

Since Macauley's arrival, Catrìona had been barely tolerable. Anna could not imagine how unbearable she was going to be now that there were two highborn men vying for her hand.

And then there was Eòsaph, and she hated to think who else might have fallen into her stepsister's snares.

"Ye know she'll play one against the other, aye?" Flora asked.

"You mean Macauley and MacMillan?" Anna nodded. "I suppose so. Everyone knows the agreement with the MacMillans was not sealed. Catrìona is still free to choose."

Flora clucked her tongue. "Aye, and she'll enjoy the game."

Without even meeting him, Anna and the rest of the islanders believed Lachann MacMillan must be the better choice. So far, Macauley had not managed to endear himself to anyone on Kilgorra other than Catrìona and her father. He was imperious and demanding at the keep, and he'd taken charge of the Kilgorra distillery, giving orders and overriding Geordie Kincaid's authority.

Had he done it to demonstrate his worth to the laird?

Anna wondered if her stepfather still had the capacity to take notice of such things. But the machinations of the high and mighty had naught to do with her, naught but Macauley's unwelcome advances, which she took pains to avoid. Catrìona had treated her with full-blown animosity when she'd come to Kilgorra as a young child and her mother had married Catrìona's father. Anna's mother had taken all the laird's attentions, leaving Catrìona to fend for herself. When Sigrid and her newborn son had died, naught had been the same for either daughter.

Anna had lost the only family she would ever have.

And Catrìona had lost any chance of gaining her father's attention, for he'd started turning to the solace of drink more often than not. Catrìona had blamed Anna for all her woes back then.

She had seen to it that every memory of Sigrid was erased from Kilgorra Keep. And she'd relegated Anna to the servants' quarters at the very bottom of the keep.

Naught had changed since then. These days, it seemed Anna's stepfather hardly remembered who she was.

Anna started for the tray Flora had prepared, but Catrìona suddenly descended into the kitchen from the stairs that led up to the great hall. She caught sight of Anna and snapped at her. "I've been looking for you, you lazy wench!"

Chapter 4

Catrìona wore a deep green gown that Anna had made just for this occasion, and she had tied her father's tartan at her waist. Her fine shoes had come all the way from Inverness, while Anna's and most of the other women's feet at Kilgorra Castle were bare.

Catrìona grabbed Anna by the arm, pinching hard. Anna yelped in surprise.

"Where have you been?"

"On Spirit Isle," Anna retorted.

Catrìona drew away from her with distaste. She was as superstitious as the rest of the Kilgorrans, and the very mention of the island filled her with dread.

Anna was careful never to tell anyone about the true nature of the isle, about the deep blue loch or the wild roots and berries that grew in the island's verdant, green interior. Some brave Kilgorran might decide to risk injury from the *sluagh dubh* and explore it.

'Twas the last thing Anna and Kyla wanted. The isle was their haven. If anyone on Kilgorra had ever known of the beautiful dell that lay within the ring of mountains all 'round its coast, no one seemed to remember it now. And if they did—well, there were the tales of the *sluagh dubh* to keep them away.

Gudrun had never believed in such things, and after the death of Anna's mother, the woman had explored the isle's rocky terrain, taking Anna and Kyla with her. Anna was the one who had discovered the long, low tunnel on the northeastern side of the isle. She'd followed the passage all the way to the interior and found a beautiful green dell within, and the loch with its healing springs.

Anna treasured her time on Spirit Isle, and she was fortunate to have a bit more freedom than some of the other servants at the castle. Years ago, Gudrun had humored her and Kyla when they'd turned one of the caves into a cozy home for them while they were away from Kilgorra and Anna's vile stepsister. Spirit Isle had become a tiny paradise unto itself for them, with nothing—not even a boggle—to spoil it.

"Bring the meal up to the hall," Catrìona hissed. "Now!"

"Let Nighean carry some of it, Anna," Flora said. "'Tis too much for one—"

"Shut your insolent mouth, old woman," Catrìona barked. "You know our guest has arrived, and there is not a speck of refreshment ready for him."

Catrìona gave Anna a stern glance, then quickly bustled up the stairs, muttering angrily under her breath. Anna knew better than to defy her stepsister, especially if she wanted to get away from the castle to hide Kyla later. She picked up the tray laden with the dishes Flora had prepared and carefully followed Catrìona up to the great hall.

At the top of the stairs, Catrìona took hold of Anna's sleeve. "Put it on the table, you fool slecher. *And be quick about it!*"

Anna felt herself teetering on the top step, and the tray started to slip. She feared Flora had been right. She should have ignored Catrìona and waited for Nighean to help her with the heavy tray. She struggled to gain her balance, afraid she was going to drop everything, and then there would be hell to pay. Her stepsister would make sure she could not get back to the village, would prevent her from getting Kyla and her bairn a place to hide away for the night.

The weight on her shoulder fell away unexpectedly, and Anna felt a moment's confusion and panic, afraid the tray was about to clatter to the floor.

Chapter 5

Anna squeezed her eyes shut and waited.

But there was no crash, no disaster. She opened her eyes, only to see Lachann MacMillan stepping away with the tray in his hands. He carried it to the table with ease, then set it down with barely a glance back.

The room grew silent, and Anna felt her face heat with embarrassment and worry. Catrìona would not take kindly to Anna being rescued by their guest, a man her stepsister might well choose to marry if Macauley had not yet fully won her. Catrìona sidled up beside Anna and gave her another painful pinch on the back of her arm to demonstrate her ire.

Anna held back a squeal of pain, jerking away from Catrìona to follow MacMillan to the table, where he left her to her work. She kept her head down, making an effort to draw no further attention to herself as she took the platters and bowls from the tray and arranged them on the laird's banquet table.

She dearly hoped her stepsister would not hear about Lachann's rescue of Kyla on the pier, but she feared 'twas impossible to keep such gossip from her. Catrìona would hear what he had done to Birk—and why.

But mayhap Anna's name would not be mentioned. She could only pray that would be so.

She finished her task as quickly as possible, then hurried back to the stairs. She would have flown down to the kitchen had it not been for her braw rescuer standing in her path. She looked up at him, unsure what to do, what to say, if anything. She knew that if the man seemed to take any notice of her, Catrìona would be livid.

"Th-thank you for your assistance, sir," Anna said, meaning more than his help with the tray. She hoped he understood she could say no more, for she needed to make her speech quick and seemingly inconsequential. Which it was. She could have no further business with the man.

She made a slight bow, wishing she could tell herself she wanted naught more than to escape the room and his scrutiny.

But she would have been lying.

His eyes were so very intense, and when they rested upon her throat and he gave a questioning glance—

Anna wasted not another second but skirted 'round the highlander and went down the stairs to the scullery as quickly as her legs would carry her.

The maid, Anna, served as a momentary and welcome distraction against Lachann's nerves, which buzzed like a hive about to explode.

He had never expected to encounter Cullen Macauley again, much less here on Laird MacDuffie's isle. He was still reeling with the news Macauley had given him of Fiona MacDonald's death, and when the fair lass from the pier had come into the hall struggling under the weight of a ridiculously overladen tray, Lachann had nearly snapped at Laird MacDuffie for misusing his servants.

What a mistake that would have been. Lachann had come to court the man and his daughter. Not to alienate him.

And 'twould not go over well if he were to cleave Macauley in two right there in MacDuffie's hall.

Gesu. Fiona was dead? She'd once been everything to him—until Cullen Macauley had come along.

The pain of losing her had faded some, but not the hatred he felt for the man who'd taken her away from him. The man who'd gone to Skye knowing full well that Lachann was to marry Fiona.

"So, ye know each other, then?"

"Aye," Macauley replied with a cockiness that made Lachann want to shove his fist down the bastard's throat. "Though 'tis been some years."

Lachann could barely stand to lay eyes upon Macauley. If Fiona was dead, the damned blighter could not have protected her well enough. Could not have cared for her as Lachann had done. As he *would* have done.

Now the bastard was here. And to what purpose? Macauley had a proprietary air about him, touching Catrìona's elbow and her lower back as a husband would do. He spoke to Laird MacDuffie as would a favored nephew. Or son.

Damn all. 'Twas clear Macauley had come for the exact same purpose as Lachann. To make Catrìona his wife and eventually become laird in her father's place. Why else would he have come to Kilgorra?

Had he learned of Lachann's intention to marry Catrìona MacDuffie and come to thwart him once again? *Gesu.* It could so easily be true.

MacDuffie had written naught of Macauley during negotiations with Lachann and his brothers. The MacMillans understood that a betrothal between Lachann and Kilgorra's daughter was a mere formality to be ratified on Lachann's arrival. And that once they wed and Lachann developed a defensive force for Kilgorra, he would become laird of the isle.

Lachann gathered his composure about him like a cloak. He had not planned on having any competition here. So far, Catrìona MacDuffie had naught to recommend her beyond being the daughter of the laird. She was as plain as reputed, and seemed equally drab in personality.

Which was just as Lachann would have it. He needed no wife to drive him to distraction, as his bonny Fiona had done. This MacDuffie woman would suit him well.

As Macauley's presence did not.

Lachann tamped down his temper and considered what mischief was afoot. Had Macauley begun to train an army of his own? Had he made an offer to MacDuffie already?

Aye, of course he had. He'd had no lands of his own at the time of his marriage to Fiona. 'Twas no secret he'd intended to become laird of all the MacDonald territory, and he'd used Fiona to advance his goal. It seemed clear her death had thwarted his designs.

Lachann would have to get rid of him, though he did not know how he would accomplish it, for old MacDuffie was quite clearly pleased with Macauley and acted on the most familiar terms with him. 'Twas almost as though Macauley had lived all his life at Kilgorra Castle.

This was a complication Lachann did not need. He wondered if the bastard had already seduced Catrìona.

"The news of your wife's passing grieves me sorely, Macauley," he growled, having some difficulty getting the words out.

"Aye," Macauley replied as though he knew naught of what Fiona and Lachann had meant to each other, " 'twas a sad day for all on Skye."

Lachann wanted to know how Fiona had died; he wanted the details. And yet he did not. He could not bear to think of Fiona dying horribly in a raid. Or worse, from bearing Macauley's child. The mere thought of it turned his stomach.

He looked to Laird MacDuffie, unable and unwilling to continue speaking to Macauley a moment longer than necessary. He needed a moment to regroup. "Laird, we were told that rooms would be prepared—"

"Aye, uh . . ." MacDuffie looked to his daughter as though he could not quite recall the arrangements. "Call for Anna to come up and take the MacMillans' bags up to their rooms."

Anna? The serving maid who'd already been taxed beyond reason today? Just as Catrìona started for the stairs where the maid had descended, Lachann objected. "Laird, there are too many, and they are too heavy for a lass. Have you no menservants?"

"Certainly we do," the laird replied in a wee huff, and Lachann realized Duncan was going to blister his ears later for his injudicious remark.

Good God, what a mess. Could MacDuffie truly be such a dolt that he knew naught of the Macauleys? That he would actually consider tying himself to this infamous clan?

What was wrong with him?

MacDuffie assumed the air of command and spoke again to his daughter. "Catrìona, send someone for Graeme and Alex. They can do the carrying. After all," he said with a sly look, "the MacMillans have come to stay."

Lachann caught Duncan's sidelong glance, a subtle

chiding for being too blunt. Lachann knew he should have *suggested* that a manservant would be better suited to carrying the luggage, rather than accuse the laird of misjudging the task. Or of misusing the serving lass.

Well, he'd never been the most diplomatic of men, although he pledged to do better, at least with MacDuffie and his daughter. He *did* want the woman to accept him as her husband.

He needed to keep his goal in mind. He and his brother Dugan had engaged in numerous heated discussions about this plan during the weeks leading up to Lachann's departure. The argument had not been about the wisdom of allying with Kilgorra, for no one had disputed the desirability—no, the *necessity*—of such a pact. It had been about Lachann's intention to wed MacDuffie's daughter.

Dugan had become a firm believer in love after meeting Maura, the woman who'd become his wife. And now he did not want Lachann to fall into a marriage for strategic purposes, no matter how important they were. He wanted Lachann to experience the same kind of madness Dugan felt for his own wife.

Lachann had come to believe 'twas far better to wed for a logical and advantageous purpose than because of some useless emotion that would only tear his heart to shreds.

Ach, aye—he believed in love. In its vast destructive powers.

Chapter 6

Catrìona came to him. Smiling coyly, she took his arm and led him to the curved stone stairs. "Come with me, Lachann. The men will bring up the bags."

Lachann felt some satisfaction when Macauley objected to the woman giving her attention to him. "Catrìona, do you not think the servants can see to—"

"No, Cullen," she said, and when she laughed, her countenance was not so dour. "'Tis a lady's duty to see to her guests."

Her words and laughter did not agree entirely with her attitude. Lachann thought Catrìona seemed more than just a wee bit put out by his request to retreat to their chambers.

But what did the lass think? That they would not prefer to settle themselves before sitting down to table? That Lachann would think naught of a rival for his position when all had been as good as settled mere weeks ago?

As Duncan and Kieran followed behind, Lachann glanced down at Catrìona surreptitiously, taking stock of his future wife, because this time, Macauley would not win. 'Twould be Lachann standing before a priest with the woman of his choosing.

And Macauley could go hang.

Catrìona's features were unremarkable, though her skin was good. Her hair was a light shade of brown, and was twisted into a complex knot at her nape with a few loose curls teasing her ears. Her eyes were a darker brown, with thick, black lashes—most definitely her best feature, especially when she turned her rapt attention upon him.

She was hardly the kind of woman a man would lose his head over, but neither was she a beastie. She seemed adequately built for childbearing, and Lachann was confident he could rouse some enthusiasm in her over that prospect. 'Twould be a chore to bed a woman who possessed no passion.

They climbed to the top of the steps, coming to a long, old-fashioned gallery much like the one at Braemore Keep, but longer and wider.

"Your chamber is down at the end, Lachann, beside the stairs to the solar," Catrìona said. "Your cousins have the rooms directly across from yours."

She moved to walk ahead of him, and Lachann followed, with Kieran and Duncan behind him. He watched Catrìona and the exaggerated sway of her hips. When she turned to smile at him over her shoulder, Lachann felt naught.

The lack of any reaction was a double-edged sword, at best.

"I hope you will not be long," Catrìona said. She gazed up at him with blatant interest, and Lachann decided Macauley must not have won her yet. "The meal is ready, and you must be—"

"Aye, famished." He gave her a smile, hoping to forge the beginnings of a short and pleasing courtship. "We'll take only a few minutes."

He knew Duncan would be pleased by the amiable exchange, and stood watching as Catrìona left them to their chambers.

"What in hell is Cullen Macauley doing here?" Kieran hissed once Catrìona was gone.

"Same thing I am," Lachann said.

"Do you think he knew you were coming here, Lachann?"

"How could he?" Lachann replied. "Though our communications were not secret . . . I suppose word could have reached him early in the summer."

"*Gesu*. The man's a—"

"I wonder how far he's gotten with a Kilgorran army," Lachann said. Much as he would like to grouse about Macauley's presence, 'twould do him no good.

"Well, certainly not far enough to provide guards at the pier when we docked," Kieran quipped.

"I do not understand Laird MacDuffie allowing Macauley such favored status," Duncan said.

"I wonder what the Kilgorrans think of him," Lachann remarked.

"It does not matter what they think, Lachann," Duncan retorted. "The man who marries Catrìona will have legitimacy."

Aye, but so would the man who established and commanded Kilgorra's army.

Lachann gave a quick shake of his head. If Macauley had begun to build an army, Lachann's arrival could well divide the isle into warring factions. He knew what an underhanded bastard Macauley was, and he'd seen enough feuding in the highlands to last a lifetime.

'Twas not what he wanted. For even if he won, he would lose something exceedingly important—the unity of the isle.

"You believe that if Macauley marries Catrìona, he will become laird?" Lachann asked. "Because she seems to favor him. As does her father."

"Macauley has come to Kilgorra to do what he failed to do on Skye," Kieran said.

"Become laird," Lachann said quietly.

"Aye," Kieran replied.

Duncan gave a slow nod. "There is a long tradition here: Catrìona's grandfather became laird when the prior laird chose him—his son-in-law. The same was done even before that. MacDuffie will choose his daughter's husband to become laird after him."

"You *will* marry the lass, will you not, Lachann?" Kieran asked. "Braemore needs Kilgorra."

"Aye. I'll marry her."

"We should get back to the hall as soon as possible, Lachann," Duncan said, glancing toward the staircase. "'Twill not do to keep the laird waiting."

"Lady Catrìona seemed anxious for our return," Kieran added.

Lachann rubbed a hand across his face. He'd never thought much of diplomacy before. Now he was in the thick of it. "She can wait while I wash my face and get the lay of the place."

Kieran stood still with his hands on his hips, looking toward the staircase.

"What?" Lachann asked.

"She is just as they said—as drab as an oatcake."

Duncan visibly clenched his teeth at Kieran's unseemly remark.

Lachann shook his head. "She'll do."

Kieran and Duncan went into their chambers, and when Lachann opened the door to his bedchamber, he discovered the maid Anna, half lying across his bed.

Chapter 7

Anna gave a startled squeal and scrambled away from the bed. She had not expected MacMillan to come up to his room so soon. And now that he was here . . .

She swallowed, her throat clenching painfully as she did so. He was so very tall, and as he came toward her, removing his sword from his belt, Anna felt an instant of panic before realizing he meant her no harm. "I-I just wanted to leave you a small token o-of m-my—"

"Aye? A token?" He set his sword on a nearby table.

Dear God, his voice was pure highland moss, thick and rich. "For helping my friend. A-and me, too!" The man had done more for her in one day than anyone had done in the past ten years since Gudrun's death.

She pointed to the bowl of raspberries she'd left on the bolster of his bed and realized she should not have been referring in any way to the man's bed. 'Twas much too forward, and he might mistake her meaning.

Herregud. She ought not to have come up here at all!

"Well," she said, taking a step to go past him to the door, but he stopped her progress with one hand on her arm. "I-I hope you enjoy them. The berries, I mean."

"I'm sure I will. How is your neck?"

"Sore, but I'll . . ."

He untied the cloth at her throat and used his thumb to tip her head up. Anna suppressed a shiver at his touch and studied his eyes and the elegant arch of his thick, dark brow as he gently touched her throat.

" . . . I'll survive."

"Aye. You will." His eyes rested upon each of her features before he dropped his hand to his side. "Did the bastard drown?"

Anna shook her head. "Not that I heard."

The air in Anna's lungs seemed to seep out of her as the laird lost interest in her, and walked past the bed to the window to look outside. Anna knew there was naught to see but a steep cliff and the sea beyond. "You must take care, then," he said, not dismissing her at all. "A bully doesn't generally take kindly to being beaten by a stranger. Over a woman."

"But you weren't—"

"'Tis the way he'll see it," MacMillan said with finality. As though he had some experience with such men. He turned to look at her. "Take care."

She wondered which man would stay—MacMillan or Macauley.

'Twould be a fine competition, indeed. For those who were interested.

Anna returned to the kitchen. There was much more work to be done with the Braemore guests arriving a day early. She tamped down her desperate eagerness to return to Janet Carnegie's cottage for Kyla, and went to work next to Flora. She hoped the healer managed to keep Kyla from leaving, at least until Anna returned and could convince her to stay at the castle that night, or, if she was well enough, in their secret cave on Spirit Isle.

"Are ye ready to tell me what happened down at the dock?" Flora asked.

Anna shrugged. "I told you most of it. Birk was drunk. He beat his wife. Kyla came to my curragh just as Lachann MacMillan arrived on the pier."

"Nay!"

Anna nodded. "He caught her before she collapsed and carried her up to Janet's cottage."

"Sweet heaven above," Flora said.

Anna began to scrub some of the cooking pots. Of course Catrìona would learn of the incident, but Anna did not see how her stepsister could possibly hold Mac-Millan's actions against her. "Tell me the rest," Fiona said. "Birk came after ye then?"

"Aye. MacMillan had already settled Kyla inside and left Janet's cottage. But soon enough, Birk stormed in and went for Kyla again."

"Dear God." Flora closed her eyes and said a silent prayer. "I suppose ye got in his way."

"Of course I did. I wasn't about to let him kill Kyla before our eyes."

"And so he attacked ye."

"Aye, I thought he would kill me in his rage. But MacMillan came back inside," Anna explained. "He must have seen Birk on the road as he returned to the pier and realized what the wily bastard was about."

"So 'twas our Braemore guest who saved ye from Birk's wrath."

Anna gave a quick nod. She did not want to think about the big man's caress, or the expression in his eyes when he'd looked at her, but she found it difficult to put them from her mind.

"He's a right splendid-looking fellow," Flora said. "As braw a highlander as ever I've seen."

Anna felt her cheeks heat, for she'd been thinking the very same thing.

"I wonder if the Braemore man knows Cullen Macauley has come to wed yer stepsister, too," Flora said.

Anna shrugged, demonstrating an indifference she did not quite feel. "Getting Kyla to safety is all I care about."

"Then ye must hie yerself down to Janet's cottage and move her before Birk regains his senses enough to understand he's been bested."

"Aye. As soon as the meal is served and cleared," Anna said. "If I go before, they'll notice my absence.

Besides, I won't leave you with all this work and only Nighean and Meg to help you."

"And wee Glenna."

Anna smiled as she glanced at the young maid. Flora had taken her under her wing, just as Gudrun had done for Kyla and Anna all those years ago.

But the lass was observant, and paid far too close attention to all that was said in the kitchen. The servants knew 'twas necessary to guard their tongues when Glenna was about. 'Twould not do to have their opinions restated elsewhere.

The laird's heavy oaken table in the great hall was full—covered with platters of food brought by the serving maid. All of Lachann's men had been invited to join in for a welcoming feast, so they sat 'round it, alongside the laird and his daughter—and Macauley.

"What do you know of fighting ships, MacMillan?" Macauley asked from his place across from Lachann. Catrìona sat beside her father, next to Macauley. She sat quietly, her eyes following a white and black cat that came into the hall and sat down to groom itself before the fireplace. She appeared to lack any interest in the conversation.

"I know that the Spaniards sailed three-masted frigates when they came to the highlands on their ill-advised campaign last year," Lachann replied.

"On their ill-adv—?"

"And that the Sassenach navy has yet to take an interest in our western shores," Lachann continued without giving Macauley a chance to interrupt. It aggravated him no end to see Catrìona seated beside Macauley when *Lachann* was to be her husband.

"Do ye think that'll change any time soon, MacMillan?" Laird MacDuffie queried.

Lachann tamped down his irritation. He was older and wiser now, and none of the bitter hatred he felt for Macauley would serve him now. "Only when the highlands have something they want," he said to the laird. "Or when the Jacobites rise again."

There was silence after Lachann's last words. He knew naught of another uprising, and frankly hoped that if there was one, 'twould not happen anytime soon. In his opinion, it did not serve the highlanders well to call attention to themselves. The northern lands might have an opportunity to prosper only if they could get through a decade or two without warfare. Only then would they be ready to bring back their king. . . .

Ever since Lachann and Dugan had located the hidden French treasure, the MacMillans had used their wealth to assist neighboring allies in paying their rents, for strength and friendship in the region served everyone. They'd helped numerous others sort out difficulties arising from floods and famines, and from the loss of diseased livestock. They'd brought in grain, and cattle or sheep for the poorest clans to help them prosper. But the MacMillan brothers had been circumspect about it, not wishing to make their newfound riches too obvious.

Dugan had not done anything ostentatious beyond his purchase of MacMillan lands from the Duke of Argyll. That secret was safe, for the old duke would never let it be known that he'd been bested by a highland laird who'd found a vast treasure while the duke had searched futilely for it.

"Let us have no talk of Jacobites tonight," MacDuffie said, raising his glass and downing a full draught of whiskey.

The laird had already swallowed more than one man's share of spirits, and Lachann had noted from the first that the man did not have the look of a robust highlander. His complexion was sallow and his eyes lacked focus. Lachann could not help but wonder whether something ailed him.

Something besides too much whiskey.

"I wholly disagree with MacMillan," Macauley said. "The clans learned their lesson in '15 and will not be so quick to go to war again. . . ."

"Mayhap, but there is always the danger of raiders. Pirates," Lachann said. He turned to MacDuffie. "Laird, do I have the authority to begin training the men to repel such an attack—as we agreed in our correspondence?"

The old man shifted in his chair. "Aye," he said quietly.

Lachann breathed a sigh of relief and leaned back in his chair as Macauley took charge of the conversation. If MacDuffie had changed his mind, Lachann would have had to make a decision: take Kilgorra by force, or return to Braemore without accomplishing the goal that was so vital to his clan. He glanced at Duncan, who shot him a look of caution.

Aye. Best to keep his mouth shut now, just as Catrìona had been doing all through the meal. She had said naught to Lachann, but as Lachann looked across the table at her, she smiled and slid one finger down the length of her neckline.

He was certain 'twas meant as a flirtatious gesture, but he found her to be as interesting as the pitcher of ale on the table before him.

Lachann took a sip from his mug and noticed Macauley looking at him with utter loathing in his eyes, which he quickly masked. 'Twas clear he held naught but contempt for Lachann.

They were even, then.

Nay, Lachann had the advantage. MacDuffie would never allow his daughter to choose the man with less wealth and fewer resources.

At least, Lachann did not think so.

But then MacDuffie drank yet another glass of whiskey, and Lachann had to wonder at the man's sensibility. MacDuffie tried to refill his glass but found the bottle at his elbow empty. "Where is that damned wench, anyway?" he demanded, his words slightly slurred. "Call for more whiskey."

Catrìona got up from her chair beside Macauley and went to the top of the stairs, where Anna had nearly fallen awhile earlier under the weight of that absurdly weighted tray.

"Anna!" she called.

"What brings you to Kilgorra, MacMillan?" Macauley asked, and Lachann realized the laird must have said naught to him of Lachann's intentions.

He gave his old rival a hard glare. "I might ask the same of you, Macauley."

The other man laughed. "To be sure, I plan to . . . *help* Kilgorra open trade with the lowlands. And perhaps England and France."

Lachann glanced at Duncan, whose expression was carefully schooled to give no reaction at all. Lachann wondered if Macauley was serious, but he was not about to question the man now.

Anna emerged from the stairs with another whiskey bottle for the laird, as well as a tray of fruit and cheese. She kept her eyes down and served the table efficiently, picking up the pitcher of ale and refilling everyone's mug.

When she came to stand beside Lachann, he could not refrain from inhaling deeply of her scent, and he thought of the raspberries she'd brought him. They were the same color as her bonny lips.

Lachann quickly turned his attention to his intended bride. "I look forward to exploring your isle, Catrìona."

"Aye?" she replied. She pushed away from the table and came to Lachann's side, easing Anna away. She reached for the tray the maid had brought and pressed her breast against Lachann's shoulder as she moved.

Lachann realized he needed to generate some enthusiasm for the woman. "Will you be free on the morrow to ride with me?"

"No, she will not," Macauley interjected. He faced Catrìona squarely, with irritation. "You are spending the day with me, if you recall."

Catrìona looked away from Macauley and smiled down at Lachann. "I regret I cannot go with you on the morrow, Lachann," she said. "But the day after?"

Lachann felt Macauley's glare.

"Aye," he said.

"I do apologize, Lachann," Catrìona said sweetly, leaning into him. "If only I'd known . . ."

Damn all if he would apologize for arriving early after altering his plan to stop at Callachulain to visit his elderly uncle. He'd wanted no delays, for his purpose on Kilgorra was essential to the protection and safety of Braemore. Leave it to a Macauley to sabotage his intentions.

Lachann maintained a semblance of calm, remembering that Macauley had had some time to court the woman, so she knew him. The only questions were how well, and whether Lachann could supplant him.

At least Macauley did not seem to have started recruiting men for an army. Lachann had the advantage there.

"Laird MacDuffie, we saw no guards when we came into the harbor," Kieran said. "Is that because you were expecting us?"

"Kilgorra is a peaceful isle, " Macauley answered for MacDuffie. He kept his eyes upon Catrìona as she left Lachann's side and returned to her place at the table. "We have naught to fear."

We?

Fury simmered just beneath Lachann's surface, and his hands were oh so ready to draw his sword. But there had been no open warfare between the MacMillans and Macauleys since that final battle when Lachann had taken Ewan hostage. Matters had quieted, even after the debacle with Fiona, but naught had been settled.

And Macauley was ahead in the game of rivalry he was playing. Lachann knew how easily rumors spread in the highlands. He was certain Macauley must have gotten wind of his intentions to come to Kilgorra and wed Catrìona. The blighter had seen it as an opportunity to thwart Lachann while he bettered his lot.

Just as he'd done on Skye.

At least this time Lachann had no intimate connection to the bride. She was merely the means to an end.

Lachann eased his hand away from the hilt of his sword and turned his attention to Laird MacDuffie.

Was the man so well jaked that he had lost all influence over his daughter? Would he actually allow her to choose Macauley?

Anna clipped down a back staircase when she finished in the great hall, then stood in the shadowy corridor outside the kitchen with her back against the wall.

Her reaction to Lachann MacMillan was unwarranted and unwelcome. She would brace herself next time she needed to be in his presence, and somehow ignore the remarkable sensations that skittered through her when she stood near him.

She wondered if this was anything like the attraction Kyla had felt for Birk when he'd first begun coming 'round to court her. He'd been such a fine young man then, strong, but attentive and sweet. And when Kyla had fallen wildly in love with him, Anna had been envious of her friend. She'd thought perhaps she might like to fall in love, too. . . .

But no Kilgorran had affected her the way Birk had done with Kyla. And now that everyone on the isle knew how well that had turned out, Anna had concluded she was far better off keeping to herself. She would live out her life as Gudrun had done, content in her small cottage behind the castle gardens. 'Twas far safer.

But Anna couldn't avoid Lachann MacMillan entirely, for he'd moved into the keep and she had duties to perform near, and even inside, his bedchamber. She would just have to figure some way to make herself immune to his appeal.

Mayhap she would picture him as the troll in one of Gudrun's tales—the horrible creature that hid beneath the bridge as the billy goats tried to pass.

Anna snorted at the very idea.

Lachann MacMillan was anything but a troll, as her drumming heart attested.

"Anna? Is that ye back there?" Flora called out.

"Aye," Anna replied, stepping into the kitchen.

"We can finish up with all the doings in the great hall without ye," Flora said. "Go on down to Janet's and see about Kyla."

"Aye, soon. I'll just take this last tray up to them," Anna said in spite of herself.

"But—"

"'Twill not delay me much."

Anna took the tray before Flora could protest any further, but she stopped before she reached the top of the stairs. She paused, balancing the tray against the wall as she smoothed her apron and slid the few loose strands of her hair into her braid before entering the hall.

MacMillan looked right at her as she crested the top step. And he looked away just as quickly.

Ach, fine then. Anna wanted naught to do with him, either.

Chapter 8

Lachann avoided looking at Anna as she placed a tray of honeyed sweets on the table, but he was unlikely to forget the sight of her comely face.

"There's little point in wandering 'round the isle, MacMillan. Macauley can show you the distillery upon the morrow." Laird MacDuffie's words had begun to slur together. "'Tis far more interesting than the land."

"The distillery?" Lachann asked, surprised yet again. What did the distillery have to do with anything? Fine spirits were brewed there, but it made Kilgorra a target for raiders, who would take the whiskey if there was no fighting force to challenge them.

"Aye. The Kilgorra Distillery," MacDuffie said. "Cullen has taken a special interest in it."

"I appreciate the offer, Laird," Lachann said, choosing his words carefully, "but I had hoped to take the day to explore the land tomorrow."

What in hell was Macauley up to?

"Ach, 'tis all the same to me," MacDuffie said into his glass. Then he downed its contents. "Do what you will."

Aye. As soon as he explored the island, he was going to recruit men who wanted to train as warriors, in spite of the laird's belief in perpetual peace.

Lachann did not know how the man remained upright after so much whiskey. But then Anna's retreating form caught his eye, and the laird's tolerance for drink became no more than a passing thought.

Anna's face and form were as fair as any Lachann had ever seen, but naught was seductive about the lass. She did not make flirtatious eyes at him, nor give any coy smiles to invite his attention. The clothing she wore was hardly alluring, no different from the attire worn by the servants at Braemore Keep. She wore no beguiling jewels, nor was her hair arranged in some intricate fashion designed to draw a man's eye.

And yet—

"Our wee isle has little to boast of," Catrìona said, thankfully breaking into Lachann's musings. But her tone and expression indicated a surprising distaste for her island home. "We have fishermen who make the pier reek of rotting fish entrails, and the paltry farms scattered among the rocky hillsides are hardly worth your time."

"The only thing of value on Kilgorra is the distillery," Macauley added, and Catrìona gave him a warm smile. An encouraging smile.

"I'll take your word on that. For now," Lachann responded, mystified by their attitude. Was it possible they did not understand the vital importance of grain in the production of Kilgorra whiskey? And that the more widely known the whiskey became, the greater the necessity of armed men to protect it?

Ach, this conversation was making Lachann's head throb. He'd have left the table in disgust, but he knew he needed to remain with his hosts and be convivial. Macauley was as irritating as ever, and Catrìona— well, she was purely puzzling.

'Twas obvious she was partial toward Macauley, and yet she flirted with Lachann. . . .

Gesu, he hoped Catrìona did not intend to play games of her own.

Mayhap he could convince her to spend time with him after supper without Macauley's unwelcome presence. There, perhaps he could declare his intentions directly to her and ask for her answer.

He had had no illusions about her comeliness or lack thereof, but he'd hoped she would at the very least be biddable. Mayhap even glad to have a suitor of her own status to woo and wed her. Without Macauley's influence, 'twas entirely possible she would be more agreeable—

"Come back here, Anna," Catrìona said. "Build up

the fire, else Father will take a chill. And take that manky cat with you when you leave."

Lachann sensed some animosity from Catrìona toward Anna, but from what he had seen, the lass performed her duties well. He found no cause for complaint. On the contrary, she moved about almost silently on her bare feet, serving the table efficiently, without intruding.

Lachann remembered the passion he'd seen in her eyes during their earlier encounters on the pier and at the healer's cottage. He could easily imagine her fiery response if he should kiss her.

Gesu!

He took a large gulp of ale and pointedly turned his attention from the maid. What in hell was he thinking? Once he made Catrìona his bride, he would reside in the keep. Anna would continue to serve him and his wife.

He needed to keep that in mind.

Catrìona did not miss the quick appraising look of appreciation that crossed Lachann's face when his eyes alighted upon Anna, and the anger that always simmered just below her surface when Anna was near threatened to bubble over.

She should have drowned the wench when she'd had the chance years ago.

Anna had been worse than a thorn in Catrìona's side since the day she and her mother had arrived on Kilgorra. Catrìona had been on the verge of gaining some fatherly attention for a change when Sigrid and her wee brat had sailed into Kilgorra harbor, looking for a home.

That woman with her Norse speech and strange ways should have stayed at Kearvaig with her dead husband's family. 'Twas entirely unfair that the fair-haired wench—a foreigner, at that—should have snared Catrìona's father in marriage.

Ach, but she'd been a comely one. And Catrìona's father had been unable to resist her wiles. He'd allowed Sigrid to distract him from Catrìona's grief over the loss of her own beloved mother, and he'd taken Sigrid MacIver to his bed. He'd married her and then thrown his preference for the woman's fair daughter in Catrìona's face.

Catrìona had not cared one whit when the Norsewoman had died birthing her bairn. And she suspected that if the woman's son had not died at birth, then she might very well have been motivated to . . .

Well, her actions likely would have depended upon how much her father had doted upon the bairn—and ignored *her*.

She watched Anna kneel before the fireplace, arranging bricks of peat on the grate and lighting the fire. When she stood up to leave and faced the table to give a slight curtsey, Catrìona took great satisfaction in the smudge of filthy ashes on her cheek. *Not so perfect now, eh?*

Her stepsister deserved that degradation and more.

Once she was given her leave, Anna picked up that horrid feline she favored and disappeared down the steps to the kitchen. Mayhap Catrìona should see to it that the foul cat disappeared. 'Twould serve the wench right.

She turned to Lachann, wishing there was a way to avoid Cullen on the morrow. Because when she beckoned him next, she wanted him to be mad with lust. Ach, she doubted she would choose Cullen for her husband, for he had nowhere near the wealth of the MacMillans. But she could enjoy him now.

She caught his eye and nearly laughed aloud. He was so easy to tease, and knowing that his cock was becoming hard under his plaid was incredibly arousing.

He was an adequate bedmate, though not half as inventive as Eòsaph Drummond. And Eòsaph did not mind when Birk Ramsay joined them in the cave for some brazenly stimulating activities. She wished Birk had come to the chapel with Eòsaph that afternoon, then mayhap she would not have felt quite so needy right now.

She felt Cullen squirm beside her, and surreptitiously slid her hand under his plaid and onto his thigh. And then up.

He made a strangled sound, then coughed to cover it when she cupped his ballocks in her hand.

While Catrìona grasped Macauley's jewels, she observed Lachann MacMillan listening intently to her father, trying to make sense of his rambling discourse on the history of Kilgorra whiskey. And she smiled, thinking about the tryst she would have with Cullen upon the morrow in the locked office of the distillery, with Geordie Kincaid shuffling his papers just outside.

Anna felt naught but relief when there was no more to do besides scoop up the cat, Effie, and escape from her stepfather's great hall.

She'd heard Laird MacDuffie's rambling blather about the distillery, and it pleased her to note that Lachann MacMillan kept his own counsel for the most part.

She'd sensed his eyes upon her, and though his gaze had not exactly unnerved her, she'd felt a distinctly warming effect on her skin. Her face had heated, and the tips of her breasts had tightened so they were excruciatingly sensitive. She cuddled furry Effie tightly to her chest to make the sensation go away.

Her gaze had been inexorably drawn to MacMillan, and she could not help but notice the shadow of a beard on his square jaw. His dark hair curled slightly at his nape, and his big hand was curled in a deceptively innocent manner 'round his mug. Anna knew how potent those hands were, and not only from the way they'd dealt with Kyla and Birk. Even now, Anna could feel the energy of his touch, the leashed power that he wielded.

Ach, 'twas best to have gotten out of there. As hard as she tried to think of Lachann MacMillan as a troll, 'twas not possible.

"Would you care to see the rest of the keep, Lachann?" Catrìona asked.

"No," he replied. "I need to see where my men will be housed."

"Of course," Catrìona said.

"I'll go with you." Macauley pushed back from the table and made to accompany them.

"That will not be necessary, Cullen," Catrìona said pleasantly. "Besides, my father is ready to retire. You know how he's come to enjoy your assistance when he prepares for bed."

'Twas a victory for Lachann, but it felt quite small after watching Catrìona and Macauley sitting close together all through the meal.

The MacMillan men rose from their seats and followed Catrìona and Lachann from the hall. Lachann did not bother to look back at Macauley. He could feel the bastard's glare through his plaid.

They left the great hall and went through a passageway to a door that led to the back of the keep. They stepped outside into a wide bailey lined by trees.

"Did you see the barracks when you came through the castle gates?" Catrìona asked.

"We did," Lachann replied. "Near the armory, adjacent to the smithy."

The barracks were located at the edge of a wide courtyard, in view of the keep. As they approached the long stone building, Lachann noticed the blacksmith standing at the open door of the smithy with his arms folded across his chest. He was red-haired and slightly slack-jawed, but his eyes stayed on the MacMillan group as they passed.

Or mayhap 'twas Catrìona he watched. There was a dullness about his eyes, and Lachann wondered if the man would be able to fashion the weapons they were going to need. It seemed quite likely Lachann would have to bring in an armorer and a good gunsmith. He'd expected no less. But parts were always needed, and a good blacksmith was invaluable.

The smithy's attention shifted when Anna walked past him, carrying a load of linens in the opposite direction of the barracks with the black and white cat following her.

"How long has the armory been dormant?" Lachann asked Catrìona.

"Oh," she stopped to think. "It has been several years. Ten, at least."

"And your blacksmith?" he asked. "Do you know if he ever fashioned swords for your father?"

Catrìona shook her head. "I don't believe so. Mungo Ramsay is not the . . . well, he's not exactly the cleverest of men."

But he was large and strong, judging by his stance and the dense muscles in his arms. He watched Anna's progress across the courtyard unabashedly.

"Does he know why I'm here?" Lachann would have thought the man would come over and make himself known to the future laird.

Catrìona shrugged. "I'm not sure."

Lachann opened the door of the barracks and allowed Catrìona to step inside before him while the rest of the men waited outside. He lit a lamp near the door and looked at the row of beds that were ready for use.

"I hope it meets your men's needs."

"Aye. It appears more than adequate."

"Good," she said, though she appeared slightly put out. Mayhap because they'd not yet had a chance to be alone. Lachann could only hope that was so.

"You can let Graeme or Alex know if there is anything else you need," she said.

Chapter 9

'Twas past dark by the time Anna was able to leave the castle and go down to Janet's cottage for Kyla. She found her friend reclining on the pallet where she'd left her, feeding her bairn. A bowl of savory broth sat discarded beside her.

"How is she?" Anna asked Janet.

"Weak. Tired. Afeared."

The skin 'round Kyla's eye had turned an ugly purple, and there was a large, lumpy bruise welling up around the gash on her lip. Anna wished she could take her to Spirit Isle and soak her in the healing waters there, but her friend was in no shape to travel across the straits to get there. Nor was it likely she would be able to crawl through the narrow stone cave that tunneled through the mountain to the interior of the isle.

"Has she any broken bones?"

"Nay, but she's bruised all over," Janet replied. "He knocked her about pretty well this time."

Anna's concern flared to anger. "'Tis all I can do to keep from searching for the miserable beast and putting a bullet into his brain."

"Anna, no," Kyla gasped. Tears shimmered in her eyes.

"And why wouldn't I?" Anna demanded, unable to contain her anger. "No doubt the bleeter went back to the pub after his dunking and he's still so jaked he wouldn't recognize a pistol if I stuck it right between his eyes. What I wouldn't give to blow the clarty monster's—"

"Well, I do'na know where ye'd get a pistol, lass," Janet said, "but ye've no time for it now, anyway. Ye need to get Kyla away before the man comes to his senses and remembers where she is."

Anna blinked back her own tears, aware that Janet was right.

She crouched down before her friend. "Kyla, do you think you can walk up to the castle?"

"No, Anna," Kyla said quietly. "I must take Douglas and go home."

"Not tonight," Janet countered. "Not until someone talks some sense into your bloody husband."

"Or beats it into him."

"What?" Kyla whimpered.

Ach, Anna knew her friend had loved her husband

once, but how could she now—after all the beatings and the horrible, harsh words? "I've made Gudrun's cottage ready for you," she said, for there was no point in arguing with Kyla about Birk's worth. She was blinded by love, and there was no telling when she'd get her sight back. "Well, at least the bed is ready. I spared little time moving the old crates aside or doing anything more."

When she'd finished her chores at the keep, she'd hurried out to the wee thatched cottage where Gudrun had lived until her death ten years ago. 'Twas Flora who'd suggested the old croft, for no one ever used it these days except for storage, but it was habitable, if crowded with crates full of discards from the castle. "Birk doesn't know of it, so he won't find you tonight. You can sleep in peace . . . and heal."

Kyla gave her a dubious look. "What about his uncle? Mungo Ramsay will be about the castle grounds."

Aye, Mungo was a large, muscular man, well suited to doing any heavy work that was required within the castle walls. There was little smithing to do these days, and Anna did not know what to make of him. But he always kept his distance, rarely even speaking to her.

But he watched her, and he kept his eyes on Kyla whenever she came up. It was unnerving, but he'd never made a move to harm either of them. Anna suspected Mungo was one of Catrìona's conquests, but she did not care to give that distasteful thought too much attention.

"No one ever thinks about Gudrun's cottage. Not

since it's been closed up all these years." Anna took Douglas from Kyla's arms and patted his back. "Please, Kyla, don't argue."

The bairn gave out a loud belch. "Well now. That's a braw lad," Janet said.

"Anna . . ."

Anna ignored her friend's plaintive tone. "You'll be fine tonight up at the castle. Can you walk up there?" Anna would borrow a horse and cart if need be.

Kyla touched her injured lip and winced. "I'll try," she said, and Anna was relieved there would be no further discussion—and no tears—about going home to her nasty turnip of a husband.

Anna handed Douglas to Janet and helped Kyla to her feet. Kyla was unsteady at first, but she managed to walk to the door.

"Come on, then. Lean on me."

Kyla took Anna's arm, and Anna took Douglas from Janet. "I'll look in on you tomorrow, lass," Janet said. "And bring ye news of yer husband."

Kyla nodded. "Thank you, Janet. For everything."

'Twas a slow walk up to the castle, with Kyla leaning heavily upon Anna. Douglas fell asleep in Anna's arms, and when they finally reached the castle keep and skirted 'round to the side gardens and beyond, Anna could see that Kyla was spent.

"Only a few steps more," Anna said, urging her friend forward across the overgrown cobbled path to the cottage. 'Twas tucked away far from the keep, so no one would hear Douglas if he cried during the night.

Anna wanted to avoid Mungo Ramsay seeing them, and she didn't want young Glenna to know she'd brought Kyla to the castle. She feared neither of them could keep Kyla's whereabouts secret.

She pushed open the door to the cottage and slipped inside. Fortunately, there was just enough light from the open window for them to see the bed beyond the stacked crates, on the other side of the fireplace. Kyla lay down, and Anna put Douglas beside her, then knelt to build a fire.

"I put an extra blanket out for you, Ky."

"I cannot thank you enough for all you've done for me, Anna. But you know I must—"

"Let's not think about what you must do. Not now."

The fire flared to life, and Anna rested back on her heels. She thought of those early days after her mother's death, when she'd been left to fend for herself.

MacDuffie had been so drunk he hadn't even noticed Anna's absence, and there'd been no one but Gudrun to object when Catrìona had ejected Anna from the bedchamber she'd been given next to her mother's.

Back then, Kyla had been no more than an orphan herself, but she'd become Anna's anchor in her time of grief. They'd quickly become as close as sisters. "Do you remember when my mother died?" Anna asked.

Kyla nodded and brushed one of Douglas's russet

curls off his forehead. "We were alone, but for Gudrun. And she was grieving your mother, as well." She lay quietly for a moment. "Anna, if anything should happen to me, I want you to promise—"

"Naught will happen to you!" This was not the direction Anna had intended the conversation to go.

"But you know it could. You and I lost both our parents at a young age," Kyla said, laying her head down. "I just want the comfort of knowing you'll see to Douglas if—"

"You think Birk will allow it?" Anna retorted. She knew what Kyla wanted, and 'twas hardly realistic. "Just be sure to take no chances, Kyla. With anything."

'Twas clear Kyla knew she should fear that Birk would one day kill her. The thought of it made Anna's blood run cold, but she consoled herself with the knowledge that 'twould not happen tonight.

Ah. So much for the madness of love. 'Twas a state that served no one well.

Anna made sure Kyla was comfortable and Douglas sound asleep. "Go to sleep now, *min kjære venn.*"

The Norse term Gudrun had taught them brought a cautious smile to Kyla's injured mouth.

"I'll just run up to the kitchen and gather some supplies for us," Anna added, rising to her feet. She tucked the extra blanket 'round her friend, for 'twas damp and still chilly in the cottage. "I'll be back soon."

She left the cottage and closed the door tightly behind

her. No one would find Kyla there. No one would even think of looking for her at the cottage. Except Flora, and she was no threat to anyone beyond trying to over-feed them.

Anna walked through the dense brush toward the keep and turned 'round to make sure the smoke from the cottage's chimney was not too thick. Reassuring herself 'twas hardly visible, she turned back—

And crashed into something entirely unexpected.

She whirled 'round.

"Anna?" Lachann MacMillan stood directly in her path. He bowed slightly, and Anna pressed one hand to her breast as though it could slow her heart. "We seem to be meeting in odd places."

"What are you doing out here?" Anna blurted, care-ful not to turn 'round again or give any other clue about the cottage.

"I could ask the same of you," he said. He stood far too close for Anna's peace of mind. One step more and they would be touching.

Chapter 10

Every nerve in Lachann's body urged him to close the distance between himself and the lass. Her damaged voice and her fiercely flashing eyes were far more appealing than they ought to have been. She was possessed of a fiery innocence that drew him like a moth to flame.

"I am a servant here, sir," she said firmly, gesturing vaguely toward the keep. "My tasks take me all over the castle grounds."

"Ach, aye?" He sensed she was not being entirely forthright, and it occurred to him there was a good chance she'd brought her injured friend to the castle and hidden her nearby. Without permission. Not that she needed to worry that he would divulge her hiding place to anyone.

"Of course," she said. "Now, if you'll excuse me, I have much to do before I can retire for the night."

Without thinking, he stopped her with a light grasp of her arm. He found himself stepping closer, breathing in her scent, a heady combination of kitchen spices and the sea. Her breath was warm on his neck, and Lachann tipped his head down, his mouth so close to hers, his body reacting like a satyr in the presence of a nymph. He wanted to taste her, wanted to—

Gesu, he must be mad. He did not take advantage of servants, especially when he was about to betroth himself to the mistress here.

He drew back, releasing her. Anna stood still for a moment, and Lachann had to clench his hands at his sides to keep from reaching for her again, for her chest rose in quick breaths, a clear sign her reaction was as potent as his own.

A complete diversion was necessary.

"Will she be safe back here?" he asked, tipping his head in the direction from which Anna had come. "Her husband doesn't know of this place?"

She looked sharply at him. "I— N-no. No one will think of it."

"Good."

She started past him, and Lachann watched as she returned to the keep, her thick plait of pale golden hair swinging seductively down her back.

He shook his head as though to clear away his momentary lunacy and followed her toward the keep. He had no intention of risking his heart again—and he was quite certain there was no chance of that with Catrìona.

There was no chance with Anna, either, for he would not allow any such thing to happen.

Still, 'twas no hardship to walk behind the lass, and he enjoyed the fetchingly ingenuous sway of her hips as she walked. And if his presence made her the least bit uncomfortable, she did not show it. There was an air of confidence about her that he'd sensed in only a few other women—in his grandmother, his sister, and Dugan's wife.

She pointedly ignored him behind her, and when they reached the keep, she disappeared down a few steps to what Lachann supposed must be the kitchens. He paused for a moment, then started for the main road that led down to the pier; Duncan was waiting for him near the gate.

They started walking together, down the path toward the pier. "Where is Kieran?" Lachann asked. 'Twas a simple question in a situation that was not simple at all.

"He's staying to see what Macauley has to say if he ever comes out of MacDuffie's room."

"Better him than me," Lachann retorted. "I've been this close to running him through ever since we got here."

"I could see it, Lachann. You held your temper very well. We all did."

"Mayhap. But I make no promises for future encounters." Nor was he sure about further encounters with the serving maid, Anna. She was so far off-limits the thought of her should not even cross his mind. But her smudged face and the intense way she cared for her friend would not leave him.

It did not take long for the two men to reach the expansive wooden pier that jutted into the water. "The harbor is as much a weakness as an advantage to the isle," Lachann said, welcoming a logistical discussion with Duncan. "'Tis deep enough for ships to sail right in and men to disembark on the pier."

"Aye," Duncan remarked. "We'll need to secure these waters and set up patrols to watch for ships passing south."

Lachann nodded. 'Twas imperative that he prevent raiders from sailing down Loch Ewe to Braemore as they'd done before. Securing these waters was the best way to do so. He stood looking out at the black waters below.

If he were at home, he would dive into the loch and swim until exhaustion drove all his questions—and bonny Anna—from his mind.

"'Tis nothing like Loch Maree, is it?" Duncan said.

Lachann shook his head. And Kilgorra was nothing like Braemore.

There was much to do here, not the least of which was to figure out what Cullen Macauley intended to do. If he had an interest in the distillery, he must also be interested in the grain production on the isle. Lachann did not believe Macauley was as foolish as Catrìona and her sire in thinking the farmland was inconsequential. A good barley crop was essential for making whiskey.

"What was it Macauley said about trade?" Duncan asked. "He intends to open up commerce with the lowlands?"

Lachann nodded.

"What of his ties with Skye?"

Lachann shrugged and made a mental note to follow up on that question. Perhaps Macauley intended to come to some agreement on trade between Skye and Kilgorra—crops or livestock from Skye for Kilgorra's whiskey.

Aye, expanding trade was part of Lachann's plan as well, though he intended to secure the island and begin training an army first.

His thoughts turned to Braemore. Already, he missed his home, missed his brothers and sister. Of course he'd been away from Braemore before. He was thirty years old and had fought in two wars. He'd gone with Dugan on a wild search for a hidden treasure. And found one.

But this was different. This was meant to be permanent.

Lachann had not expected his undertaking on Kilgorra to be easy or simple. But neither had he planned on the reality of a wife who failed to stir his blood and a father-in-law who was overly fond of his whiskey. He surely hadn't planned on having to compete once

again with a Macauley for the hand of the woman he
. . . Well, at least he did not love Catrìona. He would
never love anyone the way he'd loved Fiona.

But he'd had a distinct impression of some subtle alliance between Macauley and Catrìona. A bond that
had had a chance to develop before Lachann's arrival
on Kilgorra.

"We should have had the agreement with MacDuffie
carved in stone and sealed in blood before we came to
Kilgorra," Lachann said.

"Aye. Then this absurd competition with Macauley
would be for naught. You could kick the bastard out on
his arse, take Catrìona to the kirk, and there'd be no
more to say of it."

"I might just do that anyway."

Lachann looked toward the village, tucked into the
rocky cliffs that towered above it. There were flickering
lights in some of the cottages, and he saw a few fires
burning outside. The shops were all dark and quiet,
but he heard the faint strains of fiddle music and a few
voices coming from the public house. A dog barked.
Another one answered.

Lachann wouldn't have minded the opportunity to
take a drink with the men he would soon command,
but there was a good possibility he'd encounter the fool
he'd thrown into the sea. And he doubted the man—
and possibly his friends—would be of a favorable dis-
position toward him.

Not that it would matter in the least once he was in charge.

He looked past the public house to the whitewashed distillery looming in the distance. Kilgorra whiskey was an asset, to be sure. But the distillery needed no outside assistance to thrive—certainly not from the likes of Cullen Macauley—for it had been producing fine spirits long before Macauley's arrival.

Lachann would leave it for now. Once he trained a fighting force and became laird, he might see about expanding Kilgorra's whiskey production and increasing the trade. Mayhap to the Americas.

"What is your plan for the morrow, Lachann?"

"You and Kieran—ride to the southern end of the isle and talk to the men on the farms," Lachann replied. "See how many there are and how they are usually occupied. With fishing? Farming? Making whiskey? Sitting on their arses in the public house all day . . . ?"

"Which is what MacDuffie would be doing if he were not laird, eh?"

Lachann nodded. "By the look of it, the isle's liquid spirits are a mite too dear to the old man's heart. But 'tis no matter. I do not need his assistance to put my plans into place."

Lachann intended to establish a rotating schedule for training the island men, much the same way his grandfather had done at Braemore. It made sense to leave some of the men to tend their farms or look after their nets while the others trained with Lachann and the rest of the Braemore men.

"You need his daughter, though."

As they stood on the pier, the moon came out from behind the clouds. Lachann turned to look out at the Minch and saw the dark shadow of a small isle that lay northeast of Kilgorra. He'd noticed it earlier, when the *Glencoe Lass* had arrived. But 'twas of little interest to him now, for there did not seem to be a harbor out there or any place to land an army.

Still, he would visit the place one day soon, just to be sure.

"Duncan," he said, "send Stuart and Rob Cameron to Skye on the *Glencoe Lass,* and have them look into the reason for Macauley's departure—or exile, as the case may be."

Duncan nodded. "Aye."

Lachann assumed the Cameron brothers would also discover what had happened to Fiona.

Though he still wasn't quite sure he wanted to know.

Anna could not think about what had just happened on the path to the keep. Lachann MacMillan had nearly kissed her.

Herregud! If he had, she would have kissed him back.

He created a strange hunger in her—a sensation of

need that no meal could satisfy. She pressed a hand to her stomach and took a deep breath.

Aye. She was steady now. 'Twas all so absurd, allowing herself to be drawn to the man. Surely 'twas only because of his assistance with Kyla and later with Birk that she felt so deeply attracted. For no one had ever provided such help to her before. The protection her stepfather gave was nominal at best, and Anna had needed to fend for herself entirely ever since Gudrun's death.

Anna shook her head to clear her thoughts. She'd sensed a kindness in Lachann MacMillan, that was all. And such kindness appealed to her.

Satisfied there was nothing more to it, Anna filled a pitcher of water and collected some thick cloths to use as nappies for Douglas before going back to the cottage. She made her way to the garden path and had to quash a vague sense of disappointment that she did not encounter Lachann MacMillan again.

Not that she actually wanted to see him. But 'twould be interesting to . . . to . . .

Ach, she felt quite confused. The man had naught to do with her, nor she with him. What he made her feel was—well, 'twas unlike anything she'd ever felt before, with any other man. But of course, she'd never met anyone like Lachann MacMillan on Kilgorra.

Anna hurried to the cottage, and when she entered, she found both Kyla and her bairn sound asleep. She made her own bed on the floor near the fire and lay down, unwilling to leave her friend on her own for the night while she was so badly injured.

She felt restless as she lay on her pallet, and she distracted herself by watching the shadows on the ceiling and recalling the many hours she and Kyla had spent there with Gudrun. She felt relieved to know that Kyla had never taken Birk there. At least, not that Anna knew of.

No. Kyla would never have brought him here. This was the private place they had shared with Gudrun only. Gudrun had taught both of them to weave and sew in this very room, even as she'd told old Norse tales and instructed them in the rudiments of her language.

The fire crackled loudly and Anna turned over, missing Gudrun, wishing she'd learned more from her about her mother's family. As it was, Anna knew very little—only that Sigrid had been sent from her homeland to wed the foreign laird who'd been Anna's father.

Gudrun said her mother had come to love the man she'd married and had sorely grieved for Laird Kearvaig when he'd died. And when Sigrid had passed away delivering MacDuffie's child, he'd become despondent.

Aye, she scoffed. Marriage was a wondrous thing.

She looked over at Kyla and wondered what would happen with Birk. Kyla had wed him thinking 'twould be so much better than living in Kilgorra Keep and serving the laird and his daughter.

As everyone on Kilgorra knew, Kyla had been wrong.

Anna wished there was something she could do for her friend beyond rescuing her every time Birk got drunk and lit into her. Tomorrow or the day after, when Birk had finished his drinking bout, his head would be splitting, and he would be all apologies and regret.

For that was how it always went. From vicious drunkenness to pitiful repentance. 'Twas not how marriage should be, though any illusions Anna had ever had about the institution had long since died. And yet . . .

A new, intensely warm and shivery feeling came over Anna when she thought again of Lachann, though this time it had naught to do with his handling of Birk.

What if he *had* kissed her? The very idea caused her to breathe a little shallower.

Is this what happened when a woman lay with a man? Did her body yearn for his touch, his caress? Anna tried to think of something else, anything to divert her attention from the man's incredible appeal. She did not want this, did not want to feel aroused by MacMillan or any other man.

Yet her heart warmed when she thought of how quickly he'd reacted to Kyla's distress on the pier, and his masterful dealings with Birk at Janet's cottage. Birk was not a small man, yet MacMillan had pulled him off her and lifted him to his shoulder while Anna had lain on the floor, looking up at his tightly muscled legs with his plaid swirling about his knees.

She'd never seen a more sensual sight.

'Twas something Catrìona would soon have the right to appreciate at her leisure.

Anna shuddered at the thought of Catrìona ogling those mighty limbs and, for a moment, wished her stepsister would choose Macauley instead.

But that would be the worst thing possible for Kilgorra. After the devastating pirate raid that occurred last summer, the islanders realized they needed a strong leader. They needed to be able to defend the isle against raiders. But they did not want Cullen Macauley to take the laird's place.

It all rested upon Catrìona.

Anna had never understood Catrìona. They were supposed to have been sisters. Catrìona was six years older than Anna and knew what it was to lose her own mother. She should have understood Anna's grief. She should have helped her through it.

But she'd taken perverse delight in tormenting Anna in every possible way, from intentionally burning her arm with a hot ember when no one had been looking, to pushing her out of a small curragh when Catrìona had received permission to row her wee sister 'round the harbor.

The fishing boats just happened to have been returning at the time, and someone had seen Anna flailing about in the water. They'd fished her out of the frigid sea, and of course Catrìona had blamed Anna's clumsiness for the "accident."

Anna had not been able to contradict Catrìona's version of what had happened, but to this day, she had a healthy respect for—mayhap 'twas more a fear of—the open sea. Gudrun had helped her to master her fear to some extent, but not enough for Anna to consider taking her curragh 'round Scotland's coast and trying to sail to the Norse lands.

Anna had grown up, and so had Catrìona, whose second greatest delight seemed to be ordering the servants about.

Her first pleasure was trysting with the occasional sailor who came to the isle to trade, and a few foolish island men like Eòsaph Drummond. The thought of Catrìona taking her pleasure in Lachann MacMillan's bed turned Anna's stomach.

Wee Douglas whimpered softly next to Kyla, and Anna quickly went to the bed and picked him up to keep him from waking his mother. 'Twas pointless to dwell on Catrìona's marital choice. Anna had naught to say about it.

"Ach, my bonny lad," she whispered as she settled the bairn next to her on her own blankets. "Can you not let your poor mam sleep just a bit?" Anna did not think the bairn was hungry, for Kyla had fed him not long ago. 'Twas likely he was just restless and out of sorts in the unfamiliar cottage.

Douglas smiled and cooed, batting his wee hands at the air. Anna used to think she'd like a few bairns of her own, but she knew better now. 'Twould take a man to accomplish that, and she knew of no marriage that had either lasted or been happy.

The last thing Anna wanted was a husband. Her heart's desire was to leave Kilgorra—leave the isle that had been her prison home these past eighteen years—and find her mother's family. If only she had the wherewithal to leave, she would go in a minute.

But first she would have to convince Kyla to come with her.

Chapter 11

In the predawn light the next morn, Lachann allowed himself to imagine he could see Braemore from the window of his bedchamber. He knew 'twas only a fleeting fancy, but he also knew that Braemore lay to the southwest. Exactly the exposure of his window.

He turned away and pulled on his clothes. Kilgorra would be his home, and he would learn to love it as he'd loved Braemore. He would develop friendships here as deep and as full as those he'd enjoyed within his own clan.

And there was no reason his family and friends could not visit the island. If they were to be allies, Lachann would want his brothers to become familiar with the place.

Sometime during the night, between his moments of restless sleep, Lachann had decided he could win Catrìona from whatever influence Macauley had over her. 'Twas only a matter of being pleasant with her. More pleasant than Macauley.

Anyone with an ounce of sense would know she ought to be more interested in the suitor who had already promised a significant bride price for her.

Mayhap her attention to Macauley was merely a strategy to make Lachann desire her more. Lachann could play her game, but he preferred a more straightforward approach. In all things.

The sun's rays were just beginning to cast their light across the white peaks in the sea far below his window, so Lachann decided 'twas not too early to go down to the great hall in search of his future bride. He met no one in the gallery, and in the great hall he saw the last person he ought to feel any interest in.

Anna knelt before the large fireplace near the dining table, sweeping out the ashes from last night's fire. As she stood, she startled at the sight of him.

"Ach! I did not hear you come in."

"I did not realize my steps were so light," he said. "You appeared to be lost in thought."

A streak of dark gray ash graced her chin, and Lachann resisted the urge to move closer and rub it away with his thumb. Her shapely brows dipped over her blue-green eyes. "Aye. I was thinking of my friend, Kyla . . ."

"Her husband found—?"

"Ach, no," Anna replied, and her frown of worry was as pitiful as any he'd ever seen.

He would have liked naught but to smooth it away. With his lips.

"I made sure she stayed hidden away from him because I know what he would do."

Lachann reminded himself 'twas none of his concern. Nor was the hint of a dimple that appeared in the lass's cheek every time she spoke.

He glanced toward the staircase. "Has Laird MacDuffie come down yet?"

"Not yet," she replied. "The laird and his daughter are not early risers. And he has been suffering frequent headaches lately. If you care to break your fast, our cook will be pleased to—"

"Simple fare will do." Lachann did not doubt the old man had been having headaches. With the amount of whiskey he consumed, who wouldn't?

Anna started for the stairs that led to the kitchen, and Lachann followed. "Flora always has porridge ready for the servants. If you don't mind that, I'll bring a bowl to you."

"Aye, porridge will do, but I'll just take it in the kitchen," he said. He didn't think Duncan would be happy about him going down to eat with the servants, but Lachann had never been one to stand on ceremony.

And when he became laird, there were going to be numerous changes. The household might as well become accustomed to his ways now.

Lachann followed Anna down the stone steps and

considered the inefficient design of the keep. 'Twas archaic. The kitchen should be much closer to the hall and on the same level at least. Else the servants—like Anna—had to struggle with heavy trays as they made the climb up to the hall.

At least the kitchen was large and well appointed.

The cook—Flora?—was an auburn-haired woman at least a decade older than Lachann, and she gave him a look of surprise when he ducked under the lintel and entered her domain. "Be at ease, woman."

"Anna?" she whispered anxiously, her cheeks blushing madly.

Anna laughed, and a tightness between Lachann's shoulder blades eased slightly. He had not even realized the spot was so taut. "Our guest has come for a bowl of your famous porridge, Flora."

"Famous, hmmpf!" Flora scoffed. She stood at her table looking unsure. "Only porridge, Laird?"

"Aye," he said simply, though he was not yet laird. 'Twas a struggle to keep his eyes from following Anna as she moved on bare feet about the kitchen. She poured milk into a saucer, and when she set it on the floor by the door, the black and white cat came running silently to it.

Lachann found himself captivated by the sight of Anna's fingers sliding into the wee beast's fur, petting her while the cat purred loud enough to be heard all through the kitchen.

He swallowed thickly and turned to Flora, who took a bowl from a cupboard and spooned some of the hot, thick mash into it. She glanced in Anna's direction, but the younger woman had moved on and was busy collecting water into her bucket from the kitchen cistern. Flora wiped her hands on her apron, then took the bowl and handed it to Lachann hesitatingly.

"Thank you."

"Wait," Anna said, putting down her bucket. She took the bowl from Lachann's hand and ducked down to a low cupboard near the stove. She took out two small bags, then sprinkled some of their contents onto his breakfast. She returned the bowl to him with the hint of a smile in her eyes.

Lachann looked into it. "What did you add?"

"A few spices. Taste it and see if you like it," she said. She picked up her full bucket and disappeared up the stairs.

Lachann must have stood watching overlong, for it wasn't until Flora spoke to him that he realized he'd been staring. "Sir?" she asked. "Would you care for tea as well?"

He declined on his way to the door, where he stepped outside into the chilly morning sunlight. The waves were crashing upon the rocks below, and the sound was both invigorating and disquieting.

Lachann knew something of ships and the open sea, for he'd gone years ago with his cousin Iain MacQuarry on his trading runs to and from Ireland. Iain's crew had been well trained and well armed in case of troubles.

Pirates had come, but only once during Lachann's single season with his cousin. A pirate ship from the outer isles had attacked MacQuarry, who'd refused to yield to the rogues' demands. There'd been a vicious battle, but Lachann's cousin had prevailed because of some heavy guns and a well-trained crew.

Lachann intended to train the Kilgorrans in much the same way. If all went well, he would order another brig like the *Glencoe Lass* to be built for the purpose of guarding the isle's seaways.

But too much rested upon Catrìona's whim. Lachann did not appreciate having come this distance only to find his intended bride being wooed by a Macauley. He would set matters right as soon as he got a feel for the isle and began recruiting its men.

He walked 'round to the garden and sat down in a sunny spot, where he took his first taste of the porridge. 'Twas far more flavorful than what was served at Braemore, and he appreciated the additions Anna had made.

He also appreciated the gentle movement of her body as she'd worked efficiently in the kitchen, then hastened up the stairs to the great hall. He might have sworn off beautiful women after Fiona, but he was not unaffected by the sight of one.

'Twas clear Anna was more than just a bonny parcel. It had been quite obvious to Lachann that the collapse of her friend on the pier had taken her completely by surprise. In spite of that, she'd reacted swiftly and capably, acting with confidence in her every move.

Lachann hardened his heart. Determined to keep his thoughts focused and far from the kind of trouble the comely maid would bring him, he considered what to do. Demand that MacDuffie banish Macauley from the isle?

Nay. His pride would not allow it. Lachann was going to vanquish Macauley this time in his own way. He would marry Catrìona and become laird of his own realm. No man would take that from him.

Lachann heard a footstep behind him at the same time as a most unwelcome voice rose above the crashing waves below.

Lachann's stomach clenched when he turned and saw his adversary approaching.

"You're up and about early, MacMillan," Macauley said.

Lachann continued eating, as though Macauley's presence had no effect whatsoever. "What are you doing here, Macauley?"

"Waiting for the cook to prepare a decent breakfast for me."

Lachann ground his teeth. He'd just as soon take his dirk to the man's throat as sit there and look at him. "You are more a fool than I'd thought, Macauley," he said. "What are you doing on Kilgorra?"

Chapter 12

Anna did not know what she could possibly have been thinking, yattering at Lachann MacMillan in the great hall and again in Flora's kitchen. Her mind had been full of thoughts of him when he'd come upon her so quietly in the hall, and she hoped she'd adequately covered her inappropriate musings by speaking of Kyla.

And then she'd given special attention to his porridge. Her behavior had been perilously close to flirtatious.

Never before had she done such a thing, and she had no intention of repeating it. Lachann MacMillan had naught to do with her, and the sooner he married Catriona, the better 'twould be.

She hurried down to the pier with her basket of provisions, enough to last for several days on the isle. Kyla would be safe there for as long as Anna could keep her there. Birk would not dare come for her, as he might do at the castle. He was terrified of the *sluagh dubh,* and Anna knew Kyla had never corrected his misconception about the wicked spirit.

She heard children's voices as she headed back up toward the castle. Among the trees at the beginning of the path, she discovered Angus MacLaren battling his young cohort, Robbie Kincaid, using wooden swords. The young castle maid, Glenna, looked on in awe of their prowess, adding to each lad's bravado.

Anna laughed. "Shouldn't you be up at the castle by now, Angus?"

"We're goin', Anna!" Angus shouted with a dramatic flourish of his weapon. "But first, I must defeat my enemy and run him through!"

"Ah! I thought Robbie Kincaid was your friend!"

"Nay!" Angus growled. "He is a pirate from Lewis who's come to steal our whiskey!"

Glenna frowned. "I thought ye were fightin' fer my honor, Angus MacLaren!"

Angus lowered his sword and turned to gape at Glenna. "Yer *what*?"

Robbie took advantage of the moment and slid his own sword between Angus's arm and chest, "killing" him. "Ye know better than t' turn yer back on yer enemy, Angus!"

"**W**hat am *I* doing here?" Macauley's tone was flippant. "Same as you, I imagine, MacMillan."

"Aye?" Lachann stood and faced his rival, but he forced himself to relax. "Looking for yet another wife? Did you think this time you wouldn't have to steal her?"

Macauley bristled. "Fiona MacDonald came to me willingly—"

"What happened to her, Macauley?" Lachann growled.

Macauley put his hands on his hips and spoke in an offhanded manner. "She sickened and died." There wasn't a trace of sorrow or regret on his face.

Gesu, but he was callous. "Died of what?"

"She was *my* wife, MacMillan," he said, "and a private matter. So 'tis not your concern."

Lachann's dirk was strapped to his calf. At this distance he could draw it and throw it, skewering Macauley where he stood. And yet the heat of emotion no longer drove him.

He started to leave, but stopped dead still at Macauley's next words. "'Tis said the MacMillans have become the wealthiest clan in the northwest."

Lachann turned to face him. "So now the Macauleys have taken to listening to rumors?"

"Only the important ones."

'Twas disturbing to know that his family's enemy had been keeping track of MacMillan fortunes. That knowledge reinforced Lachann's suspicion that Cullen had learned of his plans to wed Catrìona and take control of the island.

And that was the reason the bastard had come.

"Here is an important one, and not a rumor, either," Lachann said as he walked back to stand two paces from Macauley. "If you interfere with my plans here, I will kill you."

Macauley's insouciant expression faded slightly at the threat, but he said naught as Lachann took his leave and headed for the stable. While he meant what he said, Lachann wasn't one to waste time with useless talk, and the encounter with Macauley had not only been useless, it had left Lachann with a sour taste.

He had much to accomplish, and he assumed Duncan and Kieran had already left the castle for the southern coast. Deciding 'twas time he followed his own orders and visited the farms in the highlands south of the village, he started for the stable but stopped when he saw Anna and her injured friend slowly making their way toward the castle gate.

Anna had washed her face clean, and she carried her friend's bairn in her arms, along with a heavy satchel slung over her shoulder. The friend appeared none too steady on her bare feet, but Anna led the way, step by step. Mayhap she was taking the lass home.

Which might well be disastrous.

Lachann did not—could not—allow his misgivings

to sidetrack him. Besides, he was in a foul mood and did not care to impose it upon anyone. He needed a great deal more information about the isle before firming up his plans and speaking to Laird MacDuffie about what he intended to do.

"Can you make it down the hill, Kyla?" Anna asked her friend. All she wanted was to get Kyla to Spirit Isle. There, she and Douglas could stay for a couple of days and not have to worry about Birk.

And mayhap when they were finally over there, Anna could stop ruminating on Lachann MacMillan and the shivery sensations he elicited with his touch. Or the welling in her chest when she recalled how close his lips had come to touching hers.

She needed to remember he was going to be her laird, and nothing more.

"Aye, I can walk," Kyla replied. "Birk didn't cripple me."

"No, thank the Lord."

"But I should go home."

"No. Not yet." They both knew Birk would not be sober for a few days, and he was a danger to Kyla while he was drunk.

'Twas clear that something had to be done about him, but to date, his father had been able to do naught, and pleas for assistance from the laird had gone unanswered. Laird MacDuffie had taken to sleeping at all hours of the day and leaving the management of his household to his daughter. He took no interest in the affairs of the village, and there was no other Kilgorra man who would intervene. They all believed 'twas up to a husband to discipline his wife however he saw fit.

Anna feared Birk would kill Kyla one day, for his outbursts of temper seemed to grow worse by the month. One day, he would knock her down a flight of stairs or into the sea. . . .

There had to be something Anna could do. She just had not thought of it yet. "The birlinns will be out already." Though Birk was not likely to be among the fishermen. "We ought to be able to get to the isle without anyone knowing we're gone."

"Anna . . ."

"I wish you would not argue with me about leaving."

"I fear 'twill only make Birk angrier if he cannot find me for days."

Anna swallowed hard. *This* was why she would never marry. She knew of no man she would ever trust to have such power over her—power to beat her whenever he felt the urge. The power to dictate where she would go and with whom. The very thought of being trapped the way Kyla was made her shudder.

But then there was the sweet bairn in her arms—and Anna would never have a child of her own. It caused an ache that she quickly tamped away.

"You must decide, then," Anna said, frustrated with her friend. "Come to the isle with me, or go home to Birk."

"Anna, one day someone is going to figure out that there's more to Spirit Island than they ever thought."

"Even if they did, do you really think they would risk an encounter with the *sluagh dubh* to find out?" Anna asked, confident that the long-standing tales of the horrible, restless spirit would keep every Kilgorran away.

Years ago, one of the Kincaids had gone to the isle and something had happened to him. He'd come back a beaten-up wreck, blathering about a malevolent spirit that had tormented him within an inch of his life. Anna suspected the man had always been a wee bit cracked in the head, for there was no horrible spirit on the island.

Or perhaps someone had pulled a prank on him.

Nevertheless, the superstitious islanders believed Anna and Kyla had learned how to placate the imaginary wraith and keep it from coming to the main isle, so they were never discouraged from going there.

"If you want to go home, I'll walk you up to your cottage," Anna said, though it hurt to say it. "Mayhap Birk will be contrite when next he sees you. He usually is."

As they walked through the castle bailey, they heard Mungo's hammer in the blacksmith's shop, so they circled 'round behind the building and left through the castle gate.

"I do not like the way Mungo watches me with Douglas," Kyla said once they'd reached the path. "'Tis as though . . ." She shook her head.

"What?"

"Sometimes I think he would take Douglas from me. Mayhap harm him."

Anna did not know everything Mungo was capable of, but she did not think he would have any interest in a bairn—even if 'twas his nephew's child. He was far more interested in watching Catrìona and doing her bidding, even when she ordered him to discipline the castle children.

She shuddered at the thought of it. "Come on. Let's get as far away as possible."

They'd walked less than halfway down to the pier when a single horse approached from the castle. Anna knew who it would be. Her heart gave a little trill of anticipation in her chest, but when she looked up, Lachann MacMillan merely slowed his horse slightly when he reached them.

Lachann was sorely tempted to stop and offer his assistance to Anna and her friend, but he heard Duncan's voice in his head quite clearly, reminding him that the lass was a servant in the house he would soon rule. Her problems were not his, and if he made them so, he could very well alienate Laird MacDuffie and his daughter.

In spite of Duncan's admonitions, Lachann stopped and dismounted.

"I'll take that for you." He took the satchel from Anna's shoulder and put his arm 'round Kyla's waist to assist her down the path.

Duncan and his advice could go hang. 'Twas not in Lachann's nature to let a woman in this condition struggle on without assistance. He would have lifted her onto his horse, but he feared hurting her even more.

"Where are you going?" he asked Anna. "Shouldn't you stay where—"

"Just down to the pier. Kyla will be safe."

"On a boat?"

Anna hesitated before answering. "No. I'll take her to our island."

Chapter 13

"**Y**our island?" Lachann asked. "You're referring to the small isle that lies beyond the straits?"

"Aye."

"'Tis habitable?" It appeared to Lachann as a mass of rock and nothing more.

"Barely," Anna answered. "But Kyla will be safe once we're there."

Kyla stumbled and Lachann lifted her into his arms. "Birk won't come for me on the isle."

Lachann winced at the sight of her bruised face. "Where is he now?"

"I don't know."

And Lachann had too much to do today to spend time trying to find him. If both women felt they would be safe on the isle, then so be it. He helped Kyla to the edge of the pier, where he'd caught her the previous day, and left Anna to help her into a small curragh. She stepped in and he handed her the satchel.

"Thank you."

Lachann gave her a nod, then stood watching as they settled into the boat and Anna cast off. As much as he might doubt their strategy for keeping Kyla safe, they had been dealing with her husband far longer than he had.

Anna handled the boat expertly, navigating 'round the other boats at the pier until they were in the open water. After a moment, she looked back at him.

Their eyes met, and when she smiled, he realized he'd stood there overlong. 'Twas time he went about his own business.

His horse had followed him to the pier, so he mounted and rode into the hills, up beyond the village. From the high peak that rose above the village, he could see much of Kilgorra's coast and the sea. He looked for Anna and saw that she'd already rowed a good distance.

He rode up to a large cottage at the edge of a vast field of barley. As he approached, he saw an old woman carrying a basket of laundry to the side of the house where stout drying ropes had been hung. She looked up at him. "Ye're the Braemore lad?"

"Aye," Lachann replied, glad to have his thoughts diverted from Anna MacIver. "Though 'tis been some time since I was called a lad."

"When ye're my age, everyone is but a lad or a lass," she said. "Ye look as though ye could use a draught of cool water."

'Twas true. The sun had fully risen, but heavy clouds were gathering just north of the isle. Lachann dismounted as three young men stepped out of the croft. One led the way while the other two tied their belts 'round the plaid at their waists. The woman put the basket down next to her washing tub.

"Good morn to ye," said the first of the men, extending his hand. "I'm Boyd MacPherson. These are my brothers, Tavish and Rob. That's our granny, Isobel MacRae."

Lachann gave a nod of acknowledgement as he shook the men's hands. "Lachann MacMillan. You've a bonny farm." He took the ladle of fresh water handed to him by the old woman. "You grow barley for the distillery?"

"Aye," Boyd said. "We provide more barley than any other farm on the isle."

Their prosperity gave these men good reason for learning to defend their land, though that was not so much Lachann's concern at the moment. First, he wanted to see to it that Kilgorra was capable of blocking the sea lanes to his home on Loch Maree.

"I remember you, MacMillan," Boyd said. "From Perth, 1715."

Lachann looked up. "You were there?"

"Aye," he replied. "Your brother Dugan was wounded on patrol when he came upon some of Argyll's men. He was outnumbered but put up a good fight."

"Aye," Lachann said, cringing at the memory. "'Twas only because my cousin Duncan went looking for him that he survived."

"Aye. I remember the day," Boyd said. "Just a handful of us went from Kilgorra with my uncle to fight for King Jamie."

"'Twas a long time ago," Lachann remarked, heartened to know there were at least a few men on the isle who knew how to do more than throw a net or follow a plow. He took in all the brothers at a glance. "So you've fighting skills?"

"Aye. We all have." Boyd gestured toward his brothers. "We followed our uncle Iain MacRae to Castletown. And on to Sheriffmuir."

Where Lachann knew a battle had been fought.

"I plan to raise an army here on Kilgorra," Lachann said.

"Aye, we've heard talk of it," MacPherson said, looking across to his grandmother, who nodded.

"'Tis about time," Tavish said. "Last summer, a band of pirates led by Blackburn MacGaurie raided and made away with thirty barrels of Kilgorra whiskey."

'Twas what Lachann had expected. And yet Cullen Macauley had not heard of the raid. Likely he had not bothered to ask, and no one had told him. He was well and truly focused on the distillery, as though he could make his fortune there without any protection at all.

"There were killings that day," Isobel said. "'Twas horrid."

"Our men were unprepared," MacPherson explained. "Our weapons rusty. We could not organize quickly enough to combat them."

"Now we hear of pirates raiding the outer isles," Rob said. "'Tis dangerous these days on Kilgorra."

Lachann looked out at the sea. He knew there were numerous islands west of the mainland. Plenty of places for raiders of all sorts to hide.

"One such ship attempted to invade Braemore in the spring," Lachann said.

"Aye?"

"We lost men as well." Lachann remembered the carnage that day and vowed 'twould never happen again. Now there were cannons at Braemore, and he was going to provide yet another layer of defense here at Kilgorra against encroachers on Loch Maree.

"Our men need to be trained," Boyd said. "Too few of us have any experience."

"I brought some of the best men from Braemore to provide training," Lachann said. "Our isle will be well defended in future, on land and at sea."

"'Tis good to hear it," Rob said. "Laird MacDuffie has done naught in years. I don't believe he understood the devastation of the attack last year or the threat that still remains."

"Because he's become a wee tumshie in his dotage," Isobel said with disgust.

As they spoke of raiders, they all looked toward the sea. They saw Anna's curragh, just arriving at her isle.

"'Tis Anna MacIver," Rob said.

"Aye," Lachann said. "I saw her down at the pier just before she left."

Isobel shuddered. "'Tis likely she's takin' Kyla Ramsay there to keep her from her husband for a few days. She does'na mind the boggle that haunts the place."

"The boggle?" Lachann frowned.

"Aye. The wee isle is haunted by a fierce *sluagh dubh*. Birk would never go there."

Lachann recognized the term, though he'd never encountered any such malevolent spirit in his travels. He wasn't sure he actually believed in them.

The old woman shrugged while Rob answered the question. "Anna knows a way to placate the *sluagh dubh* and goes there whenever she likes."

"She appeases it somehow," Tavish said, "so the bloody thing leaves Kilgorra alone."

Lachann had never heard such bleeting nonsense, but he didn't argue. He watched for a moment as Anna's boat floated out of sight to the northern side of the wee island. He intended to visit the place for himself to see if any part of it could hide a raiding force. He needed to know if there were any other good landing places within rowing distance of Kilgorra.

"Ramsay. Birk *Ramsay*?" he asked, remembering the name of the blacksmith at the castle. Naturally, many of the families on an isle like Kilgorra would be related. "He's the son of the blacksmith?"

"His nephew," Isobel said. "And neither one has a clever bone in his body."

Aye, that much had seemed evident.

"MacMillan," Boyd said, "we've got a harvest to bring in next month. But if you are ready now to arm and train our men to fend off a raid, we're willing and able."

"Aye," Rob added. "Count on me."

Tavish grinned. "Me, too. But you'd better take care if you give any weapons to the men at the distillery."

Lachann gave him a questioning glance.

"Because they might see fit to try their battle skills on Cullen Macauley."

Chapter 14

The sea was relatively smooth when Anna started out, far smoother than her nerves. No, she had not expected to encounter Birk before they got away. But she hadn't anticipated Lachann MacMillan coming to Kyla's rescue once again, either.

The man turned up in the strangest places, and Anna needed to get her reaction to him under control. He was to become her sister's husband—yet another reason for Anna to try and figure a way to leave Kilgorra. Mayhap she would be able to talk Kyla into it this time.

They neared the isle, but the water had become choppy and the approach to the isle was tricky, with numerous underwater rock formations all 'round. Anna nervously eyed the rough waters as she rowed, as well as the clouds that were gathering overhead. A brisk wind came up, and Anna rowed faster, anxious to get them to dry land. "'Twill rain soon," she said to Kyla, relieved when she steered her boat up onto the rocky shore. "As soon as I tie up the curragh, we'll need to hurry."

Once they got to the cave, there was no worry of getting drenched. Anna always kept it well-provisioned with firewood and blankets, so there would be no need to leave the cave once it started raining. And she'd packed plenty of food and the supplies they would need for managing Douglas while they were on the isle.

Anna steered the curragh 'round to a narrow stretch of beach on the northeast side and slid it up onto the sand. She stood and offered her hand to her friend. "Let me help you, Kyla."

As soon as Kyla was off the boat, Anna tied it to the stake that Gudrun had driven into the ground years ago, then pulled the curragh as far out of the water as it would go.

They walked further north along the rocky beach until they came to an opening in the black, moss-covered rock. From the outside, the cavity was hardly visible. But once seen, it appeared to be a deep cave, like many around it. When Anna and Kyla slipped inside, 'twas nearly pitch dark, but they knew the route well. They made a turn to the right, and then a left, and a stream of light came through from the opposite end.

The ceiling was low, so they had to crawl through to the other side, and Anna knew 'twas difficult for Kyla with all her bruises. But she'd wrapped Douglas in a sling, where he rode comfortably against Kyla's chest while Anna carried their provisions.

They finally reached the far end and crawled out of the tunnel. Standing, 'twas only a few steps to the cave where they'd spent so many peaceful hours away from the castle with Gudrun.

Once inside the cave, Anna unrolled the pallets they would use as beds, then took Douglas from Kyla and put him on one of them. She picked up an empty jug as Kyla sat down on her pallet beside her bairn. "Will you be all right while I—"

"Aye. Fresh water," Kyla said. "Go."

Anna took the water jug to the spring that fed the loch. When she returned, Kyla was lying on her side, feeding Douglas.

Anna felt Kyla's gaze upon her as she put their provisions into the covered crocks that Gudrun had brought years before. She got a fire going under the cave's outcropping and put a pan of water on to boil.

"Are you all right, Ky?" she asked. It had been a strenuous process for a bruised and battered woman, getting all the way from Kilgorra Castle to Spirit Isle.

"Mmm. I am now." She closed her eyes and rested as Douglas drank his fill.

"Are you ready to break your fast?"

"Just tea," Kyla replied.

Anna looked back at her friend. She'd eaten next to naught since the day before, when she'd collapsed on the pier, and Anna was worried. Kyla looked gaunt and pale, aside from her colorful bruises.

Anna took out a tin of tea and two cups. Mayhap she could get Ky to take something more with her tea.

"Anna . . . ," Kyla said. "You've said naught of our rescuer."

Anna noticed Kyla trying for a wry smile, but her split lip prevented it.

"What is there to say?" Besides the fact that Anna had not been able to shut him out of her thoughts and dreams at all last night, much as she'd tried. Or that a pitiful yearning for his embrace—and, Lord help her, his kiss—had plagued her during her weaker moments.

"I would say he was a hero to carry me up to Janet's cottage yesterday, and then save you from Birk's wrath," Kyla remarked. "And this morn . . . he could have ridden right past us. He probably *should* have, if he wants Catrìona's favor."

Anna swallowed, her sore neck muscles reminding her exactly how much a hero Lachann MacMillan had been. Ach, aye—he was a man among men. One who had naught to do with her. "Well, he is not a troll," Anna muttered.

"What?"

"He will be a strong leader once he weds Catrìona and becomes laird."

"What if he doesn't?"

"Doesn't what? Become laird?" Anna spread honey on a crust of bread for Kyla and handed it to her.

"No. What if he doesn't wed Catrìona?"

"Ach, you talk nonsense, Ky," Anna scoffed, even though a wee trill of pleasure skittered through her at the thought of Catrìona failing to add Lachann Mac-Millan as one of her conquests.

She sat down across from Kyla. "Everyone knows that is his purpose here, and they all want to keep Catrìona's true nature from him as long as possible."

"Aye, but what if Catrìona won't have him?" Kyla mused.

Anna reached for the water jug. "You may be injured, Kyla, but I didn't realize Birk's beatings had rendered you daft."

"I'm not daft. What if Catrìona decides to wed Macauley?"

"Why would she?" Even Catrìona must recognize the superior man.

Kyla made a grim face. "You know Catrìona as well as I, Anna."

Aye, Anna knew her stepsister well, and the thought of her clutches in Lachann MacMillan sickened her. But so did the idea of Cullen Macauley as laird of the castle and the isle. "Why would she choose Macauley over MacMillan?"

"Because she likes having her own way," Kyla said.

"So she does."

"Do you think MacMillan will be as easy to manipulate as the old laird?" Kyla asked. "Or Macauley?"

No, Anna did not think so. Lachann MacMillan was a man who knew what he was about and would not appreciate Catrìona's lies and manipulations.

"Catrìona will choose whoever suits her own purposes," Kyla said. "We both know that."

"Aye, but MacMillan wants Kilgorra," Anna said. "And there seems to be no love lost between him and Macauley."

"Really? They know each other?"

"They know they're rivals for Catrìona's hand."

Douglas slept while Anna and Kyla drank their tea. Anna had heard that the MacMillans wanted Kilgorra because of its location where Loch Ewe met the Minch. That he wanted to control what ships passed Kilgorra on their way south. Marrying Catrìona seemed a high price for it.

"The lairdship of Kilgorra is much more important to Lachann MacMillan than any of Catrìona's bad, er . . . habits," Anna said. "They say the MacMillans intend to build a dynasty here, like the MacDonalds of old on Skye."

Anna had tried to imagine it—seeing all the buildings at the castle in use. Ships coming and going from the harbor every week. The distillery expanded. Every Kilgorran would become prosperous, even the fishermen, who spoke of exporting the fish their wives preserved, and the weavers, whose wool was some of the finest in Scotland.

"With a man like MacMillan in charge, Kilgorra would be safe from pirate attacks," Anna said, remembering the previous summer's deadly raid that had caught the islanders so unprepared. "He brought cannons, Ky. And that brigantine he sailed in on—"

"Aye. I saw it," Kyla replied. She toyed with the hair on her son's head. "But if MacMillan does not wed Catrìona, he will leave Kilgorra."

Anna nodded.

"And if he goes . . . ," Kyla said.

"Aye? If he goes . . . ?" Anna would never see him again, and Kilgorra would be no worse off than it was a month ago. But at least he would not be shackled to the likes of Catrìona MacDuffie. Anna had that one small satisfaction.

"If he goes," Kyla speculated, "he might be persuaded to take you away with him."

"Ach, now I know you're daft, Ky." Anna got up and went to the fire, filling Anna's cup with more hot water. "You know I want no man to control my life."

Kyla gave her a stern look. "Aye, you'd rather just stay on at Kilgorra Keep and allow your hateful stepsister to control it instead."

Anna stared into the fire. Did Kyla think it was an actual possibility? That Lachann MacMillan would take her away to Braemore with him?

Ach, 'twas all nonsense. If she were to leave, she would have to figure a way to do it herself. And she would never leave without her friend.

Kyla laughed. "Did MacMillan actually catch me on the pier when I fainted?"

Anna nodded. "He moved so fast, 'twas unbeliev—"

"And when Birk came up to Janet's cottage and shoved you against the wall," Kyla said, "I saw Mac-Millan pull him off you and throw him over his shoulder. 'Twas as though Birk were naught but a wee lad."

Anna could not suppress the ripple of pleasure that melted through her when she remembered Lachann's heroism. If this was what Kyla had felt in those early days whenever Birk had been near, 'twas no wonder she'd married him.

He'd made her daft.

Chapter 15

Lachann was welcomed warmly by the Kilgorrans, and he felt encouraged by the number of men who'd shown up in the castle courtyard at dawn on his fourth day to begin their training. None of them wanted to be caught ill-prepared if called upon to defend against another invasion.

Lachann knew the feeling well. Even though the Braemore men had been prepared when the pirates had struck, they'd suffered too many losses. He felt quite strongly that neither Braemore nor Kilgorra should ever experience such misfortune again.

'Twould be best for Kilgorra to become known as a well-defended territory, so no raider would take the chance of coming ashore. Nor would they want to risk engagement with the *Glencoe Lass* or any other ship Lachann commissioned.

He felt invigorated after his day's labors and was

walking toward the stable when he encountered several children playing near the blacksmith's shop. He recognized Angus MacLaren and Robbie Kincaid among them as they battled others in the group, using swords they'd cleverly fashioned out of wood.

Their voices sounded in loud imitation of their elders, and Lachann smiled at the playful noise. Lads were the same everywhere. They played just as Lachann and his brothers had done years before. As he passed the group, he noticed a wagon heavily loaded with crates of cannon ball, grapeshot, and gunpowder. 'Twas ordnance the smithy had been tasked with putting away the day before, and yet there it stood on an uneven patch of ground in front of Ramsay's shop, with only a block of wood behind one wheel to keep it from rolling.

The children were playing much too close to it.

As their "battle" moved closer to the wagon, Lachann shouted for them to move away from it, but they did not hear him. He started moving toward them, but one of the lads, Davy MacDonall, bumped into it and fell to the ground. He knocked the wedge of wood from the wheel and the wagon shifted, pinning his leg beneath it.

The lad screamed, and Lachann ran. He reached the wagon seconds later and wasted no time putting his shoulder to the side of the cart and shoving hard. At the same time, he shouted to the blacksmith to come and help push the cart off the boy. But the man stood still, watching, as though the accident had been nothing out of the ordinary.

Anna MacIver suddenly appeared as though from nowhere, alone and carrying the heavy pack she'd taken with her to the wee isle. Lachann guessed she must have just returned.

"Mungo!" she screamed. She dropped her pack to come and kneel beside the injured boy. "Help us!"

As she positioned herself near Davy's head, the other children came and pushed alongside Lachann, but the cart was lodged against something that prevented its movement.

"Ramsay!" Lachann shouted.

The blacksmith came to him just as the cart moved far enough for Anna to pull Davy out from under it. "He's out, Lachann!" she cried.

Lachann dropped to the ground beside the boy, who was unconscious now, no doubt from pain. His leg was broken, the skin around the break brutally torn.

"Robbie, run down to the village and fetch Janet," she said. She looked up at Lachann with abject horror and powerlessness in her eyes.

Lachann spoke to the boy who'd made himself known to everyone. "Angus, go and get Kieran or Duncan from the courtyard. Tell them what happened and that we'll need a splint and a stretcher."

"Aye, Laird," the lad said before running off to do as he was bid.

"And don't call me 'laird'!" Lachann called after him. Because naught was settled.

Lachann's temper flared when he looked past Anna and saw Ramsay retreating, then turning to watch, with his hands crossed over his chest.

Anna caressed Davy's cheeks and forehead, murmuring words of comfort even though 'twas unlikely the lad could hear her.

"Ach, his poor leg is broken," she whispered, as though the words spoken any louder might make the situation worse.

Lachann nodded, not mentioning the fact that it was more than broken, 'twas mangled. Ramsay was supposed to have unloaded that cart and put away all the equipment yesterday. But as angry as Lachann was, he would not upbraid the man now.

His attention remained on Anna, on her windblown hair, only nominally confined to her plait. Her eyes were bright with tears and concern, and she worried her lower lip with her teeth. Her distress tugged at something Lachann had buried deep after losing Fiona to Macauley.

"You're just back from your isle?"

She nodded and wiped her eyes. "Ach, weeping will do him no good. What should we do?"

"Wait for the healer," he said.

Angus returned with the adults, who scurried to find the makings for a splint. Quickly, they managed to get the leg wrapped and put the boy on a makeshift stretcher.

"Take him to the keep," Lachann said. "He'll stay there until the healer arrives. And someone bring his parents." He turned to Anna. "Who are his parents?"

She kept one hand on Davy's arm as the men lifted him onto the stretcher. "Meg and Gordon MacDonall. He's a fisherman."

"Someone can fetch them," he said, noting that Ramsay had disappeared all the way inside his shop.

Anna let go of the boy, then rubbed her arms with her hands, still shaken. Lachann ignored the urge to draw her into his arms to comfort her. "Ach, 'twill be a blow to Meg and Gordie. Davy is their eldest, and they've three younger bairns."

They turned toward the keep, and Lachann put his hand at the small of her back in spite of himself. Touching her seemed as natural as breathing. He'd been aware of her absence every day she'd been gone—from the mornings, when he'd taken his plain bowl of porridge from Flora, to the evenings, when he'd retired to his bedchamber and sampled a few of the berries she'd given him on his first day.

"Flora will know what to do until Janet comes," Anna said. "At least, I hope . . ."

Lachann realized he had not even been this close to Catrìona, in spite of spending half the previous day with her. And today the woman was as elusive as a damned sprite, turning up at odd times, and disappearing quickly thereafter. He dropped his hand away from Anna and stopped, leaving her to walk ahead.

She turned a questioning gaze toward him.

"See that everything is done for the lad," he said. "I've business back at the smithy shop."

"Business? With . . . Mungo?"

Lachann nodded but did not elaborate. Anna could not have missed the way Ramsay had held back until she'd called for his assistance. 'Twas intolerable.

He made his way back to the heavily weighted cart that stood right beside the blacksmith's shop. He'd given explicit orders yesterday for Mungo to unload the wagon. At Braemore, he would not have had to mention it twice.

And yet here . . .

His temper was barely contained when he approached the shop and found no one. "Where are you, Ramsay?" he shouted.

The blacksmith stepped out from behind a stone wall, carrying a heavy hammer in his hand. His eyes were dark and shaded by his heavy red brows. Lachann thought them not especially sharp. But that was no excuse.

"I called to you for assistance, blacksmith." Lachann's voice was low and just as dangerous as the blacksmith appeared. "You ignored me. You ignored the plight of the child under the cart until Anna MacIver shouted your name."

"I do'na like all their noise," the man growled.

"No one cares what you *like*!" Lachann bellowed. "'Twas sheer luck I was able to move that cart!" Though he credited the children with adding just enough strength to budge the damned thing off Davy's leg.

Ramsay narrowed his eyes. "Ye do'na give orders here, MacMillan."

"What are you, a bleeting idiot?" Lachann approached the man. "'Twas not a matter of orders but common sense."

The man adjusted his grip on the hammer, and Lachann dearly wished he would raise it against him. 'Twas the only provocation he needed to lay the fool out on his arse. Mayhap a solid beating would teach him something about *orders*.

"What happened out here?" 'Twas Catrìona, coming into the shop from the direction of the stable. "Mungo?"

"Aye, *Mungo*." Lachann did not bother to temper his scathing tone. "Mayhap you can explain to your mistress what happened."

The man stood mute, looking outside, past Lachann.

Lachann managed to temper his voice and avoid roaring at the bastard. "You need not look to Anna or Catrìona or anyone else in this castle when I tell you something is to be done. Because aye—I do have the authority to give orders here."

Catrìona shot Lachann a glare as she moved toward the blacksmith. "Lachann—"

"That cart," he said, giving a curt nod of his head toward the offending wagon. "Unload it now, and see that everything is put away neatly, and in good order."

With that, he left the smith's shop and Catrìona, and trotted up to the keep. He was too angry to try and be pleasant with the woman just then. And he had no interest in spending another minute with the likes of Mungo Ramsay.

He entered the kitchen and found Davy sprawled out on Flora's worktable, still unconscious. Most of the children had been sent away, though Angus and Robbie remained, standing just outside. Davy's parents had not yet arrived.

Angus grabbed Lachann's sleeve. "Do ye think he'll live?"

"I hope so." Though Lachann did not know if the lad would keep his leg. 'Twould be up to the healer to say.

Chapter 16

Anna steadied Davy's leg while Janet washed the wound and reapplied the splint. It grieved her to know the boy was unlikely to walk again, at least not without a crutch. Of course his family had counted on him to grow into a strong young man, capable of manning his father's birlinn, mayhap even his own one day.

"Wipe yer tears now, Anna MacIver," Janet said. "The lad will live."

"I know, but—"

"Ye're too softhearted fer yer own good, lass." The healer nodded toward a bowl of clean rags. "Hand that over."

"Leave her be, Janet," Flora admonished. "A soft heart is no' the worst thing for a lass."

Anna might feel sympathy for a poor, injured child, but she did not feel softhearted toward everyone. If she could toss Birk Ramsay down a deep, dark pit, she would not think twice about it.

She'd only been able to keep Kyla on Spirit Isle for two days. And she'd had no luck in convincing her friend to go away from Kilgorra with her—if she could manage to find the means.

Which did not mean Anna was giving up on Kyla. One of these days, she was going to find a way to persuade her friend to go.

Fortunately, Birk had not been at home when they'd returned to Kyla's cottage in the village only an hour ago. Kyla thought it possible that her husband was out fishing with his father, but Anna had her doubts. He had become so useless of late that he rarely brought in anything to eat. 'Twas his father who provided for Kyla and the bairn, and Anna respected Roy Ramsay for it, even though he'd not been able to effect a change in his son.

The signs of Birk's last attack on Kyla had still been scattered throughout their cottage when they'd returned. He'd done naught to right the chairs that had been tipped over or clean up the stack of peat that had tumbled onto the floor. 'Twas unlikely he was aware that Kyla and his child had been gone for two days.

The sight of such violence in the house was nearly as upsetting as seeing what Birk had done to his wife. Anna had been unnerved by it. She'd tried to get Ky to come to the castle and stay in the cottage, but Kyla had refused. She'd insisted all would be well.

And now this.

Anna knew most of the families on Kilgorra, and she knew Davy's injury would be devastating to his family. Like the other families, they counted on their sons to take up their fathers' work. 'Twas doubtful Robbie would ever be able to work on Gordon MacDonall's birlinn. Not on crutches.

At least Lachann had acted quickly to get the wagon off Robbie's leg. The lad was alive. And as she looked at Lachann now, his face a mask of concern for the boy, she knew the man from Braemore was exactly the kind of laird Kilgorra needed.

And for that honor, he only had to marry Catrìona.

Lachann stepped outside and made arrangements for a wagon to be prepared to take the boy home. Then he took Duncan and Kieran aside. "Go to the smithy shop and make sure that wagon is emptied and the weapons are stowed properly."

Duncan nodded gravely. "I should have seen to it myself, Lachann."

Lachann shook his head. "You should have been able to trust that my orders had been followed."

What Lachann said was true, but it did not help the child who lay inside with his leg—and perhaps his life—shattered.

He went back into the kitchen right after the boy's distraught mother arrived. The healer spoke to her in quiet tones while Anna moved about, spooning some of Flora's savory stew into a large pot. She collected bread and bannocks, and even a crock of milk to take to the boy's home in the village.

When Davy's mother succumbed to her tears, 'twas Anna who embraced the woman and reassured her. "Whatever you need, Meg. You have only to let us know."

"I have a wagon ready and men to carry him to it," Lachann said. He turned to the healer. "It seems best to get him home while he's still unconscious."

"Aye," Janet replied. "Meg, stand aside and let the men carry your lad out."

Anna remained quiet through the process, her brow furrowed, clearly disturbed by the accident. She held onto Meg's hand while they moved Davy, then took the provisions she'd gathered out to the wagon.

"I'll be back later," she said to Flora.

"Do'na worry, lass. Cat— Er, no one knows yer back from the isle."

"Aye, she does," Anna said as she went outside.

'Twas clear to Lachann that Flora meant Catrìona did not know Anna had returned. He had witnessed his intended bride's harshness toward the servants and her animosity toward Anna in particular. And yet she was sympathetic to Mungo Ramsay.

It made no sense whatsoever.

The wagon started on its trip down to the village,

and Lachann went to the stable and saddled his horse, as he'd planned to do before Davy's accident. He took the path down to the pier, then walked his horse down to the beach.

He supposed he should have stayed at the castle and looked for Catrìona, but he was able to rouse little interest in talking to her, not when she'd shown so much more consideration toward the errant blacksmith than the injured child.

It did not sit well.

He headed south on the beach. To his left was a wall of rock, rising high above sea level. Numerous shallow caves had been carved out of the rock, caves that could possibly be inhabited.

But Lachann saw no signs of habitation now. And he noted that the shoreline was made treacherous by numerous channels of underwater rocks. 'Twas unlikely any boats would be able to approach in secret.

'Twas almost as though part of Kilgorra itself was underwater and lying in wait for the unsuspecting traveler to become snared upon its shores.

When Lachann finished exploring the western shore, he returned to the village and asked the location of Davy's home. He left his horse at the pier and walked up the lane, arriving just as the healer was about to leave.

Anna was inside, holding one MacDonall bairn on her hip, and stirring a pot over the fire while Meg MacDonall sat beside her injured son.

Lachann turned his attention to the healer. "You do not think the lad will lose his leg?"

The woman shook her head. "My poultice should keep it from festering. But whether or not he'll ever run on it again is another question."

Lachann hoped Janet was right about the infection. Such a wound could kill.

While the woman spoke, he was distracted by the approach of a ship out in the distance, sailing from east to west. It astonished Lachann that after being attacked by pirates the previous year, the Kilgorrans had posted no guards on the pier. There wasn't even a lookout near the harbor to warn of a hostile approach.

That had already changed. He'd given orders for men to be stationed at a few strategic points on the isle to watch for incoming ships—ships that could well be a danger to Kilgorra. He just wished he had a spyglass on his person now, in order to size up the craft that had begun to tack toward them.

Anna put down the child and came to the door, but she turned to speak to Meg before stepping outside. "I'll send Angus down to help fetch and carry for you until your husband comes home. You've enough to do with the other bairns."

"I'd thank you for that," the woman said. "Please give my thanks to Flora—for all her help . . ."

"Send Angus to the castle if you need anything," Anna said, then turned and stepped out of the cottage, closing the door behind her.

"I'll be off now," Janet said. "Meg will send Angus to me if there's any change."

When Janet left them, Anna placed her hand on Lachann's forearm and looked up at him. "Thank you. For what you did for Davy."

"'Twas only what any sane man would do."

She realized she was holding him and released him slowly. Lachann wished she hadn't. "Did Janet say whether his leg will heal?" she asked. "It looks gruesome."

Lachann gave a shake of his head. "She does not know, but the poultice is to keep it from festering."

"I wonder if there's anything more we can do. Has anyone called for Father Herriot? He'll be a comfort to Meg."

Why hadn't Catrìona come down to the village? Lachann wondered. It seemed odd that she had not bothered to look in on the child. Or offer any assistance to the family.

Yet here was Anna, doing what she could for the injured lad's family. *Who, exactly, is the lady of Kilgorra?*

Anna started down the lane as she gazed out in the direction of her isle. Lachann walked with her, observing her sun-kissed cheeks and disheveled hair.

"Look," she said. "There's the *Saoibhreas* coming into the harbor."

"You know that ship?"

"I recognize the flag she flies," she replied.

They continued toward the pier, where, Lachann knew, his men would be armed and waiting to hail the ship.

"'Tis wise to send Angus to help Davy's mother," he said.

"Only common sense."

Mayhap. "Do you take care of everyone on Kilgorra?"

"What do you mean?"

He shook his head. "Naught. You were gone two days. Is there so much to do on your rocky little isle that—"

"You noticed my absence?"

"Of course. I saw you leave, and you haven't been at the keep, so I assume you just returned."

She smiled, and the dimple in her cheek deepened. Her hair swirled about her head like a halo. "You're right."

"How is your friend?" he asked.

"Healing." She moved to stand in front of him. "I need a favor."

He raised a brow. "A what?"

"A favor. I want you to teach me to shoot a pistol."

"No." He diverted to walk past her, but she quickly caught up.

"Show me how to use a sword, then. Or a dirk."

"No."

"Why not?" A hint of a crease appeared between

her brows. "Do I not have the right to protect myself?"

"'Tis the men's duty to protect the women of the isle."

"What if I need protection against one of those men?"

"Anna—"

"What if there is no man with the mettle to deal with Birk Ramsay when he attacks Kyla—or attacks me—again?"

Damn all, the woman was right. He'd taught his sister to use a pistol as well as a knife, but she carried the dirk with her when she rode off alone to visit the outlying crofts on Braemore lands. "I won't give you a pistol."

"A knife, then. Show me how to use a knife to protect myself."

"I'll think about it," he said. *Gesu,* but she was fierce and beautiful, all at once.

He needed a distraction, so he gestured toward the ship that was fast approaching the harbor. "You're sure that ship is the *Saoibhreas*?"

She was undeterred. "What is there to think about? There isn't a man on this isle who will stand up to Birk Ramsay." Her voice became tinged with anger, and her face flushed with color.

"He will have to deal with me," Lachann said. And he meant it. 'Twas up to the laird to ensure and enforce lawful behavior. And while 'twas not illegal to discipline one's own wife, Lachann could not imagine what Kyla could have done to deserve the beating she'd received.

"But you will not always be there, will you?" Anna demanded. "When he comes for us again, you'll be up at the castle, or off somewhere, seeing to island business."

She was right. And when Lachann thought about Ramsay's size and strength, he knew he could not refuse her.

"All right. But I cannot teach you with the men."

"You'll do it?" she asked with some astonishment.

"Aye." He just hoped he would not regret it.

Chapter 17

Anna could hardly believe Lachann had agreed to her request. For once in her life, she did not feel entirely powerless. And the lessons he taught her would serve her well when she and Ky left Kilgorra. 'Twas only a matter of time—and a certain amount of badgering—before she convinced Kyla to leave.

Aye, leaving the island would be difficult, for this was the only home she knew, and she felt a deep kinship with many of Kilgorra's families. But staying and dealing with Catrìona—and her husband—every day for the rest of her life was unthinkable.

Several of Lachann's men came down to the pier to meet the *Saoibhreas* when its men came ashore. Anna started to slip away, but Lachann took hold of her hand and kept her by his side. "What do you know of this ship?"

"Only that it's a trader that hails from Inverness."

His hand was hard and warm, and swallowed hers with its size. Anna was surprised and flattered that he would seek information from her in front of his men. "They pay good coin for our whiskey and sell it all along the northern coast."

Lachann drew her away to the narrow copse of trees where the path to the castle met the edge of the pier. "We can begin your training in the morn. Early."

"Where?"

"What about the cottage where you hid Kyla Ramsay?"

Anna nodded. "I'll be there."

She started up the path to the castle and was surprised when he continued beside her.

"So, you do not fear the terrible boggle when you visit your isle."

Anna was not sure whether he was mocking her. She cast a sidelong glance in his direction, but his expression betrayed naught. "N-no. I'm accustomed to it."

"I understand you protect Kilgorra from the wrath of the *sluagh dubh*."

"Well, I don't know if it's—"

"What would it do," he asked, "if you did not placate it with your visits?"

"I b-believe it has caused madness," she said hesitantly. She did not enjoy lying to Lachann, but she could not very well tell him the truth. The secret was hers and Kyla's.

"So all of Kilgorra would go mad if you did not . . ." He stopped them from continuing up the path with one of his hands on her arm. She did not understand how it could be so incredibly strong while 'twas so very gentle. "How, exactly do you appcase it? What does it want?"

Anna cleared her throat. "It seems only to want . . . t-to want . . ."

"Aye?"

"Well, just the o-occasional visit. From me. And sometimes Kyla, of course."

"I see," he said.

"Don't you want to join your men on the pier?" she asked, anxious to get out from under his scrutiny. And his mighty hand on her arm. "The *Saoibhreas* sailors are starting to disembark."

"My men are more than capable of handling the *Saoibhreas*."

"Uh, well, I-I would love to stay and talk—"

"You were very kind to Davy's mother," Lachann said.

"Kind?"

"You love this isle and all its people, don't you?"

"Love Kilgorra?" She stopped and looked up at him, into his eyes that saw much, but mayhap not quite enough. "I would leave this isle today if I could get Kyla to leave with me."

He looked at her oddly. "Where would you go?"

She shrugged. To the Norse country, maybe—but she did not know where her kin were, and she didn't know enough of the language to make a go of it there. "Somewhere in Scotland, I suppose. On the mainland."

"What would you do there?"

"I would manage my own life there, under no one's thumb."

Lachann stopped and watched Anna run up the path ahead of him. She was right, he really should join his men at the *Saoibhreas* and meet its captain. He intended to know every trading vessel that came into the harbor, and this would be a good start.

But he had not wanted their conversation to end.

Once again, she'd managed to ease the tension between his shoulders, a knot that had grown and tightened from the moment he'd seen the children playing near the dangerous wagon. She was better than a good rubdown after a strenuous training session.

Ach, he should not allow thoughts of a rubdown to mingle with his thoughts of Anna, for the two together were like tinder to flame. He could so easily imagine her able hands on his body, kneading, caressing, pleasuring. . . .

Gesu, he was a fool.

'Twas late when he finished his duties on the pier,

and when he returned to the castle, he went up in search of Catrìona. But she was not to be found.

Her absence would not have bothered Lachann unduly, for his enthusiasm for the woman had not improved since their first meeting. In fact, he felt some distaste for her now, after her behavior with the blacksmith earlier.

But Macauley was missing as well. Which might have been an innocent coincidence. Lachann, however, was not one to believe in coincidences. Like Macauley's presence on the isle.

But he was not to be deterred. Kilgorra suited him well, and once his defenses were in place, the isle itself would be secure from attack. 'Twas the first time he'd thought of Kilgorra's well-being before that of Braemore, and Lachann realized the isle had become as important to him as his own homeland.

While there was still some light, he climbed up to walk the perimeter of the castle walls. He checked the parapets and battlements, and considered locations for his cannons. It also gave him a good overview of the surrounding lands, the beach where he'd explored earlier, and the castle grounds inside.

The keep, where Catrìona and her father lived, was massive, and Lachann assumed much of it was unused. It lay at the southwestern corner of the castle, and his own window overlooked the sea.

He looked left and saw the armory, the smithy, and

the barracks, and then an overgrown area of the castle with trees and brush that hid whatever lay there. Anna's cottage, for one thing.

He never should have agreed to teach her to defend herself. But damn all if he wasn't looking forward to the lesson.

Anna passed through the castle gates and went directly to the kitchen.

"Ah, Anna—yer back!" Flora said.

"Aye. Have you seen Angus?" She was not going to think about that conversation with Lachann. She could not tell whether he'd been teasing her about the *sluagh dubh* or if he'd been genuinely curious.

And then there was that blurting of her desire to leave Kilgorra. Well, mayhap that was best. If Lachann and Catrìona did not wed, he would leave the island. And now he knew she wanted to leave, too. Kyla's prediction that he would take her away might well come true.

"Angus? He's playing in the close with Robbie," Flora said.

"Climbing the Bruce Tree, no doubt, and right after Davy's broken his leg," Anna said. They'd been told so often to stay out of that tree. "I'm going to send him down to Meg MacDonall until her husband comes in on his boat."

"Aye, she'll need the extra help," Flora responded. "'Tis a miracle the Braemore lad was able to move that cart off Davy's leg."

"Aye. While Mungo Ramsay stood and watched," Anna said.

"What? Mungo was there but did not help?"

Anna shook her head. "I do not understand that man. Never have. Even when I was a small lass he favored Catrìona—"

"Ach, that one!" Flora said with an expression of acute distaste. "Well, ye're best to stay clear of him, I can guarantee ye that." Aye, Anna knew it. 'Twas why she always avoided the smith's shop. There was no telling what strange thoughts went through the man's mind. And the control Catrìona seemed to have over him—'twas just wrong. "I'm going to Gudrun's cottage to clear it out."

"Then off with ye," Flora said. "There's naught fer ye to do here."

Anna stopped in the close and found Angus sitting at the base of the Bruce Tree, thank heavens. She sent him down to the MacDonall house, then walked through the garden to Gudrun's cottage. Once inside, she lit a few candles and got a fire started to take the chill out of the air.

Then she turned to look at the room where she'd spent so many peaceful hours with Gudrun. A wave of nostalgia came over her, thinking about the old Norse maid. No doubt some of Gudrun's belongings were in the boxes and crates that were stacked there.

Anna began to wonder what else was stored inside the boxes she had shoved aside to make room for Kyla's bed. She had to stand on a wobbly chair to lift the highest one down, then she found an old metal hook to pry off the top.

Inside were several moth-eaten gowns, small enough to be meant for a child. There was one wee pair of leather shoes with miniature buckles, as well as an arisaid made from MacDuffie's plaid.

She sat back on her heels as the blood drained from her head. These were *her* clothes! She remembered the shoes very well—as well as the fact that they'd been taken from her soon after her mother's death. By Catrìona.

What else was there?

Folded neatly was a flag of red with a blue cross and what appeared to be a coat of arms in one corner.

Beneath that was a beautiful, golden silk *tonnag*. Carefully, she lifted the *tonnag* from the box, realizing that her mother must have worn the delicate shawl on special occasions. Mayhap it had been draped over her head and shoulders during her wedding to Anna's father. Surely Sigrid had worn it when she'd married Catrìona's father.

Anna took out the finely woven gown of dark blue that lay beneath the *tonnag*, and she felt a pang of grief so sharp it seemed to cut right through her heart. It had been so long since Sigrid's death, and yet Anna could *see* her mother in this gown. She could remember every detail of Sigrid's face, the sparkle of her eyes, the warmth of her smile.

Anna's life would have been so different if her mother had lived. And Catrìona's, too. Mayhap Sigrid's influence would have softened Catrìona's cruel edges. Mayhap the care of a wee brother would have assuaged her anger over her father's new family.

Anna cradled her mother's clothes to her breast for a moment, then packed them away again. She had no time for ruminating on the past. She was about to learn to defend herself, and that was all that mattered.

She fastened the top of the crate and began to clear a space where Lachann could teach her what she wanted—needed—to learn.

Lachann noticed right away that Anna was not serving their evening meal. He'd thought about going down to the village for a hearty supper with his men in the local tavern, but he'd hoped to see her in the great hall. Now that he knew she was not here, he wished he hadn't been, either.

These were not the best thoughts to have when he was preparing to take a wife. He had a responsibility to do all in his power to win Catrìona as a willing bride, so he and his two cousins supped with her in the great hall, along with her father and Macauley. The MacMillans all watched in awe as the laird drank copiously from his bottle of Kilgorra whiskey.

Lachann grew tired of listening to the old man's drunken blather and decided to speak of his strategy for defending Kilgorra. "We are going to mount two cannons on the castle walls, Laird."

"Cannons?" MacDuffie's brows came together. "On my walls?"

"Aye, and one near the harbor."

MacDuffie muttered something unintelligible as he took another swallow from his glass. The old man glanced down the table. "What d'you think of the idea, Macauley?"

"Ever the warmongering MacMillans," Macauley said with a sneer. "Cannons will only give rise to rumors of wealth we need to defend. And possibly—"

"Has no one told you the isle was attacked just last summer?" Kieran interjected, while Lachann tamped down his temper. The MacMillans had never begun a feud or attacked a neighbor. Any warring they engaged in was purely in defense of their lands.

"Kilgorra was attacked?" Macauley scoffed. "By whom?"

"You're not especially well informed, Macauley," Kieran said. "Some pirating clan from the outer isles attacked Kilgorra last summer."

Macauley looked first to MacDuffie, then to Catrìona. "No one spoke of this to me."

Lachann felt a small satisfaction in that.

"'Tis only by luck that they have not returned to steal more Kilgorra whiskey," Duncan said.

"Or murder more islanders. Kilgorra will not be unprepared next time pirates come raiding," Lachann said with finality. "The cannons go into place tomorrow. I've already got patrols near the harbor and men stationed at watch points on the high grounds."

He felt Catrìona's measuring gaze upon him and knew he should take it as a positive sign. But he had far more interest in organizing the Kilgorran men into effective troops that were capable of defending the isle than wooing the woman who was to become his wife.

And meeting Anna in the morn to show her how to use a knife.

Lachann focused his thoughts. He had much to accomplish on Kilgorra, and in a short time. A serving lass could not help him in the least. On the contrary, she could become a hindrance.

On the morrow he would teach her to wield a dirk, and that would be an end to it. 'Twas time for him to court Catrìona in earnest, marry her, and take the reins of lairdship from her father.

Lachann liked Kilgorra. In only a few days' time, it had become more than just a strategic location for posting armed warriors to protect Braemore. He was coming to know and respect the people of the isle, and the island was beginning to feel like home.

MacPherson's affable introductions proved invaluable. The Kilgorrans all agreed the laird had allowed the island's defenses to weaken until they were barely existent. They'd prepared themselves to some extent against another raid, but their weaponry was outdated, and swords would be of limited use against a well-practiced enemy. To that end, Lachann recruited islanders to train with his men, while Duncan and Kieran organized those who came to the castle courtyard to volunteer.

The men—fishermen and farmers alike—began their training at the castle that morning. And while the men who'd come from Braemore were responsible for the training, Lachann chose two Kilgorran leaders to assist them: Boyd MacPherson and his cousin, a fisherman named Donald MacRae. Both men had the respect and loyalty of every Kilgorran, far more than they showed their own laird, whom they saw as a failing old man.

Everything was falling into place. Almost.

When supper ended, Lachann asked Catrìona to walk out to the gardens with him. She agreed, and he escorted her from the keep by way of a passageway just outside the great hall. 'Twas time to overcome his indifference and woo her in earnest, for he suspected Macauley would not wait much longer to make her his own.

Unless he had already done so.

It made her somewhat less appealing, but Lachann would do what he needed to do to secure the lairdship. Lachann would take her to wife, but there was naught about her that would ever put his heart at risk. She was not the kind to do that.

As far as Lachann could tell, she'd been indifferent to Davy MacDonall's injury, which had taken place in her own realm—the castle. She was callous and demanding with the servants, and she possessed not a shred of . . .

Lachann sighed, shrugging off his concerns. He would have a few words with Catrìona after they were wed, and she would gain an understanding of what was expected of a laird's wife. Of *his* wife. Certainly 'twas not to stand at the smithy shop and question that dolt of a blacksmith while a child lay injured in her courtyard.

'Twas Anna, not Catrìona, who had brought food from the castle for the MacDonalls. Anna who had gone to the village to give comfort to the injured lad's mother.

Lachann hoped 'twould be merely a matter of instructing Catrìona on her duties as lady of the isle. She'd had no mother to show her, and only a drunkard of a father to support her.

She took Lachann's arm as they walked. He guessed she was not much younger than his own thirty years, old enough to have married and borne a few bairns. Old enough to have become set in her ways.

But she could be taught.

"The blue of your gown is quite fetching, Catrìona," he said, though as soon as he'd seen it, the color had brought to mind the pale color of Anna's eyes.

Catrìona looked up at him with an expression that was more than slightly unsettling, though he was unsure why it struck him so. If she'd been a man, he'd have been wary of her drawing a weapon. "Thank you, Lachann," she said.

They strolled on and Lachann swallowed his misgivings. "Have you ever traveled away from Kilgorra?"

She shook her head. "No, never."

"Never visited relatives on the mainland?"

"We have no relations ashore," she said. "I've never before had reason to leave."

Lachann felt fortunate to have had grandparents and numerous cousins at Braemore, for he'd been hardly more than a bairn when his parents had met their deaths at Glencoe. Soldiers had murdered his father and eldest brother in cold blood, and Lachann's mother had died of exposure in trying to get the rest of the family to safety.'Twas Dugan, a mere lad at the time, who'd managed to get his younger siblings away in the midst of that hell.

They'd been taken to Braemore and become Mac-Millans, welcomed by the clan that had been his mother's. When he'd come up with his plan to protect Braemore by sea, he'd been thinking only of his own clan. Now he knew that Kilgorra needed him, too.

Dusk came upon Lachann and Catrìona as they continued on a path past the lush beds of flowers at the far side of the courtyard, the path where he'd encountered Anna that first evening on Kilgorra.

Where he'd wanted naught but to kiss her.

Lachann felt no such urge with Catrìona, even though the moment was conducive to a romantic interlude. Catrìona clung to his arm and pressed her body against him as they walked. The heavy perfume of the flowers surrounded them.

"I understand you have a great number of relations at Braemore," Catrìona said. "And now your brother is laird of the MacMillans."

"Aye. He became laird when our grandfather passed away a few years back."

"'Tis a grave responsibility."

"Aye." One that her father had not taken seriously for a good many years, it seemed.

"Shall we walk to the chapel?" Catrìona asked. "'Tis much quieter there."

"Quieter?"

She looked up at him with a lazy smile. "No one will disturb us out there."

Lachann swallowed. He needed to go, just to seal the betrothal agreement. He wanted her father's lands, she wanted a husband. Either him or Cullen Macauley.

"Aye. Lead the way."

Catrìona took a tighter hold of his arm and drew him away from the garden and onto an overgrown path toward the southern wall. In the gloaming, he could make out the silhouette of a tall stone steeple, but it appeared to be in ruins. The castle wall extended some distance past the chapel grounds, and Lachann was able to make out a metal gate breaking the solid line of the wall.

"What's out there?"

"Naught. A cliff," Catrìona said.

"The chapel is no longer used?" he asked.

"No," she replied offhandedly. "There is a kirk in the village."

She gave a furtive glance 'round the area, and Lachann allowed her to pull him to a thick elm tree. She circled 'round him, and with the gleam in her dark eyes that had bothered him only a few minutes ago, maneuvered him back against the tree and stood close to him. Very close.

For the moment, Lachann believed it prudent to allow her to think she was in charge.

"This is what you wanted, is it not?" she asked sweetly. "To be alone together?"

She reached up and unfastened the MacMillan brooch that held his plaid in place at his shoulder.

Aye, that was exactly what he should have wanted,

though as he stood with his back to the tree, he felt naught but an uneasy tension. After all her flirting with Cullen Macauley, this seemed slightly . . . arbitrary.

Not that that made any difference in the long run. Mayhap she was just weighing her options. Lachann believed he ought to be pleased that she was willing to test the waters with him. He certainly had no intentions of marrying for love, but he did not want a wife who recoiled when he kissed her. Or bedded her.

"What do you desire, Lachann MacMillan?" she asked in a hushed voice. "Tell me."

Chapter 18

Lachann felt the coarse bark of the massive elm tree at his back and the warm length of Catrìona's body against his. What he desired ought to have been completely clear. And yet he was unmoved.

Catrìona slipped her fingers into his belt, and Lachann had the distinct impression she would actually disrobe him where he stood. There might have been a time when he'd enjoyed this kind of seduction, but that time was not now.

"Mmm. We have no braw warriors on Kilgorra like you, Lachann."

He caught her hand before she reached vulnerable territory. "Catrìona—"

Something hit Lachann on the head, and he looked up. A quiet giggle came from somewhere within the higher branches of the elm. Catrìona let out a squeal and jerked away from Lachann as more pelting occurred. 'Twas small twigs that were hitting them.

"Is that you, Angus MacLaren?" she hissed. "And Robbie Kincaid! Get down here!"

The giggles turned into chuckles, and then childish cackles. And suddenly, a small body came crashing down and would have hit the ground had Lachann not managed to catch the lad.

But as soon as he put him on his feet, Catrìona scooped up a stout branch and gave the lad a nasty clout on the backs of his legs. Then she took hold of his ear and started pulling him back to the keep, forgetting Lachann altogether. "You are a nasty wee devil, Angus! Your father shall hear of your skulking about where you do not belong!"

Aye, the lad was in trouble for being where he should not.

Lachann had the uneasy sense that he did not belong there, either.

On her way back to the keep from Gudrun's cottage, Anna nearly collided with Catrìona, who was rushing forward. She held a bellowing Angus MacLaren by the ear and used a stick to herd a worried-looking Robbie Kincaid at her side. Lachann MacMillan followed behind at a more leisurely pace.

They were coming from the direction of the chapel, Catrìona's favorite trysting place. 'Twas isolated and romantic, with the ruins of the beautiful old chapel and the thickest, bonniest elm tree Anna had ever seen. All the servants knew better than to venture to the spot when Catrìona was on the prowl.

Anna just hated the thought of what Catrìona had been doing with Lachann in the old churchyard. And yet here were Angus and Robbie, and Catrìona was clearly livid. Anna could not imagine what horrible transgression the lads had committed.

"Hie yourselves to the blacksmith and wait for me there."

"Ach, no, m'lady!" Angus cried.

"We were havin' naught but a bit o' fun!" Robbie wailed.

Lachann's deep voice cut through the lads' terrified clamoring. "Catrìona." Suddenly, all was quiet. "Release them."

Catrìona hesitated for an instant, but then she let go of Angus's ear and slowly turned to face Lachann. In the short space of time it took for her to turn, she composed herself, wiping away the vindictive expression everyone at the castle knew so well. Particularly Anna.

"Lads, go home," Lachann said. "And play no more pranks. I would take it amiss if you hurt yourselves, as Davy MacDonall did today."

The two ran off as quickly as their legs would carry them, and Catrìona shot a malevolent glance at Anna before sliding her hand into the crook of Lachann's elbow. Anna's chest burned at the sight of the two of them together.

Ach, she was being worse than an idiot. She'd known better than to dream of an escape from Kilgorra. At least with Lachann MacMillan.

"'Tis about time you returned, Anna MacIver," Catrìona said in a tone of feigned affability. "Flora has need of you in the kitchen."

"I'm sure she does," Anna replied without looking up at Lachann. She just couldn't, not while he was in the midst of courting Catrìona. She did not want to think of how many trips to the chapel he'd already made with her while she'd been away on Spirit Isle. "I'm on my way there now."

"You have time to make up for, Anna," Catrìona said as Anna started to move past them.

"Aye. And I will."

Anna scurried down to Flora's domain, and when the older woman saw her, she said, "What's happened to ye, lass? Yer face is as red as a brined herring!"

"Naught," Anna retorted. She took an apron and tied it about her waist. "What chores are left to do? Shall I knead the dough for you?"

Flora was in the midst of preparing dough for their bread on the morrow, but she shook her head. Anna looked 'round to the other maids and saw Nighean scrubbing the pots Flora had used for cooking, and Meg, who had finished putting the oats in a pot to soak for the morning porridge. Red-haired Glenna was sweeping the floor.

"We're managing here, lass," Flora said. "The laird was'na feeling well, and Alex just came down from helpin' him into bed. Catrìona has gone walkin' with MacMillan."

Anna nodded, desperately looking for something to do—something to occupy her hands and her mind. "Aye. I saw them. They are just outside."

"Ah." Flora looked at her curiously.

"What?"

"Naught," Flora said in an odd tone, nodding toward a low shelf at the back of the kitchen. "Ye might gather those empty whiskey bottles and take them out to Graeme's cart to be carried back to the distillery."

Anna frowned. "There are so many. Far more than what the laird usually drinks."

"Aye. Ever since that arse Macauley brought him the specially aged draught from the distillery, he's been drinkin' more."

"'Tis not good for him."

"Nay, but I would'na know how to discourage him from it."

Neither would Anna.

But she was glad to have something to do. She'd managed to shove all the crates to the walls in Gudrun's cottage, clearing a large space for her morning lesson with Lachann. She put the empty whiskey bottles into a burlap sack and carried them outside. Effie caught up to her, missing her, no doubt, after two days away. "Aye, you'll get your platter of milk on the morrow, my wee friend."

The sky was full of stars to light her way, but Anna knew the path so well she could have found her way to the stable even if it had been pitch dark. Even with Effie trying to wrap herself 'round Anna's legs as she walked.

Anna was just grateful she would not have to encounter Lachann and Catrìona again tonight.

Once Catrìona was occupied with her husband and children . . . Surely the woman would have more important things to do after her marriage than to harass Anna every time their paths crossed.

And Lachann would have no time for lazy conversations on the island's pathways.

Anna ignored the burning in the pit of her stomach at the thought of Catrìona bearing Lachann MacMillan's children. Of having to wait upon the two of them, mayhap preparing Catrìona in her bedchamber as she awaited her husband.

She dreaded seeing the disgust in Lachann's eyes when he learned what kind of woman he'd married, and knowing that anyone on the isle could have informed him before he'd become shackled to her.

"*Herregud.*" Anna pinched her lips together at the injustice of it all, then remembered her resolution never to belong to any man.

Mayhap she could get the *Saoibhreas* to take her and Kyla to the northern coast. And from there, they could figure a way to get to Norway and her mother's people.

She wondered if Lachann had made his proposal to Catrìona tonight. He must know that Cullen Macauley had his own plans and purpose here. And it was not merely to seduce the serving maids.

Macauley wanted to be laird, too.

Chapter 19

"**W**hy were you going to send the lads to the blacksmith?" Lachann asked Catrìona. Angus had had a long day after the trauma of seeing Davy MacDonall injured, then spending the whole afternoon helping his friend's mother.

"To give them the thrashing they deserve."

In spite of her indifferent tone, he could tell she was still angry.

"Catrìona," Lachann said, keeping his voice low and even. "Do they not have parents?"

"Of course they do. But—"

"Ramsay is hardly an appropriate disciplinarian," he said.

Catrìona stiffened next to him. "He follows his orders well."

"No, he does not. The man is a fool. Do not send any more children to him. *He* should be thrashed for standing by and watching Davy MacDonall being crushed by that cart today."

"He said you moved it before he could get to you."

"He's a liar, then," Lachann said. "None of the castle children should go near the man in future. As lady of the land, you might consider taking a more positive interest in them." As Anna had done.

"Why, I know them all."

"I am sure you do, Catrìona," he said, though he had his doubts.

He managed to extricate himself from the woman's grasp and send her into the keep without him. And ach, but his excuse had been lame—that he needed to speak with his men in the barracks. But the incident with the lads had put him off as much as her inappropriate interference with Ramsay had done.

He took the path toward his men's quarters, but kept on walking past it, in the opposite direction of the old chapel.

Lachann understood the necessity of maintaining the authority of the laird and his family. And he knew discipline. But the lads in the tree were merely two children having a bit of fun. Their prank had been harmless. Catrìona had reacted as though they'd rained boiling oil down on their heads, rather than a few innocent twigs.

MacMillan parents had always meted out punishments according to the crime. At Braemore, Angus and

Robbie would have been sent to the massive elm tree and instructed to rake up every leaf, twig, and branch on the ground 'round it, then clean up the entire area near the old chapel.

He did not like to think what the blacksmith would have done to them.

He scrubbed one hand across his face and wondered what in hell he was doing there, so far from everything and everyone he cared about.

Ach, right, he reminded himself. *He was creating a protective barrier for Braemore, and securing a laird-ship for himself.*

Gesu, but he'd never thought 'twould be so difficult, and he could not help but wonder whether there was any way to wrest the lairdship from MacDuffie without marrying his daughter.

He doubted that would ever happen, not when Cullen Macauley so obviously had the laird's favor. And her thwarted seduction at the elm tree gave him to suspect Macauley had wheedled somewhat more than Catrìona's favor from her. Lachann was going to have to fight for his position. Win the daughter, win the lairdship.

He suspected no amount of soldiering would win MacDuffie's support.

Lachann stopped pacing. In the failing light of dusk, he saw Anna approaching from the stables. She did not see him as she came toward him, stopping once to pick up the white and black cat whose presence offended

Catrìona when it wandered into the hall. But Anna obviously favored the wee beast.

Lachann could not hear Anna's words, but the sound of her voice came to him, low and quiet. Pleasing.

She let the cat go and continued toward him, stopping abruptly ten paces away when she saw him. "Oh!"

"Anna."

"I . . ." She looked past him, toward the keep. "I thought you'd gone in. With Catrìona."

Lachann's instincts told him to walk the other way, but he ignored them and closed the distance between them. She smelled of kitchen spices, and his fingers fairly itched to touch the thick flaxen braid that trailed down her back. He wanted to smooth away the fine blond tendrils that curled at her ears.

"No. I . . ." He hesitated, then looked up at the sky. "'Tis a fine night. Better spent out here than inside."

"We've had some fair weather."

"It must have been fine on your isle," he said. "Tell me more about your *sluagh dubh*."

Anna shook her head, and when she smiled, all the pent-up tension in Lachann's body relaxed, all but in one very sensitive part, and he willed his unwelcome arousal to subside.

"I've said all I will on the subject."

Lachann laughed, a sound unfamiliar to his own ears. She loosed something in him that was wholly agreeable. "Who would have thought the bravest person on Kilgorra would be a woman?"

"You jest. There are many courageous women on the isle. You only have to know Meg MacDonall. Or watch the wives who send their men out to sea in their birlinns of a morn to see that—"

"Aye, lass," he said with a laugh. "I was only jesting. I am entirely impressed with the Kilgorrans I've met." And captivated by her defense of them.

She appeared taken aback by her own blunt statement, and when she spoke again, her tone was apologetic. "'Tis just that I-I know most of them. And they are v-very—"

"Of course." He caught a few wisps of the hair at her temple between his fingers and quickly found himself cupping her face in his hand. "But I doubt very much any of them have ever thought of asking to be taught to use a pistol."

"Well, most—"

"I very much enjoyed the berries you left me on my arrival," he said quietly in an attempt to put her at ease.

"I am glad to know it." Her voice was hardly more than a reserved murmur now.

Lachann stepped closer as he lowered his head and tipped hers up. He closed the inches between their mouths, brushing his against the soft, sweet warmth of her lips.

Lachann felt her sharp intake of breath, but she did not pull away. Her eyes drifted closed, and so did his an instant later. He slid his hand 'round to the back of her head to capture her lips more fully.

She made a slight moan when he wrapped his fingers 'round the thick plait of her hair and pulled her deeper into the kiss. Ach, but she was as sweet as the berries she'd given him, and as innocent as her friend's wee bairn.

Her body was soft and warm, and molded perfectly to his. And though Lachann knew this fruit was forbidden, he had no desire to stop. He would have pulled her fully into his embrace but for a sharp call that split them apart.

"Anna! Are ye there, lass?"

They both turned to see one of the menservants approaching. "Aye, Alex! I'm coming!"

Anna spun away so quickly that Lachann had to wonder if they'd actually shared that mind-searing kiss.

Alex MacRae had come for her just in time.

"The mistress wants you in her bedchamber," he said.

Somehow, Anna found her voice. "Aye. I'll go to her right away."

She left Alex near the servants' quarters and went up the stairs to the great hall, where she stopped and pressed her hands against the cold stone of the wall. Her heart was beating like the wings of a moth, and she needed to gain some control before going up to Catrìona.

She took a deep breath, and though she tried to put

that kiss from her mind, she could not. 'Twas at the forefront, and she feared 'twould likely remain there forever.

Anna had never felt anything so wondrous, and she could only imagine how much better it might have been had Lachann pulled her fully into his embrace. His touch had been gentle, but even now her body burned with a mad desire to feel all that leashed male power around her.

Her dreams of the man had not come close to the reality of his kiss. And she feared she would think of it every time she laid eyes on him.

She climbed the stairs to the bedchambers and braced herself to meet Catrìona's demands.

Her stepsister sat at her dressing table with her hairbrush in hand. "'Tis about time."

"My apologies, Catrìona," Anna replied, hoping to assuage some of her stepsister's annoyance at her absence of late. "I was running an errand for Flora."

"You seem to have far too much time to loiter about."

Anna felt her face heat. Catrìona could not possibly have seen her with Lachann. The path to the stable was not visible through the trees. She took the brush and forced herself to remain calm as she started on Catrìona's hair. "What do you mean?"

"Do not play the fool, Anna," Catrìona said with her usual ire. "You were gone two days to your horrid wee isle. *Two* days, and here we have guests!"

"You seem to have managed," Anna replied in a far lighter tone than she felt.

"Not with my clothes. Not with my hair," she spat. "Have you forgotten I have suitors?"

Ach, if only she *could* forget. "Your hair looked as bonny as ever when I saw you in the courtyard, Catrìona."

The kiss had not made her forget the way Lachann had contradicted Catrìona to save Robbie and Angus from a beating at the hands of Mungo Ramsay. Anna could not imagine what the two had done to warrant such ill treatment, but her heart warmed at the thought of Lachann's firm voice staying Catrìona's hand.

Catrìona's lips pinched tightly together at Anna's mention of the courtyard. No doubt she was still annoyed by Lachann's interference.

'Twas hardly a consolation that Catrìona would have to become accustomed to more such meddling once she wed him.

"What heinous offence did the lads commit that had you sending them off to the blacksmith for their punishment?"

"'Tis none of your concern."

Mayhap not, but Anna dearly wished she knew what had transpired out near the chapel between Catrìona and Lachann. "You know Mungo Ramsay is a brute. He did not lift a hand to help MacMillan with the cart that hurt Davy MacDonall. Not even Kyla will ever allow him near her bairn—his own nephew."

"What do I care of a worthless peasant's opinion?"

"Naught, I suppose," Anna replied, forcing herself to be gentle with the hairbrush. There were times when she wished Catrìona could be the recipient of Mungo's brutality. Then mayhap she would understand not only the pain but also the humiliation of such treatment.

Anna was anxious for the morn, for the lesson Lachann had promised her. Mayhap it would take more than one session. . . .

Catrìona blathered about some imperfections in the way her laundry had been done, while Anna took a deep breath and tried to force Lachann MacMillan from her mind. It couldn't possibly take more than one or two sessions for him to teach her how to wield a knife. And in any event, he had more important matters to deal with. She could not expect him to spend too much time with her.

Or to kiss her again.

"What is the matter with you, Anna?" Catrìona demanded. "Have you heard a word I said?" She shoved Anna aside, got up from her dressing table, and stalked across the room to the window. Her movements were grim and deliberate. She was clearly unhappy.

"Yes, I heard. Give me your sark and I'll wash it again tomorrow."

Catrìona picked it up from the end of her bed and tossed it to Anna.

"Is there anything else, Catrìona?"

Catrìona put her hands on her hips and narrowed her

eyes. "Did you see Cullen Macauley when you came in?"

Anna gave a shake of her head. "No one was about but the servants." And one entirely too fascinating man from Braemore, but Anna had no intention of divulging any more information than was absolutely necessary. "Do you want me to ask one of the men to look for him?"

Catrìona pulled on a shawl. "No. 'Tis late."

The lateness of the hour had not stopped Catrìona before. Everyone, except perhaps Laird MacDuffie, knew she slipped away from the keep on occasion to meet with her lover of the moment. Anna had never understood why she would do it.

Until now.

If Catrìona's lovers kissed her as Lachann MacMillan had kissed Anna, 'twas no wonder her stepsister sought out such intimacies. 'Twould be so easy for Anna to let herself yearn for Lachann's sensuous touch.

And absolutely disastrous.

Anna managed to get Catrìona to return to her dressing table. She plaited Catrìona's hair and bound the end with a piece of ribbon. "If there's nothing else, I'll go to—"

"The fire. 'Twill go out before the night's half done."

Anna knelt before the fireplace and added another brick. She made sure 'twould catch, then got up and started for the door. There were times when her servant's role galled her. After all, Anna's rank was no different from Catrìona's. Her father, Gillean MacIver, had been laird of his own clan. Gudrun told her he'd been Laird of Kearvaig until his death, and the only reason Sigrid and Anna had left his lands was because of a falling-out with the wife of her father's brother.

According to Gudrun, the rift had been due to jealousy, for when the uncle had made unwelcome advances toward Anna's mother, his wife had blamed Sigrid and seen to it that Sigrid and Anna were driven from their own home. Sigrid had taken her wee daughter and her maid, and traveled to Kilgorra to wed MacDuffie, a man she'd met and liked well when he'd made an earlier visit to Kearvaig.

"Take all this, too." Catrìona pointed to a heap of clothing on the floor for Anna to carry down to the laundry.

Without a word, Anna picked up Catrìona's dirty clothes and started for the door, but Catrìona tripped her. Intentionally, of course.

Anna scraped her elbow when she fell. She should have known Catrìona would do something spiteful. She always did when she felt slighted by Anna.

Biting her tongue, Anna got to her feet and went through the door. She needed to keep the peace, for she had nowhere to go, at least not yet. One kiss from the man who was promised to her stepsister was anything but a sure passage away from Kilgorra.

Chapter 20

Lachann needed to get away from the castle before he did something so completely daft . . .

Something more than merely kissing Anna MacIver.

What he would not do to give in to his body's demands. He wanted the fair lass with a passion he had not felt since—

He muttered a low curse. He could not remember ever feeling such intense desire for a woman—certainly not since he and Dugan had found their fortune and neighboring lairds had brought their kinswomen to Braemore with the hope that he would marry one of them.

Not even Fiona . . .

She'd been a sweet and beautiful woman, no more than a lass, really. But her passion had been spent upon following her father's dictates. Not on Lachann, the man she'd claimed to love.

The path to the pier was dark, but Lachann had no

difficulty seeing his way to the harbor and then finding the public house where he knew Duncan and Kieran and the others had decided to go after supper, while he'd gone off to the chapel yard with Catrìona.

And what an odd circumstance that had turned out to be.

Her wild fury at being thwarted by a couple of children was disturbing. No harm had been done, and yet she would have sent the two lads to the hulking blacksmith for an undue punishment.

Mungo Ramsay had no business seeing to the discipline of the castle children—of *any* children.

Again, Lachann had to wonder what kind of wife *and mother* Catrìona would make, and whether he could remedy her unsuitability. *Gesu,* thinking of it made his head ache.

He arrived at the public house, tied up his horse, and stepped inside. 'Twas not a large room, and by the light of a few meager candles, he saw several long tables with benches and a number of Kilgorran men sitting at them, talking with Lachann's clansmen.

Lachann recognized most of the men, and several voices called out their greetings. He gave them a nod and picked up a mug of ale from the barkeep, then went to one of the long benches where he took a seat next to the priest, Father Herriot.

"We were just talking about the pirate attack last year," Duncan said.

"Aye?"

"We had naught to fight them with," said Donald MacRae. "The men who tried to stop them from raiding the distillery were killed."

"They had pistols and rifles," another man added.

"Against our puny swords." MacRae took a long pull of ale.

Father Herriot spoke. "The fishermen were all out to sea when the pirate ship sailed into the harbor. By the time they managed to get back 'twas too late."

"Will your brigantine return to Kilgorra, Lachann?" MacRae asked.

Lachann nodded, even though his future on the isle was far from certain. He had not anticipated Catrìona being quite so . . . inapt.

"Well, with the guns on the *Glencoe Lass* and those cannons you brought, we'll not be so vulnerable next time," Rob MacPherson said.

"If there *is* a next time," someone argued. "They got what they wanted. Why would they return?"

"Do'na be daft, Ferguson. Of course they'll be back!"

"Aye, 'tis a surprise they've not come sooner . . ."

Lachann gave only half his attention to the argument. It reminded him very much of the heated discussions that took place in the public house at Braemore, whether the stakes were high or low. The men were opinionated, and vociferous, especially as the ale in the pitchers diminished.

Lachann felt right at home.

If only Catrìona could be slightly more amenable. He did not look forward to another walk to the chapel grounds with her.

But Lachann was nothing if not a determined man. He had goals to accomplish that were no less than those of his brother three years before, when he'd gone after a cache of gold that had only been rumored to exist. No one had expected Dugan to succeed. And yet he had.

Lachann owed his clan no less than the protection he could provide them through this alliance with Kilgorra. If Dugan could keep the MacMillans from being evicted from their lands, Lachann could see to it that no enemy ever succeeded in raiding Braemore from the sea.

He would figure a way.

"What of the distillery?" Lachann asked. "Who is in charge there?"

"Geordie Kincaid," said one of the men. "And he is no' a happy or contented man at the moment."

"All would be well if no' for that blathering neep from the castle," Donald MacRae remarked in a disgusted tone.

"Macauley?" Lachann said.

"Ach, aye."

"What's he done?"

"Only taken a thirty-year barrel of brew and had it put into special bottles for the laird."

Lachann frowned. "Is it not the laird's right to—"

"Aye, most definitely. 'Twould'na be a problem,

MacMillan," MacRae said. "But that barrel and two others like it were promised to the MacDonald chieftain of Skye."

Lachann understood the problem instantly. The MacDonald laird was Fiona's father. And reneging on a promised shipment of whiskey was a deliberate slight of the man, an insult Kilgorra could ill afford. Lachann wondered how this related to Macauley's time on Skye. Or his departure from that isle.

No doubt he would find out when the *Glencoe Lass* returned with the Cameron brothers from their visit to Skye.

"I suppose there are no other aged whiskeys that could be substituted."

The men shook their heads. "Nay, Laird. Those were our oldest, and without a doubt our best."

"Mayhap we can find some way to appease the MacDonald."

"Aye," MacRae said. "The laird of Skye has been wanting an alliance with Kilgorra, but our laird has put off any talks of an alliance."

That made no sense to Lachann. "Why?"

"Because he has no one of good sense to advise him," MacPherson said.

Lachann considered this as a large, bald-pated man Lachann did not recognize came into the public house. All became quiet when the man sat down at the table across from Lachann and looked him directly in the eyes.

"Ye're the one that chucked m' son into the sea?"

Chapter 21

Lachann braced himself, and he could see that his men were doing the same, putting their hands on the hilts of their swords. Aye, Lachann felt he'd made headway with the Kilgorrans, but who knew where their loyalties would lie when it came to an outsider against one of their own.

"You're Ramsay?" Lachann asked in a deceptively calm manner. Now he saw a resemblance between this man and the blacksmith at the castle. Ruddy complexions, thick russet brows. He wondered if Birk's father was as crackbrained as the other Ramsays he'd met.

Frowning fiercely, the man gave a quick nod. "Roy Ramsay."

"Aye, then. I did," Lachann said. "If he's got the gumption to beat his wife bloody, then he can stand a wee dunking."

Every breath in the tavern seemed to stop as

Ramsay stood. Lachann stood too and faced the man, though he hoped he would not have to do anything drastic.

Ramsay wiped his hand on his plaid, then extended it toward Lachann. "Then I thank ye, Laird, fer showing my fool of a son the error of his ways."

Lachann took Ramsay's hand and shook it. He wasn't sure what to say, but fortunately, Duncan stepped in at exactly the right moment.

"We haven't seen him since Lachann tossed him into the sea, Ramsay."

"Nay," the older man replied. "He went away to the beach. Thinkin' about his drunken ways, I hope. But ever since he took a nasty fall a couple of years ago, he's been as unsound as my brother, with even less conscience."

Lachann wondered at that. The blacksmith had a conscience? "What beach?" he asked. "Why did he not go to the isle where his woman went with Anna MacIver, and beg her to come home?"

"Ach, because he is a proud lad," Ramsay said. "Too proud. And a bloody neep, t' boot. Besides, no one can go t' the isle without injury—no one but Anna MacIver and my son's wife."

"Because of the *sluagh dubh*?"

"Aye," Ramsay replied. "Years ago, old Wallace Kincaid broached Spirit Isle and returned a poor ravin' lunatic."

The other men at the tables muttered and nodded their assent.

"But Anna and Kyla go there—and stay—without ill effect." Lachann did not believe in malevolent spirits, but he'd enjoyed his banter over it with Anna. He didn't think she actually believed her own tale.

"Aye. 'Twas the strange old Norse woman from the castle who taught them some sort of potent magic to keep the spirit away."

Lachann felt a shudder go through the men around him. Graeme MacLaren—one of the servants from the keep—pinned him with a deadly serious gaze. "Anna learned how to keep the bloody *sluagh dubh* from comin' to Kilgorra for us."

Lachann refrained from laughing and gave credit to Anna and the Norse woman Ramsay spoke of. They'd figured an excellent method of keeping the isle to themselves.

On the other hand, he knew little of the Norse warriors who'd raided, then inhabited, the western isles centuries ago. A tiny piece of him could not discount the possibility that they'd brought some wicked sprites from their own lands to inhabit the wee isles in the Minch for some unknown purpose. Mayhap they'd brought them unknowingly.

The Kilgorrans believed *something* had happened to Kincaid to make him go mad on the isle—something Anna and Kyla knew how to prevent.

"What beach?" Lachann asked Ramsay, returning to reality. "Where did Birk go?"

"He likes a cave on the western shore, a few miles south of the harbor."

"There are a good many caves down the western shore," MacLaren added. "He could stay there for days."

"Aye," someone added, "and sometimes he does."

"I rode the western beach today," Lachann said, "but I didn't see any inhabited caves."

"Did you go 'round the tip to the southern shore?"

Lachann shook his head. "Not that far."

"He'd have been farther down the coast. 'Tis where he usually goes."

"I saw that the waters down that way are rocky and impassable," Lachann remarked.

"Aye. 'Tis what makes our harbor so valuable," MacRae said. " 'Tis the only safe approach, even for the fishing birlinns."

Lachann had much to consider as he and his men returned to the castle, not the least of which was what Macauley was about at the distillery. Merely thumbing his nose at his father-in-law on Skye?

He did not doubt it, for the Macauleys were an implacable lot. The only reason there'd been peace between the Macauleys and the MacMillans was that the MacMillans had kept Cullen's cousin hostage. If there had been a falling out after Fiona's death . . .

Ach, there was no point in conjecture now. Lachann would know soon enough, when Stuart and Rob Cameron returned with news from Skye.

When Lacann and his men rode back through the castle gate, his thoughts turned to a certain bonny maid who resided there. And he could not stop himself from wondering where she made her bed.

Anna did not sleep well. If her nights on Spirit Isle had been fraught with dreams of what Lachann's embrace—what his kiss—would be like, she knew now.

And her dreams all through the night reflected it.

She focused her attention on the skills he was going to teach her, and not on the way his arms had felt 'round her, or the heat of his lips on hers.

Because thinking about that kiss would be disastrous.

Anna scrubbed her face the next morning at dawn, and brushed her hair until it gleamed before putting it into her usual tight plait. She put on a light blue gown that was nothing special, except for being not yet threadbare.

She saw no one as she took the back way to Gudrun's cottage and let herself inside. There was very little light inside, so she lit a few candles, then got a fire started to take the chill out of the room.

She pushed a few more crates out of the way so

there was a large space in the center of the cottage for Lachann to demonstrate the best techniques for wielding a knife. She was just pushing the low bed that Kyla had used to the wall when Lachann arrived, carrying a leather satchel. His face was freshly shaved, and his hair tied neatly in a queue at his nape. He wore his usual plaid, but somehow it seemed more vibrant today. More . . . masculine.

Anna felt tongue-tied. How did a woman approach the man who had kissed her senseless the night before? Did she speak of it, or—

"What's in the crates?"

"Ah, just some discarded clothing and things from the keep," Anna replied.

He put the satchel on one of the lower crates and opened it, taking out several dirks.

"So many?"

"We'll find one that suits you," he said. "But first . . . Have you ever . . ." A crease appeared between his brows. "Has a man ever attacked you? Anyone besides Ramsay, when he tried to strangle you?"

"Only . . ." Anna shook her head. "Not really, no." Macauley had grabbed her and tried to kiss her a couple of times, but Alex or Graeme had intervened each time, and that had been an end to it. Fortunately, Catrìona had not learned of it. She would surely blame Anna for taking away her beau—as though Anna was even vaguely interested.

"Because there are things you can do to thwart a man without drawing a weapon."

He came to stand directly in front of her. "If I were to grab you like this . . ." He took hold of her upper arms. "Open your eyes, lass."

Anna looked up at him and found him gazing at her mouth. Her heart was pounding in her chest, and they hadn't even begun. She swallowed. "Sorry. I'm just a little nervous, I suppose."

"Aye, 'tis understandable," he said, tightening his grip on her arms. "Look. When Birk Ramsay took hold of you, you could have brought up your knee—hard— right between his legs. 'Twould have kept him from doing any further harm."

Herregud. Anna felt her cheeks heat.

"Try it on me."

"No! I couldn't."

"Aye. You must. You cannot learn to defend yourself if you are not willing to practice."

"But what if I . . ." She cleared her throat, feeling acutely self-conscious.

"I'll not let you hurt me, Anna," he said. Then he shook her slightly and made a low growl in his throat. "I'm Kyla's husband. And drunk. What do you think I will do?"

He put his hand around her throat, and Anna re-acted. She brought up her knee, aiming for his groin, but he dodged the blow.

"Aye," he said with a laugh. "If I hadn't been expecting it, you'd have unmanned me."

"Do not jest about such a thing," Anna said, averting her gaze from his knowing eyes.

"You're embarrassed, my bonny warrior." Lachann tipped her chin toward him so she had to look at him. "You did well. Shall we try it again?"

"No!"

He ignored her and came after her again. Anna tried to avoid him, but he caught her 'round her waist and pulled her close. The air went out of her lungs, and all she could think of was the way he'd held her the night before.

She could almost taste his kiss.

He held very still for a moment, and Anna could feel his heart beating in his chest. His breath was warm on her cheek.

"Wh-what should I do now?"

She felt him swallow. "Go for my nose." His voice was low and quiet.

"For y-your—?"

Anna hesitated, and Lachann pulled her closer, turning so they faced each other. His eyes were a rich, dark blue, with lashes even blacker than his hair, and his gaze was so very intense.

He tipped his head down, and Anna's entire body tingled with awareness. She wanted naught but to bask in the warmth of his strong arms 'round her while his mouth took hers in a searing kiss. She wanted him to—

Anna pushed away suddenly and ducked under his arms. *This is wholly wrong.*

"I have the idea." She wasn't entirely certain she *did* have the idea, and her voice sounded slightly shaky. "What about one of these knives? It will take more than just a jab at Birk's nose to keep him from killing Kyla next time."

She felt Lachann's eyes upon her, but she could not bring herself to look at him as she went to the leather satchel he'd brought. She picked up one of the dirks and weighed it in her hand.

"This one suits me." She turned and saw that Lachann was right behind her.

"Aye," he said after a moment's hesitation. "We can try it."

"What do I do?"

"Hold it this way," he said, his big hand dwarfing her own as he guided her fingers up to the hilt of the handle. "'Twill give you greater control."

Ach, but she wished she had more control over the attraction she felt. 'Twas the last thing she needed. The last thing she *wanted*!

"Where do I strike?"

"First, you must bear in mind that your target is much larger than you and is likely to take the knife from you before you can do any damage."

He lunged suddenly and took the knife from Anna's hand.

"I was not ready, Lachann!"

"No one is ever ready when they're attacked, Anna."

"Let me try that again."

"In a moment," he said. "You cannot show your weapon until you mean to use it."

"How will I do that?"

"The same way my sister does."

"You have a sister?"

He laughed, and the corners of his eyes crinkled. He looked exceedingly charming when he smiled. "Aye. Did you think I came from nowhere? Alexandra is our healer at Braemore and often goes about our lands alone," he said. "She knows how to protect herself."

"Did you teach her?"

"Aye. Along with my brothers."

"She carries a knife?"

He nodded. "In a sheath she wears on her leg."

Anna gave a shake of her head. "How?"

He coughed slightly. "Like mine." He gestured to the dirk he wore over his stocking, just below the knee. "Raise your skirts and I'll show you."

Chapter 22

Lachann knew better.

But he could not help himself.

Anna looked at him dubiously. "Raise my . . . ?"

"You'll need to strap the knife to your leg," he said. "Up high or below the knee like mine—whichever works best for you."

He reached into his pack for a knife sheath and a garter, then knelt before her. She was still hesitating. "You can't wear it on your belt in full sight, now, can you?"

"N-no. You're right. I'll need to surprise him."

She took hold of her skirt and lifted it to her knees. Lachann forced himself to ignore the shapely limb before him and wrapped the garter just below her knee.

He heard her breath catch and looked up at her. *Gesu,* but she was beautiful. And the way her teeth pulled at her lower lip was beyond alluring. Lachann slid his hand up past her knee and rose to his feet. He put one arm 'round her waist.

"Anna." He pulled her against him and took her mouth in a searing kiss. Sliding his hand down to her hip, he pulled her against his arousal.

Raw sensation shot through him when her body melted against him. Her hands slid up his chest, then 'round to the nape of his neck, and Lachann deepened their kiss.

He parted her lips and slid his tongue inside, relishing the heat of her mouth. She made a low, breathless sound and tipped her head to give him greater access.

Lachann feasted on her as he cupped her breast in one hand. He knew that slight touch wasn't enough when he felt her shudder against him. They both needed more.

Breaking their kiss, he pulled open the laces of her bodice and moved the cloth aside. "You are so very bonny, Anna MacIver . . ." She arched against him and Lachann lowered his head to take one hardened nipple into his mouth. He skimmed his hand up her leg, then placed her foot on the low mattress near the fireplace. He drew her skirt up behind her until he touched the bare skin of her bottom.

He slid his hand into the cleft. . . .

Anna moved against him, increasing the contact. She was hot and damp, and so very ready for him.

Lachann was as hard as his claymore and aching for her touch. "Anna . . ."

He took one of her hands and placed it on his burgeoning erection. Her touch was tentative, but as she ran her hand along his hard length she trembled even as she tightened her grasp.

"Aye, lass. That's it."

Lachann kissed her again, his tongue mating with hers as he laid her down on the bed and partially covered her with his body.

He slipped the hand under her skirt higher and touched the sensitive flesh between her legs.

She gasped and closed her legs against his hand.

"Anna, let me show you . . ." He used his thumb to trace a circle 'round the sensitive nub and slipped one finger inside her. Ach, she was so very tight, and Lachann was desperate to slide into her.

"Oh!" she cried. Her body jerked, the muscles of her legs tightening as she grabbed hold of his shoulders and pulled him down to her.

Her reaction to his touch was as explosive as the gunfire going on outside.

Lachann shoved his plaid aside, beyond ready to—

Gesu. Gunfire?

His arms shook. Desire, hot and pulsing, shot through his veins. He was on the verge of the most intense moment—

Another shot rang out, then shouts.

Lachann pushed up and off the bed. Somebody was shooting inside the castle walls!

His responsibility was clear, and yet . . .

"Lachann?"

Gesu, but he wanted her. Her eyes were hazy with passion . . . as well as confusion as he pulled away, righting his clothes.

"Anna . . . I am sorry . . ."

He dashed from the cottage, heading for the courtyard, where the sound of the gunshots had come from.

For no one on the isle—*no one*—had been issued a firearm.

Anna could not escape the cottage fast enough. She laced her bodice and grabbed a dirk, jamming it into the garter at her knee.

She did not want to see Lachann just now, did not want to run into him while he dealt with whoever was shooting in the courtyard. She took the overgrown path to the chapel and pried open the rusty gate in the castle wall behind it. Then she climbed down the rough rocks that formed the caves, as well as a natural staircase that led to the beach below.

Herregud! Her thoughts were muddled, but she knew there was naught to compare with what had just happened to her. Lachann's touch had taken away her will and her common sense, and replaced it with some kind of lunacy.

She thanked the heavens the seduction had gone no further.

Anna reached the sandy beach and dropped to her knees, holding her stomach as tears welled in her eyes. She could never allow anything like that to happen again.

As incredible as it had been.

She got to her feet and started running toward the village, feeling a little desperate, and more than a little bit foolish. Only a madwoman would dally with the man who would become her sister's husband.

Only a fool would leave her heart unguarded with such a man.

She'd had her doubts before, but now 'twas certain she could not stay at Kilgorra Keep and continue to serve Catrìona and her new husband after they married. She couldn't bear to attend him at meals or when he stopped for an informal breakfast in the kitchen; couldn't pretend that naught had passed between them.

'Twas not possible to feign an indifference she did not feel.

Worst of all would be knowing Lachann and Catrìona shared the pleasures of his bed, and having to watch her stepsister grow large and round with his bairns.

Thinking of those bairns trapped the breath inside Anna's lungs. She did not want to care, but 'twas all too clear that she did. Very much.

She arrived at the pier and saw that the *Saoibhreas* was anchored and its men were carrying crates of Kilgorra whiskey up the gangway. Well, at least something was going right. The whiskey trade kept Kilgorra a prosperous isle.

A young crewman who could not have been more than twelve or thirteen years of age started on his way up the path to the village. The mad idea she'd entertained in passing yesterday struck her once again, and Anna ran to catch up with him.

"Hello!" she called, and the lad stopped and turned to wait for her.

"Might I ask you a question?" she asked when she reached him.

"Aye?"

"Does your ship ever take on passengers?"

"Ach, nay," the lad replied, apparently appalled by the question.

"What if she worked for her passage?"

"*She?* A woman?" His already pale face went white at the very idea. He shook his head vigorously. "Nay. The captain allows no women aboard the *Saoibhreas*."

Anna glanced back at the hull of the ship. Mayhap she could sneak onboard and hide somewhere inside.

Aye. *She* might. But not with Kyla and Douglas.

And she did not know where the *Saoibhreas* was headed. "Ach, well," she said to the lad. "I only thought I'd ask."

He nodded absently, then started to cough, covering his mouth with his hand.

"Are you all right?" she asked.

"Aye. 'Tis naught but a wee catarrh," he replied, though he frowned when he swallowed thickly, wincing as he did so. It seemed to Anna he was sicker than he wanted to let on. Mayhap 'twas best that she did not get on that ship—especially with Kyla and Douglas—if there was sickness aboard.

"Well," Anna said, "if you need a tonic for it, our healer is well known for her remedies. She is the best in the isles."

He gave a nod, then continued on his way to the public house, where the rest of his shipmates might well have stopped before sailing out again.

Anna took the path to Kyla's cottage, acutely conscious of the knife strapped to her leg. Could she use it on Birk? She was fairly certain he would stay away at least another day. After that, Kyla and her husband would reconcile.

'Twas something Anna had never understood before—the bond of belonging.

Aye, she thought, coming to her senses. *And beatings from a man who was supposed to protect and care for her.*

Lachann knew he should have been grateful for the interruption at the cottage, but his body screamed for release even as he ran in the direction of the gunfire. He had to put the interlude with Anna in perspective. It had been a mistake.

A liaison with a well-loved serving maid could do naught to enhance his credibility on Kilgorra. Which did not alter the fact that he wanted her with a passion that was unmatched in his memory.

As he approached the back of the blacksmith's shop, it seemed every Kilgorran who'd come to the castle to train was heading in the same direction. He pushed his way through the group of men to where Cullen Macauley was standing with Catrìona, pistol in hand.

"What in hell is going on here?" Lachann demanded. "Is that one of my pistols?"

Grinning, Macauley shrugged.

Catrìona smiled sweetly at Lachann. "Cullen was just demonstrating his shooting skills, Lachann."

Lachann took the pistol from the bastard's hand and gave it to the closest Braemore man. "See that the weapons—all of them—are locked inside the barracks when we're not using them for training, Malcolm."

He faced Cullen and Catrìona, his anger at Macauley's stupidity palpable. "You think 'tis acceptable to play at target practice when you know full well that anyone might walk into the line of fire? We had a near disaster yesterday from one man's negligence."

"Surely you do not mean—"

"Aye, I do," Lachann snapped at Catrìona. "Davy MacDonall was nearly killed because Mungo Ramsay did not unload and put away a cart loaded with gunpowder and cannon balls. I'll have no more accidents here."

Catrìona looked as though she would shoot him a retort, but apparently she thought better of it and closed her mouth. Pointedly ignoring Lachann, she took Macauley's arm and led him away from the crowd. "Come along, Cullen. I thought your shooting was quite impressive."

The men returned to the practice area in the courtyard, and Lachann turned to Kieran. "How did Macauley get his hands on that gun?"

"He might have taken it while our men were unloading the supplies right after we arrived," Kieran replied.

Lachann muttered a low curse. "From now on, I want the weapons locked in the barracks, and the gunpowder in one of the empty buildings nearby," he said. "No one is to have access without our permission."

"Aye. I'll see to it."

Lachann glanced at the path to the cottage and wondered if Anna was still there. He'd left her abruptly, even rudely.

He closed his eyes and took a deep breath. *Gesu.*

The lass did not deserve the kind of treatment he'd given her.

"Lachann," Duncan said, tipping his head in the direction of Catrìona and Macauley. "This does not bode well."

Lachann did not know how to answer. No, it did not bode well, but neither did a marriage between himself and Catrìona. He did not want a woman who stood on the wrong side of everything that made any sense.

Lachann rubbed the back of his head. "Do you know Catrìona did not bother to go down to the MacDonalls' cottage yesterday to see how Davy fared?"

"She didn't?"

Lachann walked with Duncan toward the courtyard, ignoring the powerful draw to return to the old cottage. He knew how unlikely 'twas that Anna would be there waiting for him.

Still, the allure of finding her, wherever she might be—of seeing her *now* and finishing what he'd begun—was strong.

"Lachann . . ." Duncan glanced toward Catrìona's direction. "You know your wealth alone will not be enough to secure the lairdship."

"Do not worry, Duncan." Lachann tightened his belt 'round his waist. "When it comes down to it, 'tis up to her father."

"Aye, but—"

"He must know he needs our protection."

"One would think so."

"The old man gave me leave to make what changes I deem necessary on the isle," Lachann said. "I take that as a positive sign."

"Aye, but he's likely still thinking of you as his daughter's betrothed."

"Mayhap," Lachann said. "So I'm going to make myself indispensable in every way."

"What are you going to do?"

"I'm going to the distillery to see what other mischief Macauley is up to." Lachann told himself 'twould be highly impractical to go searching for Anna in the keep. She had her chores to perform, and he had duties as well.

Besides, Anna MacIver was a complication he could not afford.

Chapter 23

Lachann rode down to the pier, then turned up the village lane and made his way to the distillery, where he dismounted and tied his horse.

A well-dressed older gentleman came out of the building and greeted Lachann. He spoke loudly, to be heard over the sound of the waterfall. "I'm Geordie Kincaid. I've been hoping ye'd soon visit us here."

Lachann remembered hearing the name of the chief distiller, who, by all accounts, had run the place successfully for years. Lachann walked alongside him, breathing in the scent of the peat fires that dried the fermenting barley. He took note of the river that flowed past the distillery and on into the sea.

"The isle has more than one freshwater spring," Lachann said, nodding toward the steep mountain behind the village. He'd seen the spring on one of his earlier rides, so he knew where the source of the river was. And he'd seen yet another spring in the hills on the southern rim of the island.

"Aye. Sweetest water in th' western isles," Kincaid said, though he seemed distracted as he led Lachann into the huge building.

They made no whiskey at Braemore, so Lachann's knowledge of the distilling process was limited. But he knew the freshwater as well as the waterfall had to be an advantage. As they walked past two men who were at work shoveling a large stack of peat into what appeared to be an oven, Lachann took in the vast space on the ground floor, which was filled with barrels stacked as high as they could go.

"Is that the kiln?" he asked Kincaid.

"Aye. We've just laid out our last batch of mashed barley until the new harvest. We'll dry it with the peat fires for a day or so, then clear the floor for the new crop."

Lachann heard footsteps on the wooden floor above. "You've got men up there in all that smoke?"

Kincaid nodded. "Aye, but only fer a few minutes. We'll let the fires die while they turn the barley as it dries."

They came to a large, old, well-used table, with sheaves of paper stacked neatly upon it, along with an ink bottle and quill. A small, unlit lamp stood on its corner.

"What's this?"

"My office," Kincaid said with a frown.

Lachann glanced to the right, where a stout door stood closed. "What's in there?"

"Ah. *That* was my office for the past twenty years," he said. "I am now forbidden access to it."

"By whom?" Lachann asked, though he had a feeling he already knew the answer.

"Cullen Macauley," Kincaid replied, his temper simmering just below his surface. "He has installed himself as the manager of the distillery."

Lachann tried the door and found it locked. "Macauley has the only key?"

A satisfied look came over Kincaid's face when he drew a set of keys from a fold of his plaid. "Ach, no. He does'na know it, but I enter as often as I must."

"Open it, Kincaid."

The man did so, and they went into the small office. Lachann found it sparsely furnished with a desk and two chairs. Papers were scattered about the desk, and Kincaid clucked his tongue as he looked at the jumble of ledgers and correspondence.

"Ye can'na run the business this way," he said. "Look a' this mess."

Aye, the desk was untidy, and so was the top of an ancient, locked chest that stood against the opposite wall. There were several empty whiskey bottles lying upon it, exactly like the ones Lachann had seen at the castle, full of the laird's thirty-year malt.

"Does Macauley actually handle any business?"

Kincaid gave a nod. "Tradin' ships have come in, and they've dealt with *him*."

"You were cut out of the transaction?"

"Aye. I have no idea whether he's gettin' a fair price or if he's givin' it away. I've seen naught written in these ledgers."

Lachann knew the whiskey trade was rarely a simple business with cash in and whiskey out. The whole system was far too complex for an outsider—an inexperienced outsider—to come in and take over.

"I hope ye can do somethin' about that bastard—beggin' yer pardon, sir," Kincaid said. "He's takin' all our best whiskey an' wastin' it on Laird MacDuffie, who would'na know a thirty-year malt from a three-year barrel. He can'na read a ledger to save his soul, and"—Kincaid unlocked the safe behind the desk—"he's kept naught to pay the farmers."

Lachann picked up a few of the empty bottles. "Why are these here?"

"Exactly the point!" Kincaid said in a tight, angry voice. The color rose to his cheeks as he spoke. "I do'na keep bottles in my office . . . and aye, this is *my* office, not his!"

"I understand your predicament, Kincaid," Lachann said, "and I will do what I can. For now, though—"

"Catrìona can'na marry that rogue," Kincaid cut in. "He's a bloody weasel, and full of secrets. He is up to no good, I can tell ye."

Lachann already knew that. "What do you think he's—"

"I do'na know, MacMillan!" Kincaid shoved his fingers through his graying hair. "But, I tell ye 'tis most irksome to know there's a plan afoot with *my* distillery, and yet not know what it is."

Kincaid's hands were balled into tight fists. "We all see his plan is to win Laird MacDuffie's favor by fillin' him with our best whiskey. He keeps the old man fully jaked and barely sensible, and one o' these fine days, the bloody dobber will wrest the laird's consent to marry his daughter. Unless you can do somethin', 'twill be only a matter of time before there's a Macauley laird in MacDuffie's place."

Aye, Lachann suspected the same. He needed to get rid of Macauley as soon as possible.

"The ship in the harbor," Lachann said. "Is its business with the distillery concluded?"

Kincaid shook his head. "No money has exchanged hands yet, if that's what yer askin'."

"Good. I'll go talk to her captain," Lachann said. "And I'll put a stop to Macauley's access here."

"I thank ye, MacMillan. Fer all ye can do."

Lachann left the distillery, leading his horse toward the pier. He had a plan for keeping Macauley out of the distillery, but he'd yet to come up with a way to eject him from Kilgorra without causing offence to the laird and his daughter.

But he would think of something.

Anna felt more than a little shaken by what had happened in Gudrun's cottage. She needed Ky now.

She took the path up to her friend's cottage. She guessed Birk was still lying about in one of the caves on the beach, imbibing excessively, as was his wont these days.

"What's wrong?" Kyla asked as Anna came into the cottage and took Douglas from her friend's arms.

"Naught."

"Anna . . ."

"Have you seen Birk?" Anna could not speak of what had just happened in the cottage. Not even to Kyla.

Kyla crossed her arms over her chest, and her questioning gaze made Anna turn 'round and bounce Douglas in her arms.

"I've not seen him yet today."

Anna's feelings were so very raw that she did not know what to say. That her heart was in jeopardy? That Catrìona did not deserve a man like Lachann MacMillan? That she would consider breaking her vow of perpetual maidenhood for him . . . ?

If 'twas not already broken by their actions in the cottage.

"I got you a weapon," Anna said. She sat down and reached under her skirt for the dirk strapped at her knee. "Hide it in this garter, and when Birk tries—"

"Anna, no."

"Aye. You must protect yourself."

Kyla sat down across from Anna. The bruise 'round her eye was mostly green now. Fading.

"Next time he goes for you, knock him hard between the legs. Use your knee, or your fist if you must."

"I-I do not think I can."

"Aye. You can and you must," Anna said, deadly serious. "If he grabs you so you cannot damage his privates, then go for his nose. Use the heel of your hand, or your knuckles."

Kyla looked askance at Anna. "How do you know all this?"

Anna shrugged. "I asked someone."

"Who?"

"It does not matter who," she said. "He gave me good advice, and now I'm passing it on to you."

"He? Lachann MacMillan, aye?"

"What if it was?"

Kyla observed Anna's face, which she struggled to keep composed. She reached across the table and took Anna's hand. "He cannot marry Catrìona."

"Aye? Well, he must," Anna retorted, feeling perilously close to tears. "Kilgorra does not deserve a laird like the one we have. Or Cullen Macauley in his place."

Kyla did not disagree, and Anna's sense that her friend was quietly assessing her was confirmed by her next question. "What happened when you asked MacMillan for the dirk?"

"He gave me a lesson on how to defend myself."

"Is that all?"

Anna felt her face flush to the roots of her hair. "Of course."

"Mayhap you can lie to yourself, Anna MacIver," Kyla said. "But I know you too well."

Anna blinked back the moisture gathering in her eyes. "Naught can happen between Lachann and me, Kyla. Absolutely naught."

The look of pure disgust Catrìona had seen in Lachann MacMillan's eyes worried her. Aye, she supposed it had been foolish for Cullen to shoot off his pistol so close to the courtyard where someone might walk by. But Mac-Millan took too much authority upon himself. Chastising Mungo after that stupid boy had been hurt, berating Cullen . . .

Catrìona had not yet consented to wed him, and he was not yet laird.

He might never be. A controlling husband was not what Catrìona wanted, though his wealth was said to be immense. Far more substantial even than that of the Duke of Argyll.

She thought about what she might do with such riches. She could have a house on the mainland, at Inverness, perhaps. Or Fort William, where hundreds of men were garrisoned. She could socialize with others of her status. The wee wren could choose far more sophisticated lovers than the ones available to her on Kilgorra.

With MacMillan's money, Catrìona's wardrobe would be the finest anyone could order from France, not these homely gowns Anna sewed for her. *Ha!* Which would require a trip to Paris, she thought with glee, something Catrìona had never before thought possible.

Cullen was not a poor man, and he was far less controlling, far more amenable than Lachann MacMillan. Catrìona did not think he would mind if she went off to Inverness for a few months. Or spent time socializing in Paris with exciting, fashionable friends. As long as he had lairdship of the isle, he would be content.

She watched him sleep on the narrow bed in the chapel room and decided he was far easier to manage than MacMillan would ever be. But did he have the funds she wanted for this new life she envisioned?

If she wed Lachann MacMillan, would he ever agree that she could live the life she wanted while he stayed behind and built Kilgorra into the military bastion he wanted?

'Twas something she needed to find out before she made her decision.

Lachann settled the issues of payment with the captain of the *Saoibhreas,* then returned to the castle to handle

the problem of Macauley and the distillery. He strode
into the courtyard and signaled for Kieran to join him.
"Come with me to the blacksmith's shop."

"You have business with that simpleton, Lachann?"

Lachann nodded. "I just discovered to what extent
Macauley has been interfering at the distillery. I'm
going to lock him out of the place as soon as the blacksmith can make a new lock."

"Aye? You think Ramsay has the skill to do it?"

"I'm going to assume so. I want you to stay with him
while he fashions it and installs it. Make sure there are
only two keys. One is to go to Geordie Kincaid. You
keep the other."

"I foresee Catrìona objecting to this, Lachann."

"Aye, she might," Lachann said simply. But he did
not care. "After I talk to Ramsay, I want you to stay on
him until he completes the task."

They continued in silence to the blacksmith's shop,
where they found Ramsay, digging for something on
one of the deep shelves in his workshop.

"Ramsay."

He turned and made a deep growl, glaring at
Lachann as though he had some grievance.

"I want you to put a new lock on the door at the distillery," Lachann said.

"Ach, aye? And why should I do that?" The man
crossed his beefy arms over his chest.

Lachann walked up to the man and stood directly

in front of him. Ramsay was a few years older than Lachann, but they were both of a size, though Lachann would bet every barrel of whiskey stored at the distillery that the blacksmith could not best him in agility. Ramsay hadn't gained his brawn by moving swiftly in battle, as Lachann had.

"I thought I made myself clear yesterday." Lachann spoke quietly and evenly.

Ramsay leaned slightly forward at the waist so that his face came close to Lachann's. Clearly, the man was accustomed to using intimidation to accomplish his ends.

The man narrowed his eyes. "And if I'm too busy to get to it?"

"My cousin Kieran will help you make sure the new locks are a priority."

Kieran leaned back casually against the doorjamb, as though the blacksmith's decision to cooperate was of no concern. But Lachann was sure Ramsay had seen him in the courtyard, practicing with sword and pistol, as well as hand to hand. Ramsay would be a fool to tangle with him.

"Do it now," Lachann added without blinking. He waited for a sign, and when the man swallowed heavily, Lachann knew he'd won. Mayhap the burly blacksmith had learned his lesson yesterday.

Chapter 24

With an eye toward moving forward with his plans, Lachann took a ride up to Roscraig Peak, the cliff that rose above the village and overlooked the harbor. He was not exactly avoiding his return to the keep, but he knew 'twas best if he did not see Anna MacIver for a while. He needed to put some distance between them.

He had to stop reliving the moments before he'd heard the gunfire, when she'd come apart, just from his touch. Lachann had been seconds away from paradise when Macauley's gunshots had interrupted him.

He should be thanking the bastard for his timing.

Lachann chose a spot where he would station a lookout, then located the best place to perch a cannon. There was a clear view from there to the castle, and a good place to ignite a signal fire if an enemy approached from the harbor.

The sea was quiet, and Lachann saw Kilgorra's fishermen anchored far in the distance.

Then he saw Anna walking on the beach west of the village.

He knew it could only be she, for he'd seen no other woman on the isle with such pale hair. And the thick plait down her back swayed in time with her purposeful stride. Lachann's entire body quaked at the sight of her.

He forced himself to look away. What he might desire and where his duty lay were two entirely different things. He thought of Duncan's earlier query about Catrìona and knew he needed to work on a strategy for gaining the lairdship without marrying the woman.

He could not tolerate a life shackled to that woman.

He'd already offered his gold to shore up Kilgorra's defenses, and he hoped 'twould be enough. But Macauley was not without resources. His own wealth, along with marriage to the laird's daughter, could be persuasive to a drunken old man.

Gesu. It had all become far more complicated than it ever should have been. Lachann hoped the Cameron brothers returned from Skye with some useful information about Macauley. Soon.

Drawn to Anna in spite of himself, Lachann rode back to the village and stepped off the pier, retracing the path he'd taken yesterday. He could not help but wonder what she was doing on that isolated stretch of beach.

Gesu, was she making her way to the caves further south, where Birk Ramsay's father had said he would be? By the determination in her step, Lachann feared she was about to go after him alone.

With the dirk he'd strapped to her leg.

He rode down the beach, quickly catching up to her. He jumped down from his horse to walk beside her and managed to speak calmly to her. "Anna. I hope you are not on your way to look for Birk Ramsay."

She looked surprised. "You know the man is a menace."

" 'Twould not be wise for you to confront him alone."

"I realize that," she said, resuming her quick pace down the sandy beach. "But *someone* needs to!"

The thought of her doing it filled him with dread. "Anna, he is dangerous."

"Aye." With her expression set, she resumed walking.

He took hold of her arm and stopped her. "What if he attacks you? What will you do?"

Her eyes were clear and guileless, and her mouth was a temptation he found difficult to resist. He drew her close.

"I'm not going for Birk," she said, but he hardly heard the words, not when his body was demanding that he lift her into his arms and carry her to some secluded spot and remind himself just exactly how delectable those plump lips were.

She breathed deeply, and his arousal grew to impossible proportions when her chest moved against his. He wanted her, wanted to explore every sweet inch of her.

He tipped his head, determined to savor at least one kiss, when she suddenly tugged away.

"Sorcha," she called out, the name wrenching Lachann out of his sensual haze.

She slipped out of his grasp and turned toward an old woman he'd not noticed before, not when 'twas Anna who'd held his complete attention.

The crooked old woman was walking toward them from one of the caves, a large basket hanging from her arm. She seemed to be in her own world, walking toward the surf, bending every now and then to pick up something and place it carefully in her basket.

Somehow, Anna managed to make herself step away from Lachann, but her breath felt tight in her chest and a heated flush of pure sensation flowed through her veins. She did not know how she succeeded in speaking to the old midwife, Sorcha Carnegie, while Lachann still had his hand on her.

This white-hot attraction that flared between them must not continue. She would not be able to bear it later, when . . .

She swallowed back her unwise yearnings and looked up at him. His jaw was tightly clenched.

"I . . . I must go," she said.

For an instant, she thought he might protest, but then he gave a brusque nod of his head and moved away. He mounted his horse but did not take off for the pier right away.

"Anna . . ."

She felt the intensity of his gaze through her entire body, pooling in the womanly heart of her—right where he'd touched her and created a maelstrom of sensation.

She let out a shaky breath and turned to Sorcha. Because she knew better than to dwell upon what could never be.

She hurried away from Lachann, toward the old woman who was walking alone down the beach, bending periodically to collect a shiny shell from the sand and put it into her basket.

Sorcha had attended Anna's mother at the fatal birthing of her bairn, Laird MacDuffie's son. These days, the woman often lost her way, and 'twas feared she might one day walk into the sea—and not return. Somehow, she'd gotten past her niece who usually kept an eye on her.

"Sorcha!" Anna called again.

The woman straightened up and looked back at Anna. She smiled broadly. "Anna? 'Tis a joy t' see ye, lass!"

"Aye, and you," Anna replied. "It looks as though your basket is full, Sorcha. I think 'tis time to go home. Màili will be worried about you."

"Màili? Nay, she's workin' at her loom. She will no' miss me."

Ah, but she would. Anna took the old woman's arm and started walking up toward the pier. Toward Lachann, whose retreating figure was not so very far away.

Anna's chest ached. Her resolve faltered, and for a moment, she entertained the impossible wish that everything could be different. That Sorcha had not been there on the beach, that she had taken Lachann to Spirit Isle, where they could be alone to—

"Is that yer man, Anna lass?"

"What?" Anna's face infused with an impossible heat.

"Yer husband." The old woman took hold of Anna's arm. She had a surprisingly strong grip.

"No, Sorcha. I have no husband, and I . . . I do not plan to marry."

"Ach, then, a lover," Sorcha said, embarrassing Anna even more. "Ye must take a man t' yer bed—"

"I do not think that would be wise—"

"Blatherskite," she retorted. "Wisdom plays no part in what takes place betwixt a woman and her man."

Anna nearly choked, for 'twas absolutely true. What had happened in Gudrun's cottage between her and Lachann had not been the least bit wise. "Sorcha, I'm sure you're right. But I—"

"What are ye afeared of, lass? Gettin' a bairn?"

Anna felt mortified by the conversation. Luckily, Lachann was too far away to hear what Sorcha was saying. 'Twould only magnify her embarrassment at such talk. "Please, Sorcha, you must not speak of such things."

"And why ever not?" the midwife demanded. "I might ferget a wee task now and again, but I remember every bairn I brought into this world. And I know a thing or two about keepin' one from startin'," she added with a wink. "How d'ye think Catrìona MacDuffie has gotten by all these years without one?"

As Lachann returned to the pier, he wondered why naught could ever be as simple as planned.

He did not like leaving Anna on the beach when he knew Birk Ramsay could be nearby, but he didn't really believe Ramsay would come out of his lair and attack her. He was likely so hungover he could barely walk.

Besides, Anna had an old woman to deal with, and he knew she would not just abandon her. Not his fair Anna. She was so much a part of this island that he found her desire to leave impossible to understand.

He rode up onto the pier, where all roads seemed to meet on Kilgorra, and saw Catrìona coming down the path from the castle. She was alone, and not paying much attention to her surroundings.

But at least Macauley was not with her. Lachann wondered what new mischief he was up to.

Catrìona stopped abruptly when she saw him. "Lachann! You . . . you are just the man I wanted to see." She looked past him and up at the ship, causing Lachann to believe otherwise. He wondered what business she had with the *Saoibhreas*.

"Aye?" he said, dismounting. "You thought you would find me here on the beach?"

"Of course not," she responded. "But you were not up at the castle with your men, so I thought possibly . . ."

"You grew bored with Macauley?"

"You must forgive him, Lachann. He did not think."

"Mayhap," Lachann replied. "But if you believe that's a fair excuse for a man who thinks he ought to be laird—"

"Well, he *does* want to marry me."

She said it as though a proposal from Macauley was the greatest honor that could have been bestowed.

If Lachann had had any doubts about taking Catrìona to wife, the answer to that question became clear at that moment. But he was not going to tip his hand just yet. He would say naught of the matter until he discussed it with Duncan and Kieran. There had to be a way to wrest control of the island without marrying MacDuffie's daughter.

The first order of business would be to get rid of Macauley. He would attempt to do it peacefully. But if the stoat would not leave, then Lachann would deal with him in whatever manner was most expedient.

'Twould be greatly satisfying to tie him to one of the small boats, tow him out to the open sea without a paddle, and leave him there. In a storm.

Catrìona put her hand through the crook of Lachann's arm, but she stopped suddenly when Anna and her elderly companion came onto the pier and up into the village. Lachann winced when Anna's eyes caught sight of Catrìona's arm in his. He felt like pushing Catrìona aside and following Anna to the village.

But circumstances did not allow it. Not yet. He turned his attention to Catrìona. "Where is Macauley now?"

"I have no idea, Lachann." She turned a bright smile upon him. "But I do know the bonniest point of all Kilgorra. I'd like to show it to you."

"Mayhap some other time, Catrìona." Lachann disentangled himself from her grasp. "I still have much to do this morn."

"Are you saying—"

"I will see you later, at the castle," he said. He took his leave of her, leading his horse up the path to the public house. He wondered which direction Anna had taken, for she was nowhere in sight.

He passed numerous shops as he rode through the village, and soon he came to a cobbled street that was lined with modest stone dwellings, all bordered by a low, stone wall. Some had small gardens in front, and there were pots full of colorful flowers on the wall. At the top of the lane, Lachann saw Anna standing with the old woman she'd met on the beach, talking with yet a third woman.

Her smile was stunning, as was her regal stance. She was gracious and sweet, and at the same time so very sensual that every muscle in his body clenched tightly as he observed her.

All three women were laughing and enjoying the swift breeze and early afternoon sun. Anna smiled and looked up at the sky as if she hadn't a care in the world, though when she caught sight of Lachann, she blushed to the roots of her hair. Just the sight of her charming dimple high up on her cheek was enough to make him as hard as the stone wall that edged the lane.

He blew out a long breath, reminding himself that he needed to tread carefully, at least until matters with MacDuffie were settled.

He dismounted and walked up to the group.

"Ach now, are ye no' the braw lad?" the old woman said in greeting.

Anna blushed to an even deeper red, but she collected herself and made the introductions. "Lachann, these are my friends, Sorcha Carnegie and Màili Carnegie, cousin to Janet, whom you've met."

"We've all heard of yer wee clash wi' Birk Ramsay," Màili said. "Has he come lookin' fer ye yet?"

"Ach," Sorcha scoffed, looking up at him with canny gray eyes. "Birk has no' the wits God gave a sparrow. He's no match fer the likes o' ye."

"Sorcha—"

"Anna," Sorcha said, turning to the object of Lachann's interest, "ye would do well to take this one t' yer bed and see what kind of braw sons he can give ye."

Chapter 25

Lachann did not seem to hear Sorcha's incredibly embarrassing words, for his attention was wholly directed on something behind Anna.

"*Gesu,* the distillery is on fire!" he rasped.

Anna turned to look back and saw black smoke rising from . . . "'Tis not the distillery, Lachann," she said, just before he mounted his horse and took off at a gallop. "'Tis the granary!"

The bell at the kirk began to clang just as Lachann turned and raced down the lane.

"Màili, take Sorcha inside," Anna said. "Then we need to get everyone to the granary with their buckets."

She shouted the alarm as she ran, and people hurried out of the shops and cottages, prepared to fight the fire. By the time Anna arrived at the granary, Lachann was there with Geordie Kincaid and the other men from the distillery, who were already trying to douse the fire with pails of water from the river.

But the back wall of the building was nearly engulfed in flames.

Lachann climbed a stout oak that stood behind the granary. A group of men gathered to form a line from the river to the granary, handing buckets of water, one after the other, to Lachann, who tossed it on the flames. Another man brought out a ladder and stood at its top on the far side of the granary, doing the same thing.

Anna organized the village women into yet another brigade to fill the buckets and quickly pass them down a line of hands that got the water to Lachann and the others who were closest to the fire.

The smell was horrific, and the work was backbreaking as well as desperate. They could not allow the fire to spread outward, else several shops and homes would be destroyed, as well as the distillery itself. Losing the granary was going to be bad enough.

Anna hastened 'round to Lachann's position and saw how perilous it was. He was far too close to the fire! His face and arms were filthy, and he was covered in sweat. Burning ash flew about his head, and Anna worried one of the embers would land in the brush nearby and start another fire that could easily engulf him.

Men handed buckets to him, one after the other, and he tossed the water at the fire as quickly as he could. But the flames spread and licked up toward him.

Panic engulfed Anna, much like the flames that were so very likely to overcome Lachann. She shouted at him to come down, but he kept at his task.

Anna interrupted the flow of buckets, taking one to throw its contents on the ground 'round Lachann, wetting it to prevent a spark from catching beneath him.

Men from the castle soon arrived and threw their backs into the fight, some carrying water, others climbing to high points behind the granary.

"We must pull down the walls before it spreads!" Lachann shouted to the men.

"Aye!" they responded, though they continued pouring water on the fire.

Finally, Lachann climbed down from his perch and disappeared into the distillery with Geordie. When they returned a few moments later, they carried several long poles with hooks attached to their ends.

"Clear the field!" Lachann shouted, distributing the poles to several of the men.

Anna and the others with buckets scurried away and watched as Lachann and his men stepped as close as they could, hooking the ends of the poles into any crack or crevice in the fiery wall.

On Lachann's count, they started pulling down the burning building. After much straining, it came crashing down, crumbling into embers while the other three walls fell into it.

The fire ebbed, but the work was not done.

People continued throwing water on the collapsed building, and the men all pitched in to dig a trench 'round it. Hours after Lachann first saw the smoke, the granary was reduced to a mere stinking, smoldering mess. But at least it posed no threat to anything else on the isle.

The tavern keeper brought out a few benches and a barrel of ale, which he poured liberally into the mugs of everyone who'd helped with the fire. Lachann drank deeply, looking 'round the crowd for Anna.

He was sure he'd just seen her.

Mayhap she'd gone back to the castle. Or to her friend's cottage.

"Kincaid," he said, catching sight of the distiller. "Walk with me. Duncan and Kieran, come with us."

They stepped over the rubble left by the disaster and soon came upon the pile of wood and stone that was left of the granary. "Do you know how the fire started, Kincaid?"

The man shook his head. "I can'na think how, Mac-Millan. The weather has been fair damp most days, not a dry timber anywhere on the isle."

Which was exactly what Lachann thought. They'd had a few rays of sun that afternoon, but the days had been misty in the morn, and there had been some rain as well. "Kieran, did you see the blacksmith return to the castle after he changed the locks?"

Kieran nodded. "He went back a long time ago. Hours." He glanced at Kincaid, who nodded. "Lachann, do you think the fire was started intentionally?"

Lachann gave a nod. "Unless 'twas an accident of some sort."

"What sort?" Kincaid asked, his forbearance obviously wearing thin. He paced back and forth next to the destroyed building. "What kind of accident would it be? No one has any business hanging about the granary. No one would be lighting a pipe back there . . ." He shook his head, obviously unable to figure how the fire might have begun.

"Aye. That's what I thought, but I wanted to make sure you agreed." Cullen Macauley had to believe his chances of gaining the lairdship of Kilgorra were slim if he was trying to interfere with Lachann's plans to build a fighting force here.

Macauley's strategy might be to mount an attack and try to take the isle by force, for what better way was there to ensure success than by keeping Kilgorra preoccupied with rebuilding the granary and therefore leaving itself undefended?

"But I can'na think of any purpose to burning down the granary," Kincaid said. "The harvest does not take place for at least two more weeks. If someone wanted to harm the whiskey business . . . well, there was very little barley inside, and we do'na store our barrels there."

"Lachann," Duncan said, "I did not see Macauley in any of the brigades."

"Nor did I," Kieran said. "And the man knows naught about distilling. He likely did'na know the granary was empty."

Lachann met Kincaid's eyes and knew the man shared his own suspicions about Macauley. "I'll go up to the castle and see if I can find him."

"You'll question him?"

Lachann gave a nod. "And I'll find out if anyone saw Ramsay in his shop."

"Do you want us to come along?" Duncan asked.

"No, I'll handle this alone."

Anna had never been so terrified. When Lachann had perched so precariously in the tree behind the granary, she'd realized she might lose him to the fire.

'Twould be far worse than losing him to Catrìona.

Ach, she felt torn in every direction as she made her way back to the castle.

It had been a horrid afternoon—*a horrid day all 'round,* Anna thought as tears filled her eyes. It had become clear that there was no solution to her predicament. She did not know how she was going to get away from Kilgorra, and Lachann was not about to leave.

No, after seeing him fighting the fire, she realized how firmly dedicated he was to becoming laird.

She trudged up the path to the castle and had nearly made it to the gates before she heard the sound of horses' hoofs trotting up behind her.

Lachann swung down beside her. He did not hesitate but pulled her into his arms. They were both hot and filthy, but naught had ever felt as good as his body pressed tightly against hers. He kissed her hard, then released her.

"You are unharmed?" His eyes were reddened from the irritation of being so close to the fire, and his face was sooty. She supposed hers must be the same.

She nodded, swallowing hard, just as Angus and Robbie came running up the path.

"Anna!" Robbie shouted. "Did ye see it?"

"Aye." Her voice was as shaky as the rest of her.

"Laird MacMillan! Ye pulled the whole wall down!" Angus cried excitedly.

"Lads," Lachann said, "were you in the village when the fire started?"

The two boys looked at each other. "Aye. O' course we were!"

"Did you see anyone up near the granary? Or the distillery?" Lachann asked, as several of his men rode up alongside them.

Angus shook his head. "We were fishin' off the pier. I did'na see anyone. Did ye, Rob?"

Robbie shook his head, then Angus grabbed his friend's sleeve and pulled him along to the castle gate.

"Do you think—"

"Lachann!" His men came up behind them, engulfed him, asking questions.

Anna had no business there, and she ran ahead to catch up with the boys as they went through the castle gate. She hurried past the keep and the courtyard, taking the path through the garden to Gudrun's cottage. Once inside, she shut the door and sat down on the bed.

Ach, she seemed to have come full circle, all in one day. From those exquisite moments in Lachann's arms, to her terror as he'd fought the fire. She *was* going to lose him.

Kilgorra needed a leader such as Lachann.

She could not stay and witness Catrìona's marriage. The *Saoibhreas* would not take her, and she doubted any other ship would, either. But she needed to get away from the keep, away from Lachann and his wife.

Aye, she could go to Spirit Isle for a time, but she could not live there permanently.

Anna glanced 'round the cottage and thought mayhap it could be her home. Gudrun had lived there for years after Sigrid's death. All Anna needed to do was to clear out the boxes and crates, and she could make it her own.

'Twould mean she would not leave everyone she knew and loved on the isle, though she would need to take pains in order to avoid Lachann and Catrìona. She decided it could be done.

She got up and went to the window. She pushed the shutters open and gazed out at the bench, now overgrown with moss and mold, where Gudrun used to sit. She could so easily picture her mother's old servant, living alone out there for so many years.

Anna quickly pulled her head inside and closed the shutters, unwilling to think about what that reality meant for her.

Anna managed to slip away from Lachann far too easily, but he let her go for now.

He checked on Ramsay and discovered numerous people had seen him hanging about his shop after returning from changing the locks at the distillery. Which left Macauley. Lachann intended to find the bastard and give him the thrashing he deserved.

"The men would like to resume their training this afternoon, Lachann," Duncan said.

"I want to meet with them back at the distillery in an hour," Lachann replied.

"Aye?"

"We'll need to rebuild the granary right away," he explained. "'Tis nearly harvest time, and the barley must be stored somewhere so the distillery has what it needs for this year's brew."

Kieran nodded. "We can get a new one up quickly. All we'll need is the timber."

"And the hardware," Duncan said, frowning. They were going to need the blacksmith's skills.

"Aye. And manpower," Lachann said. "Training must be suspended until there's a new granary to store the grain." *Damn all.*

"This sets us back, Lachann."

"'Twas likely the point," Lachann said angrily. "If Macauley wanted to distract us from creating a fighting force, he succeeded."

"'Tis quite a diversion from what we intended to do here," Duncan said.

Lachann was furious. If that was what Macauley had intended, he'd succeeded. Lachann wanted nothing more than to ram his fist down the bastard's throat and then shove him off the battlements to the sea below.

But he reined in his temper and rode through the gates, quickly dismounting at the keep, leaving his men to take his horse to the stable.

He went into the keep and up to the great hall, where Graeme was replacing the candles in the lamps.

"Have you seen Macauley?"

"No, I haven't seen him all day," Graeme replied.

"Do you have any idea where he might be?"

The man's color deepened—with anger or embarrassment, Lachann could not tell. "Ye might look . . . er, try the old chapel, sir."

"The chapel?" Lachann asked. "Beyond the stable, out by the castle wall?"

Graeme nodded. "Aye, that's it."

The place where Catrìona had taken *him*. The information did not sit well with Lachann. If Catrìona had also taken Macauley out there . . .

He was doubly glad of his decision regarding their marriage. "What about Laird MacDuffie?"

"He is in his bedchamber, sleeping," Graeme replied.

"Has he heard news of the fire in the village?"

"I do not think so, sir," Graeme replied. "Is the granary completely gone?"

Lachann nodded. "But nothing else in the village caught."

Graeme crossed himself. "Thank the Lord."

"Aye."

Lachann took the stairs to the bedchamber two at a time and went to MacDuffie's room. He knocked softly, and Alex MacRae came to the door. Lachann stepped inside and saw that the laird was indeed sound asleep.

Alex returned to the fireplace, where he'd been building up the fire.

"He complained of the cold when he had a waking moment," the servant whispered.

Lachann looked at the old laird. The man did not look well, and though there was a wee chill in the air, 'twas certainly not cold in the room. "What ails him, Alex?"

Alex shrugged. "He's always enjoyed his ale, sir, but so much whiskey is no' good fer him. And these days, he does'na always keep his food down."

All the more reason for Lachann to settle matters with him. If he died before he made Lachann his heir, Lachann would have to return home, leaving Kilgorra under dubious leadership.

It would also mean he had not secured the isle for Braemore's protection. 'Twould be an entirely unsatisfactory result of all his planning.

He left the keep and made a quick run out to the chapel, where he found no one, not Macauley, not Catrìona. His confrontation would have to wait.

But it was coming, as soon as he found the filthy stoat.

Chapter 26

Anna spent the rest of the day working in the cottage without interruption. No doubt everyone was busy at the granary, cleaning up after the disaster.

But she could not go down there, could not face Lachann again—not until she managed to overcome her bewilderment. She'd been so very certain she would never succumb to a man's seduction, and yet she had completely surrendered to Lachann's touch. Her body still tingled with the aftereffects of that last kiss, and she yearned for the strength and security of his arms 'round her.

And yet she knew how illusive those were. Hadn't her mother—*hadn't Kyla*—proved that? To love someone so desperately was to invite disaster. 'Twas an invitation Anna would never give.

She would think no more of Lachann MacMillan but concentrate on making her refuge habitable, at least for the near future. She knew 'twould be best to get away altogether. Just because the *Saoibhreas* was not inclined to take on passengers did not mean every other ship was the same. One day, she might be able to make Kyla see reason, and they would make their escape.

Kilgorra could go on as before—without them—and with a new laird in charge.

She swallowed back the unwelcome surge of emotion that rose up in her chest and pored through the crates. She found so many children's clothes inside, garments that could have been put to good use through the years. Anna recognized some of the small garments as her own, and she believed some must have been Catrìona's.

She did not know who had packed up all the clothing, but she intended to make it her business to see that it was distributed among the island's children.

By the time she finished at the cottage, 'twas far later than she thought. No one was up and about in the keep, so she went up to the bathing chamber to soak off the dirt and grime from the fire in the large metal tub her mother had brought from Kearvaig. Catrìona forbade Anna to linger up near the bedchambers unless she was performing her chores, and Anna had been soundly chastised whenever she'd used the tub.

But what her stepsister did not know would not hurt her.

As she sank down into the water, she'd assumed she would be sufficiently exhausted that her mind would just drift into innocuous thoughts. But the tips of her breasts tightened into sensitive buds, and her muscles felt taut with anticipation.

Of Lachann's touch.

When she closed her eyes, she could see every dark whisker on his face, and the specks of green in his dark blue eyes. A shudder of pure longing came over her. A longing to feel Lachann's hands upon her body, a yearning for the kisses he'd given her in Gudrun's cottage.

She let out a groan of frustration over the obvious foolishness of such desires, and because the maddeningly acute yearning between her legs did not abate when she stood up and stepped out of the tub.

She wrapped herself in a thick cloth, and as she tucked the end between her breasts, she forced thoughts of Lachann MacMillan from her mind. 'Twas beyond irritating that the man had such a deep hold on her faculties. She wished she knew how to dispel it.

She took another cloth and vigorously dried her wet hair with it, even though 'twould be a mass of tangles to comb. Mayhap the pain of that would help her get her thoughts in order.

She collected her clothes and her shoes in one hand and opened the door a crack. No one was about, so she blew out her candle and stepped out.

A loud crash stopped her before she made it to the stairs. The sound came from the vicinity of the solar on the floor above, so she dropped her belongings and ran to the steps, where she encountered Lachann Mac-Millan coming out of his bedchamber, just as she was about to climb.

"Anna . . ." Even in the shadowy passageway, she saw his eyes sweep over her, and her heart lurched with that impossible yearning she'd spent so much effort to eradicate. "What was it?" he asked.

"I-I'm not sure."

She started for the steps, but Lachann stopped her. "I'll go first."

She hastened up the curving stone steps right behind him. They reached the top and found Anna's stepfather lying on the floor with his whiskey bottle smashed at his side and the sweet, grainy-smelling liquid splattered everywhere.

"Watch your feet," Lachann said.

They were bare, as usual, but Anna felt more than slightly naked. What she wore covered her body only from her chest to an inch below her knees.

"Fetch one of the menservants, Anna," Lachann said as he crouched down beside the moaning old man. He lifted him to a sitting position, but his head lolled to one side. 'Twas bleeding profusely.

Anna hastened down the steps and stopped at Catrìona's door. She knocked lightly, and when there was no answer, she opened it. Catrìona was not inside.

Anna did not stop to question where her stepsister

might be, but held onto her towel and hurried all the way down to the servants' quarters. She flew past her own room and knocked on Alex's door. "Alex, come quickly! You're needed!"

She heard the rustling of a mattress and a low groan, then Alex opened his door, wrapping his plaid about his waist. He looked her up and down, clearly astonished by her state of undress. "What is it, lass?"

"MacDuffie fell and Lachann needs help getting him down from the solar."

"How did he get up there?" Alex asked. "Ach, never mind. He's taken to drinking his whiskey in strange places."

Anna's only clothes were lying on the floor upstairs near the gallery, for she'd left her spare gown in the laundry. She had no choice but to return to the solar dressed as she was. She found that Lachann had propped up MacDuffie against a wall.

He'd tried to contain the bleeding with an edge of MacDuffie's plaid, but the gash bled relentlessly. And the laird was moaning insensibly.

"Help me get him down to his bedchamber, Alex," Lachann said.

The two men managed to lift MacDuffie, and between them, they got him down the steps and into his chamber. Anna went ahead, aware that the cut on her stepfather's forehead would likely need stitching.

She gave a fleeting thought to Catrìona, who should be found and told of her father's mishap. But there was no time to mount a search for her. Anna opened MacDuffie's bedchamber, then pulled down his blankets and lit the lamp next to the bed as the men put MacDuffie onto the mattress.

"I'll need to go and get my sewing box," she said.

"I'll get it," Alex replied. "You stay here with the laird."

"Alex, I—"

But Alex quit the room, and Anna felt Lachann's eyes upon her. She tried not to feel self-conscious when she poured water into a basin and brought it to the laird's bedside. But Lachann did not take his eyes from her as she moistened a cloth and began to clean the wound. "There is no need for you to stay, Lachann," she said. "I'll—"

"You may need help holding him down."

"Alex can—"

"I'll do it," Lachann said.

Anna did not argue. Nor did she pay any attention to the wave of heat that slid through her as she stood half naked with the man she'd spent most of the day trying not to think of.

Anna concentrated on cleaning MacDuffie's wound and wished she could hide her red, chafed knuckles. But he seemed not to notice.

His gaze was fully focused on her face, moving from her eyes, locking upon her mouth for a moment, then down.

He cleared his throat and looked away, and only then did Anna feel as though she could breathe again.

"Does this happen often? MacDuffie drinking himself insensible?"

"Only of late, though he does not usually fall and bring himself such grief."

"He seemed on death's door when I looked in on him earlier. 'Tis a wonder he was able to climb those stairs."

Anna dabbed the wound, eliciting a groan from her stepfather.

"At least he seems a peaceful drunkard," Lachann said. "Unlike your friend's husband."

"Birk wasn't always like that," Anna said, though she did not know why she bothered to defend the man. "When he and Kyla wed, he was . . ."

"Aye?"

She shrugged. "No one ever thought he would become a husband who beat his wife."

"Least of all Kyla, I imagine."

"She was a happy bride," Anna said. "She bore a bonny son for her husband seven months ago. One would think he'd have been pleased, but his drinking worsened after he fell and cracked his head on the deck of his father's birlinn. Now, no one on the isle seems to have any influence over the blasted stoat."

Until Lachann MacMillan had tossed him into the harbor. Would Birk change once Lachann became laird and he had to fear his wrath?

Alex returned to the bedchamber with Anna's sewing

box, which used to belong to Gudrun, and perhaps even to Anna's mother before her. Every time Anna opened it, she hoped it had once rested in Sigrid's hands, that her mother had used the needles inside to make her own daughter's clothes—the very same items Anna had found tucked away in Gudrun's cottage.

She lifted the cloth from her stepfather's forehead and blood oozed out from the deep cut.

"Aye. 'Twill need sewing," Lachann said. "Alex, you take his legs and arms. I'll restrain his head."

Alex draped himself over the laird as Anna quickly threaded her needle. She began to stitch, rousing Laird MacDuffie from his stupor. Lachann and Alex managed to hold him still enough for her to complete her task.

Lachann nearly groaned when Anna bit her lower lip and let it slowly slide out again. He barely noticed her making each careful stitch, but watched as she winced a little when the needle pierced the old man's skin.

He should tell her to go and clothe herself, but he could not bring himself to do so. He was enjoying the view far too much for that.

He could not stop thinking about the advice old Sorcha had given Anna. *Ye would do well to take this one t' yer bed.*

Aye. He did not disagree.

Her eyes were lovely. And all that bonny, bare skin smelled like pure sunshine. The waves of her damp, wheat-blond hair were so very sensual, framing her beautiful face.

Every male nerve in his body yearned for the length of toweling that covered her body to come loose. And yet the last thing Lachann wanted was to share the sight of a naked Anna MacIver with Alex MacRae.

He wanted her alone, by God. And he wanted her now.

Every grimace she made as she sewed reminded him of her soft heart. She was very much the lady of the isle, taking Sorcha back to her family in the village, and pitching in to help fight the fire without hesitation. And then there was Davy MacDonall and the rest of the children of the castle—

"The old man will'na leave his bed upon the morrow," Alex said, interrupting Lachann's thoughts.

"He's done this before?" Lachann asked, for Alex sounded as though he spoke from prior experience.

"Not as bad as all this, Laird," Alex replied. "But after a bottle or two of Kilgorra whiskey, especially the old brew Macauley has been bringin' him of late . . ."

"Where is Catrìona?" Lachann asked. "She should be told of her father's accident."

Alex shrugged, and Lachann looked at Anna.

"Er, she is a sound sleeper," Anna replied.

"She must be half dead not to have heard that crash."

Anna ducked the question and tied the last stitch in the laird's head. She gently dabbed a tiny ooze of blood from MacDuffie's forehead. Then the man relaxed, settling down to his drunken sleep, snoring loudly.

"Well done, Anna." Alex pulled MacDuffie's bloody plaid out from under him and carried it to the door. "I'll be takin' my leave now."

Anna looked sharply at him. "Alex—"

"Aye?"

"Naught," she said, taking a quick, shy glance at Lachann. "I can finish here. Go back to bed."

Lachann watched her pull the blankets over MacDuffie, then move two chairs away from the bed, shoving them against the wall. She reached under the bed for the chamber pot and put it on the floor within easy reach of the laird's hand.

"What are you doing?" he asked.

"Just making sure he suffers no other mishap during the night," Anna replied. "Do you think I ought to sit up with him?"

Lachann took her arm and drew her away, to the door. "No, I do not," he said quietly but firmly. "I think you should get some sleep. You are so weary you can barely stand."

"No, I'm—"

Lachann silenced her with his mouth upon hers. She stiffened in shock, but as he gathered her close, her body softened against his. She fit him perfectly, her curves against his hard planes, just as he remembered. Just as he'd thought about all day, despite the fire and the resulting difficulties.

He eased her back against the wall and deepened their kiss, shifting his body slightly to relieve the ache in his loins. She opened for him on a quiet sigh. Lachann sucked her tongue into his mouth and slid his hand between them, to the tenuous fastening of the cloth she'd wound around her body.

It slipped loose absurdly easily, and when it fell to the floor, Lachann felt her shiver.

But not from any chill. The room was warm enough, so he suspected her bare breasts were exquisitely sensitive to the light brush of the cloth as it fell away.

She clutched Lachann's shirt to steady herself, and his hands drifted to the sides of her breasts. Then he cupped their fullness and created a firestorm of need.

In both of them.

Lachann barely touched the tips of her breasts before they became tight peaks of arousal. He could not help but break their kiss and slide his lips down to her throat. He moved further down, then touched his tongue to one taut nipple while he teased the other with his fingers.

She made a low sound of pleasure, inciting him to reach 'round to her bonny backside and pull her fully against him.

Chapter 27

Catrìona paced before the fireplace in her sewing room. Not that she ever did any sewing there. But she'd never had a man there, either—not until Cullen Macauley had come to Kilgorra.

"For heaven's sake, Cullen, go out there and see what's happened." They'd heard a crash and some voices. Clearly, something was going on.

It infuriated her when he rested lazily against the cushions of the settee and watched her. "Why? Unless the keep is on fire—which I doubt very much, since it is made of stone—I don't see why we should care about a wee, pucklie clatter."

He swore he'd had naught to do with the fire at the distillery, and Catrìona believed him. Why would he want to destroy the very thing he thought was most valuable on the isle? He intended to expand the whiskey trade and make Kilgorra's brew the most coveted in all of Britain and France.

She narrowed her eyes at the man. "Cullen . . ."

"'Twas likely a servant dropping something heavy. Come over here, pet. I'm not through with you."

"I should go back to my bedchamber," she said. Without anyone seeing her, of course. Then she could come out as though she'd been there all night, and start asking questions. What if something serious had happened?

"You'd risk someone seeing you?"

Catrìona crossed her arms over her breasts, so very thinly covered by a pretty sark Anna had made her. She would never tell Anna how very much she prized the thing, for it had played a large part in many of her seductions. Catrìona was always very careful never to let any of her men remove it from her body—it was far too delicate, and could easily tear. The garment was nearly transparent and so beautifully made that it tempted every man who'd seen her in it.

She chewed her lip, trying to decide what to do. Would MacMillan leave Kilgorra now that the granary was gone? Suddenly, Cullen did not seem so very appealing. He seemed small and petty compared to Lachann. . . .

"Come now, Catrìona. You know you want to."

No, this time, the wee wren did not want to.

He got up and pulled her into his arms, nuzzling her

neck as he skittered one hand down her back to her buttocks.

"When are you going to tell MacMillan that you're going to marry mc? And not him?"

"You know I have no choice in this, Cullen," Catrìona said, lying a little, hoping 'twould put him off for now. "'Tis really my father's decision."

Gesu, but the press of Anna's bare body against his arousal was as near to heaven as Lachann had been in many a month. He'd come so very close that morn, and his need for her had not abated in the least.

She slid her hands through his hair and held his head in place, and Lachann surrendered his own groan of pleasure.

Next, she would reach beneath his plaid and—

Lachann quickly bent to retrieve the towel cloth he'd removed from her. He wrapped it 'round her and then lifted her into his arms. Pushing open the door, he carried her through it and did not stop until he arrived at his own room. He went inside and set Anna on her feet, then reached behind him to latch the door.

Naught was going to interrupt him this time.

Lachann slid his hand 'round her waist and pulled her close. He pressed his mouth to her throat, then moved lower, removing the toweling cloth as he went. Her lips parted and he moved up to touch his mouth to hers. He slid his tongue inside, deepening the kiss as she leaned into him.

Lachann grazed her flushed skin with the back of his hand, relishing how sweetly soft she was, from her narrow shoulders, down her back, reaching the curve of her hips, then 'round to the peaks of her breasts.

As Lachann's hands explored, Anna made a quiet sound of pure surrender, grabbing hold of the plaid at his shoulder and shoving it down. He cupped one of her breasts, then bent to lave it with his tongue.

Ach, 'twas the sweetest thing he'd ever tasted.

"*Lachann . . .*" She put her hand on his chest, and when her fingers slid across his nipple, his cock throbbed in anticipation.

He took her to the bed, then lifted her onto it, coming down over her. He felt her tremble, and then her arms went 'round him as her eyes drifted closed. Lachann felt her fingers knife through the hair at his nape as he trailed kisses down her throat and to her breasts.

Naught had ever pleased him so well, except perhaps when he slid one hand down to the crux of her legs and found her moist and ready for him.

"Sweet Anna."

Lachann was as hard as his claymore, and aching to slide into her. But he wanted so much more. Wanted what they shared to be as incredible for her as he knew 'twould be for him.

Moving down, he skittered kisses across her belly

while he traced his fingers 'round her feminine sheath, using his thumb to fondle the sensitive nub at its apex. She let out a startled sound when he put his mouth to the spot and licked.

"Lachann!"

"Aye, love."

She shuddered, and her breath quickened.

He entered her with one finger while he continued to pleasure her with his tongue. She moaned, and Lachann suddenly felt all her muscles tighten 'round him.

"That's it, my bonny one. Come for me."

He heard her breath catch, and then she made a quiet whimper of complete and utter satisfaction.

He shifted his position and came over her again, settling between her thighs. His cock grew impossibly harder as it nestled against her warm cleft, and Lachann groaned with need. "Now, Anna."

She was so incredibly tight. Lachann entered her slowly, then stopped, feeling nearly mad with need. "*Anna.*"

She lifted her hips, and suddenly he was fully inside her, inside heaven. "Oh, Lachann . . ." She wrapped her arms 'round him and pulled him close.

Lachann closed his eyes against the sudden flood of sensation, then moved against her in a rhythm that she met, stroke for stroke.

The pleasure was deep and intense, and Lachann prolonged it until he felt Anna tighten 'round him once again, crying out softly with pure sensation. "Aye, lass."

His own climax shuddered through him then, and she moved with him, wreaking every intense drop of pleasure from his body.

Keeping their bodies joined, Lachann propped himself on one forearm and looked down at her while caressing her ear with his other hand. "You are so very beautiful, Anna lass."

Uncertainty touched her eyes, but Lachann dipped down to kiss her lips.

He rolled to his side, pulling her with him. Unable to get his fill of looking at her, of touching her, he gently caressed her cheek, then her chin. He slipped his arm 'round her waist and drew her flush against his body, relishing the press of her bare skin on his.

They lay together quietly, with only the sound of a sudden rain squall breaking the silence.

Lachann held Anna in his arms long into the night, cocooned in the snug bedchamber while the rain drenched the world 'round them. 'Twas as though not another soul existed on their island.

If only life could have been that simple.

Before dawn, Lachann left Anna sleeping and went to search for Macauley. No one had been able to find him last night after returning to the castle, but the man had to sleep, didn't he?

Without standing on ceremony, Lachann pushed open Macauley's bedroom door, prepared to confront him. But the room was empty. And it appeared not to have been slept in. The bed was undisturbed and the fireplace was cold.

Lachann scratched the back of his head, wondering what rock Macauley had climbed under. The bastard was devious, and Lachann should have assumed he'd stay clear of anyone who might accuse him of the fire. *Gesu*. What other nefarious plans were afoot?

Lachann was afraid he already knew.

With Macauley absent and unavailable for questioning, Lachann looked in on Laird MacDuffie. He needed to make it clear to the laird that he would not wed the man's daughter.

He stepped quietly into MacDuffie's bedchamber and found the old man sleeping soundly. His skin was pale, making the gash on his head and Anna's stitches stand out grotesquely.

Again, Lachann had to wonder if something more ailed the laird than his continuous drunkenness. He'd known many a man who'd died of the jaundice and bloating that went along with too much whiskey, but Lachann detected no yellowness of MacDuffie's eyes or skin. The old man was as white as a phantom, though, and clearly ailing.

What if he died before naming his heir?

Deciding 'twas pointless to remain in the laird's

bedroom, Lachann went down to the kitchen and found no one else up and about. No one but Anna's cat.

"You're looking for your mistress, are you?" he muttered.

The cat mewed.

"Aye. I can understand your affection for the lass." Lachann's entire body clenched with pleasure at the thought of her. He'd never known such a fiery woman as his Anna, nor one as passionate and generous. She'd worked hard yesterday alongside the other islanders trying to put out the fire. She needed to rest today, and Lachann would talk to her later—about Kilgorra, about Braemore, about Catrìona.

While the cat wrapped itself 'round Lachann's legs, he found bread and a piece of cheese for his own breakfast, and he cut a sliver of cheese for the wee creature. Then he tightened his belt and was about to set out for the stable in the rain when Duncan came into the kitchen.

"You're up early," Lachann said. "Didn't you stay late in the village?"

"Aye." Duncan rubbed a hand over heavy whiskers. "We're going to start on the new granary this morn. But with all this rain . . ."

"Aye. It might be better to wait," Lachann said. "See what the carpenters say."

Duncan nodded.

"Macauley was not in his room this morn," Lachann said. "Everyone needs to keep an eye out for him."

Duncan let out a low sound of disgust. "I don't trust the bastard any further than—"

"Aye. He's up to something, and I have a feeling the granary was just the beginning. If anyone sees him, I want him detained. By force, if necessary."

Duncan raised his brows.

"In the meantime," Lachann said, "I want the cannons up and into position today, ready for firing. The island is too vulnerable—especially with the men occupied with rebuilding the granary."

"That's a good point, Lachann," Duncan said. "If a pirate ship came into the harbor . . ."

"Aye, the harbor," Lachann said. "Our most vulnerable point. I'm going up to Roscraig Peak to make my decision on a location for one of the cannons."

"Aye," Duncan said as he headed for the stairs. "We'll meet you there soon."

"Oh, and Duncan?"

The man stopped and turned.

"I've decided not to marry Catrìona MacDuffie," he said. "Find another way for MacDuffie to make me his heir."

Chapter 28

Anna awoke alone. In Lachann MacMillan's bed.

Herregud! She must have fallen asleep in his arms. She clambered out of bed and reached for the towel she'd used last night, and found that someone had picked up the clothes she'd left on the floor outside the bathing room.

It had to have been Lachann. He'd hung them over the back of a chair to be ready when she awoke and wanted to leave his room.

She lay back on the bed and covered her eyes with her arm. Ach, what could she have been thinking last night?

She had *not* thought. That was the problem. Just like yesterday, she'd allowed the attraction she'd felt to rule her actions . . .

Except what she felt for Lachann was nothing as simple as a mere attraction. What she felt was far more than was sensible or prudent. She would not have given him her maidenhead otherwise.

Feeling more than a little bit desperate, she got up again and dressed quickly. Dashing down the stairs, she flew past the main floor and down to the servants' quarters. She pushed into her room without delay and closed the door tightly behind her as tears welled in her eyes.

Dear God, she had done it again. Allowed her heart to rule her actions.

But she could not allow it to happen again. A few days on her wee isle, and her good sense would return as sound as ever. She would let the healing waters of the loch restore her, and when she returned . . .

Well, she would deal with Catrìona's marriage to Lachann then.

But a shudder of desire rippled through her, and she feared her body would not soon forget the sensation of Lachann's touch—of his mouth on her, of his body joined to hers. . . .

Anna swallowed and closed her eyes tightly. She ached in odd places—places that would receive relief only from Lachann's manly caress, which was absolutely the last thing she should have wanted.

And yet, if she was honest, she knew 'twould be all she could think of, even when she was away on Spirit Isle.

When Lachann arrived in the village, men were already working to remove the charred remains of the granary. The rain had let up, but it was messy, muddy work.

Lachann went into the tavern, where Geordie Kincaid was already discussing the new building with a handful of carpenters. He took the man aside.

"Have them build it to your exact specifications," Lachann told him, "with an eye toward increasing your production over the next few years."

"But the cost—"

"I will cover the cost, Kincaid. This is an opportunity to modernize, and we must make the most of it."

"Aye. I will, sir."

"When the *Glencoe Lass* returns, I'll send her for any supplies not available on Kilgorra," Lachann said, for his ship should return with news from Skye within a day or two, at most. "And if improvements are needed at the distillery, include those, as well."

Lachann had decided Macauley would never become laird here. Even if the dolt wed Catrìona.

He left the building wondering not for the first time what Macauley's purpose was in keeping Laird MacDuffie drunk. If it was to make the old man ill and unable to make reasonable decisions, it seemed to be working. Sometimes the laird seemed not to know where he was, or in whose company.

Macauley's machinations might have worked if Lachann had not arrived on the isle. The man was welcome to Catrìona, but not to Kilgorra or its people.

Lachann met the three MacPherson brothers when he rode up to the top of Roscraig Peak. As they looked down, they could see the devastated area 'round the granary site, and the men working to clear the area. 'Twas bad, but it could have been so much worse. The distillery was not far from the granary, and there were other buildings nearby, as well. If the fire had been allowed to spread, they might never have managed to stop it.

"Good morn to you, Lachann," Boyd said. "Ach, 'tis a dismal sight, is it not?"

Lachann nodded.

"Will we continue our training until the lumber and the rest of the supplies are ready for the rebuilding?" Boyd asked.

"That is a very good idea," Lachann said. The better to thwart Macauley's plan. He looked out at the sea beyond Anna's isle. "No need to waste these few days. As soon as the men are gathered, I'll talk to them about what we're going to do."

Tavish tipped his head toward the devastation. "Granny says it could have been Birk Ramsay who started the fire."

"Aye? Birk Ramsay? What reason would he have for destroying the granary?"

"None at all. Nor did he have reason to destroy his own birlinn last year. But his temper has not been the same since he cracked his head. And now that he drinks . . . well, a drunk is not always in full possession of his reason."

Lachann had not thought any of the islanders would create such havoc. But someone like Ramsay would not need a reason.

"Do you know where he is?"

All three shook their heads. "You know he lies about in one of the caves on the western shore."

"Aye, I've heard." 'Twas where he'd believed Anna had been going the previous day, and the thought of her facing the man alone had been more than a tad alarming.

He'd given her only the most rudimentary of lessons in self-defense, and Lachann seriously doubted she was any kind of match for an angry Birk Ramsay. He needed to talk to her about avoiding the man altogether. *Gesu,* the last thing he wanted was for her to be hurt.

"What do you think?" Lachann asked. "Is Birk responsible?"

Rob shook his head. "I just don't see it. He's more likely to set fire to his own cottage than go about ruining his chances for another drop of the *uisge beatha.*"

Which was equally unnerving to Lachann. He disliked the thought of further harm coming to Anna's friend.

"He'll go home once he's sober and can face Kyla," Tavish said.

"Is he violent when he's sober?" Lachann asked.

"Not usually," Boyd said. "But his sober days seem to come less often now."

Anna threw on a cloak, picked up her basket, and went into the kitchen, where Flora and the other maids were at work.

"Where are ye off to in such a rush, lass?" Flora asked.

"To my isle," she said.

Flora took her by the arms and faced her. "Ach, ye look flushed. Are ye all right, Anna?"

"Aye. I just need to get over to the—"

"Ye will'na be crossin' the straits today," Flora said. "The seas are rough and will likely stay that way through the day and all night, too."

Anna swallowed her chagrin.

"What's got into ye, lass? Ye're all a'flutter this morn!"

"The laird suffered a mishap in the solar last night," Anna replied. "I'm just worried—"

"Anna," Graeme interrupted as he came into the kitchen, "yer wanted by Lady Catrìona."

"Well, *that one* is up early," Flora said. She turned to Anna. "Was the old man hurt?"

The thought of seeing Catrìona right now made Anna's stomach roil. "Aye. He split open his head. No doubt Catrìona got up to see about him." She turned to Graeme. "How is he?"

"I know naught," he replied, putting up his hands to ward off her questions. "Alex is with him. Catrìona merely stuck out her head from the laird's room and told me to fetch you."

Anna calmed herself and put her things back into her bedroom, then climbed the steps to the great hall and made her way to the main staircase. All was quiet above, and she felt more than a wee bit of trepidation in returning to the room where she had succumbed to Lachann's seduction.

Herregud, she could hardly believe she'd actually stood naked in the laird's chamber, with Lachann Mac-Millan's hands upon her.

Or that she would do it again, given the chance. She feared she could go away to Spirit Isle for a month and come back to Kilgorra still wanting him.

She paused on the stairs and pressed a hand against her chest. Mayhap she should just have Graeme tell Catrìona that he could not find her. Or that she'd gone for Janet Carnegie. Aye, that would be best—

"Anna!"

Too late. Catrìona saw her. "I'm coming."

Anna reached the top of the stairs and followed Catrìona into her stepfather's bedchamber.

"What is it?" Anna asked. "Is he—"

"Go and look at him."

Anna stepped up to MacDuffie's bedside. His forehead near the gash was red and swollen, but the stitches she'd made had held. The man cracked open his eyes and frowned at her. "Anna?" His voice was but a thin rasp. "Where . . . where is Fenella?"

"He knows *you*!" Catrìona gasped.

Anna glanced at Catrìona, who stood with her arms crossed against her chest, her face turning a deep shade of red. Anna shrugged. "Why wouldn't he know me?"

Catrìona made an incoherent sound but did not answer the question.

"Who is Fenella?"

"His sister. And he called me Lilas." Anna knew that was Catrìona's mother's name. So *that* was what upset her. The laird had recognized Anna but not his own daughter.

Anna closed her eyes for a moment and swallowed. *Ach, Laird, what have you done to me?* "'Twas obviously just a moment's confusion," Anna said. "Did he recognize Graeme? Or Alex?"

Catrìona shook her head. "No."

"Well, 'twas a nasty blow to his head. No wonder he's confused. Shall I send someone to fetch Janet Carnegie?"

Catrìona dropped into a chair and covered her face with her hands. "To think only a month ago he was as hearty as any other man his age."

"Where were you last night?" Anna asked. "We could have used your help."

Catrìona suddenly abandoned her show of grief. "'Tis not your place to question me," she snapped.

Anna sighed. Naught had changed. Her life was just as it had always been.

If not worse.

"I'll send Graeme down to Janet's cottage," she said. "Mayhap she'll know what more we should do."

"Aye. And then you must clean up that mess in the solar. I don't know why you left it overnight."

Anna tried not to seethe. She did not want to feel any sympathy for Catrìona, who'd harassed and beleaguered her for most of her life. But she knew Catrìona felt as lonely as she, no matter how many men she'd seduced. Her stepsister had doted excessively upon her father, but the old man had never taken much notice of his only child.

Flora always said that if Laird MacDuffie paid Catrìona the least bit of attention, she would not go looking for it from any man who was too daft to know better than to dally with the laird's daughter.

Anna took a half-empty bottle of whiskey from the laird's table before leaving the room. She encountered Graeme in the great hall, carrying in a load of peat for the fires.

"How is the laird?"

"Ill. Confused," Anna replied casually, as though

her life had not been irrevocably changed. As though she had not given her heart and soul to a man she could have only in secret, and only when his duty to his wife did not prevent it. "He does not look good, Graeme. Will you run down to Janet Carnegie's cottage and bring her back? I don't know what to do for him, and Catrìona is useless."

"Aye. After I finish stackin' all this."

Anna went down to the kitchen to collect the supplies she needed to clean the solar.

"So, the laird fell?" Flora asked.

Anna picked up Effie and held the cat under her chin, listening to her purr. "Aye. In the solar, smashing one of his precious whiskey bottles on the floor."

"Ach, no! The thirty-year blend?"

Anna put Effie on the floor and picked up the half-full bottle she'd removed from the laird's chamber, emptying it in the thick grass outside the kitchen. Thirty-year or three-year—she had no use for any of it.

"Ach, lass! What're ye doin'?" Flora cried when she saw the amber liquid spilling out of the bottle.

"The laird won't remember whether he drank it or not. Not in his present condition."

Flora put one hand to her breast. "Ye could have saved it fer us. A wee dram would'na be amiss tonight, when 'tis time to lay a body down."

"I am sorry, Flora. I didn't think." Anna had begun to hate the stuff. Birk was not the only drunkard in the village, and her stepfather—who had always imbibed too much, in her estimation—was incoherent more often than not these days. "I've sent Graeme for the healer."

"Aye? The laird's that bad off, then?"

"I sewed the gash in his forehead," Anna replied, refusing to think what else she'd done. "Now he's calling Catrìona by her mother's name."

"That can'na be good."

"But he knew me."

Flora placed a hand upon her breast and cast a wry look at Anna. "I'm sure that pleased Catrìona."

Anna could do naught but shake her head helplessly. "I cannot imagine why he knew my name and not hers."

"Whoever knows when such . . ." The cook frowned as she tapped one finger against her mouth.

"What is it?" Anna asked.

"'Tis just so strange. The laird was well enough afore that arse Macauley came to our isle. I wonder . . ."

"I don't understand."

"Ach, 'tis naught. What d'ye suppose will happen if the laird dies?"

Anna shuddered. Catrìona would marry one of her suitors. If she chose Macauley, the island would languish. It would be subject to more attacks like the one that had occurred the previous summer.

Of course Catrìona would marry Lachann MacMillan, and life on Kilgorra would improve. For all but Anna.

Flora tapped her fingers on the table, frowning, deep in thought. "Lachann MacMillan still knows naught of Catrìona's men, does he?"

Anna felt as distraught as Flora seemed to be. No one on Kilgorra wanted to scare Lachann away with tales of Catrìona's promiscuity. The people had made their decision about Macauley, and they wanted Lachann to toss the pompous neep from the isle, marry Catrìona, and assert his rights as her lawful husband.

"Ach, if Catrìona has the sense God gave her, she will choose MacMillan," Flora said, wiping her hands on her apron, "much as I know the lad does'na deserve such a fate."

Aye, 'twas exactly what Anna feared. But if she hoped otherwise, she would be betraying everyone on Kilgorra.

Chapter 29

The afternoon had turned warm, and the mist had burned off the higher lands by the time Lachann got back to the castle. The first person he saw on his way to the stable was Catrìona, coming toward him from the old chapel.

"Catrìona!" he called to her as he dismounted.

She stopped and gave him a wan smile. "Lachann! Did you know my father was injured last night?"

"Aye. I've seen him."

"And did you—"

"What I'd like to know is when you saw Cullen Macauley last."

"Cullen? Why, I—"

"Did you leave him just now, back at that chapel of yours?"

"How dare you!" she cried as she whirled 'round and started to walk away.

Lachann grabbed hold of her arm. "Just answer the question, Catrìona. Where and when did you see Macauley last?"

"I . . . I don't remember," she said petulantly. "Sometime yesterday."

"Before or after the granary fire?"

She yanked her arm away. "I don't know."

Lachann wanted to tell her to go to the devil, but he needed to settle matters with her father first. He wanted to know what his prospects were going to be on Kilgorra before he spoke of the future with Anna.

"Where is Anna?" he asked.

"You mean my *servant,* Anna?" she asked with clipped words. "Why do you need to know?"

Lachann waited.

Catrìona's lips thinned and her eyes narrowed. "What does it matter to you?"

Lachann did not answer. He hoped Anna had not gone across the rough straits this morn. But she was familiar with those waters, and he could not spare the time to look for her now. Not when their future was at stake.

Resigned to staying at the castle for the time being, Anna climbed up to the rarely used solar, treading carefully, for the shards of broken crockery still lay all over the floor. She collected the larger pieces of Laird

MacDuffie's bottle, then swept up the rest before getting down on her hands and knees to wash the sticky mess from the floor.

When that was done, she went to the window and looked down at the courtyard. Her gaze was instantly drawn to Lachann's half-naked figure, parrying sword to sword with one of his men.

He'd pulled his shirt from his shoulders and tied the sleeves 'round his waist while engaging in the strenuous battle games. His well-muscled chest and arms gleamed with sweat, and his damp hair curled at his nape. He called out brisk instructions to the Kilgorran men who stood watching as he clashed swords with his kinsman, Duncan.

Anna pressed one hand against her breast. All at once, everything she'd felt the night before slammed through her entire being, and she had to struggle to catch her breath.

She loved him.

He looked up at that moment and their eyes locked, causing him to misstep.

"Anna!"

Anna whirled 'round at the sound of her stepsister's voice and her footsteps marching up to the solar. Catrìona came into the room and glanced about with a critical eye, her gaze stopping at the window and landing on the warriors in the courtyard.

Anna wrestled to regain a modicum of composure,

hoping that Lachann had turned away from the window before her stepsister noticed him looking up. Catrìona would not take kindly to him paying any sort of attention to her *undeserving* sister.

When Catrìona took a sharp breath and slowly turned to face Anna with ice in her eyes, Anna knew her hopes had been in vain.

Catrìona approached her slowly, and Anna felt her dagger strapped to her calf. Did she dare draw it out? Protect herself from her own kin?

Catrìona shoved her shoulder. "Those windows need a good vinegar wash," she said in a vicious tone. "You know 'tis your responsibility to see that the keep is maintained."

"And *you* know I do all I can." Anna ducked away from another of Catrìona's pushes.

She headed for the stairs, refusing to think about her stepsister and all her demands now, not when she'd seen Lachann's expression and the hint of a smile just before he'd faltered.

She knew what the lairdship meant to him, and yet that trace of a smile gave her an unexpected glimmer of hope. Did he mean to forsake the lairdship and return to Braemore as Kyla had predicted?

Would he take her with him?

"Look at this." Catrìona kicked out a pile of old peat and ashes from the fireplace onto the clean floor. "From last winter, I imagine."

Anna needed to talk to him.

"Are you listening to me?" Catrìona demanded.

"No." Anna removed her apron and went down the steps while Catrìona railed behind her.

"I'm not finished with you, Anna MacIver!"

"Ah," Anna said under her breath, "but I am finished with you, Catrìona MacDuffie."

Lachann kept his concentration firmly focused on his demonstration of offensive technique with his claymore.

Until he caught sight of Anna through a tower window in the keep. Then his attention deserted him and Duncan managed to slice him.

'Twas merely a scratch—but 'twas one that should never have happened.

He forced a laugh and stepped forward, clapping Duncan on the shoulder, making light of his carelessness. He looked up at the window again, but Anna was gone. Lachann turned his attention back to the practice field and finished his demonstration, but it could not end quickly enough. The vision of Anna through the solar window drew him irrevocably.

He took his leave of his men and strode to the well, where he drew up half a bucket of water, then dumped it over his head. He shoved back his hair, and when he looked toward the close, he saw that Anna had come down.

He started for her, intending to steal a kiss.

Or two.

And then Cullen Macauley walked brazenly into the enclosure and approached her, as though he had not been suspiciously missing ever since the fire.

Lachann felt his jaw clench. He jogged forward as the bastard moved in close to Anna, blocking her path.

Anna tried to slip around him, but Macauley made it impossible.

"Mayhap you would join me in the garden down by the chapel?" Lachann heard him say. "'Tis cool there, and naught to do. Naught but lie back in the grass and watch the clouds. Or . . ."

Before Lachann could get to her, Macauley put his arm 'round her waist, his hand dangling dangerously close to her bottom. Just as Lachann reached them, Anna pulled her hand back and clouted him in the nose with her knuckles.

Macauley yowled, releasing her as he covered his face with both hands. Blood quickly covered the bastard's hands.

Lachann would have pummeled him if Anna had not. The lass had learned well. "Serves you right, Macauley," he said as he pulled up his shirt and shoved his arms through the sleeves. "Catrìona is not enough for you?"

"Your interference is not welcome here, MacMillan," Macauley said, clearly shaken by the unexpected turn of events.

Lachann confronted him, putting himself between Macauley and Anna. "Where have you been, Macauley?"

"Where have I been?" Macauley made a rude sound and started to walk away, but Lachann took hold of his shoulder and yanked him 'round.

"No one has seen you since the granary caught fire. Where were you yesterday afternoon?"

"You have your nerve, accusing me, MacMillan."

"I haven't accused you. Yet. Answer the question, Macauley. Where were you, and can anyone vouch for your whereabouts?"

"Cullen!" Catrìona shouted as she ran into the enclosure. She narrowed her eyes at the sight of Anna standing behind Lachann. "Cullen! You said you were going to the distill—"

Macauley turned to face her.

"Oh Lord!" she cried when she saw the blood. "What's happened?"

"This bleeting wench shoved her fist up my nose when I did naught but pass by."

"Anna?" Catrìona's face turned a vivid shade of red, and she made a grab for Anna. "Why are you still here? I gave you—"

"Leave her be, Catrìona." Lachann stopped her, taking hold of her shoulders. *Gesu,* but she was harsh.

She gave out a strangled sound. "I am in charge of my servants, Lachann MacMillan. And in case you have forgotten, 'tis my father who is laird here!"

"And he is incapable at the moment," Lachann said. He held onto Catrìona to keep her from going after Anna again. "Answer the question, Macauley. What were you doing yesterday when the fire broke out?"

"I wasn't anywhere near the granary yesterday." Macauley spat blood.

"Of course he wasn't," Catrìona said.

Lachann wasn't inclined to believe either of them. "Does that mean you were with him all day?" he asked her.

She raised her chin in indignation. "Well, I . . ."

No, she would not want to admit to an intimate relationship with Macauley, not while she still thought she could play her game with Lachann.

"I'm not answering any of your questions, MacMillan. I'm going to the distillery," Macauley said. "Your father is asking for a drink, Catrìona, and someone took away all his whiskey."

Gesu, the man was slime.

Lachann glanced back at Anna, whose eyes were cast down, as though she did not dare look at him— or at anyone. He'd have released Catrìona, put his arm 'round Anna, and taken her to a quiet spot for those stolen kisses he'd been thinking of, but he had not yet settled matters with the MacDuffies.

And he certainly wasn't done with Macauley.

"You no longer have access to the distillery," he said to his nemesis.

Blood streamed from Macauley's nose even as his face twisted into a mask of pure hatred. He lunged for Lachann. "You have no right, MacMillan."

Lachann pushed Catrìona behind him and stepped aside. "Aye, I do. Every right. Which you would know if you understood the agreement signed by Laird MacDuffie weeks ago, before I ever left Braemore."

"You cannot keep me out, MacMillan." Macauley struck a fist at Lachann, but Lachann let go of Catrìona and brought up his arm to block the blow.

"You cannot do this!" Macauley roared. He struck again, but Lachann caught the bastard's fist and twisted his arm behind him. He shoved him face-first into the wall, and none too gently.

Catrìona made sounds of protest behind Lachann and tried to pull him off Macauley, but Lachann ignored her. "You are banned from the distillery, Macauley. The business—which was on the brink of ruin even before the fire—has been returned to Geordie Kincaid's capable hands."

"Why, he's no more than a—"

"Competent distiller and manager, aye. Which you are not. Your tenure at the distillery is done."

He released Macauley and stepped back, battle-ready. The man would be a fool to try to attack now, but Lachann was ready for him. He felt Anna's surprised gaze upon him and heard more of Catrìona's protests.

"Stay away from the village," he said to Macauley just as Duncan came into the close, looking for him. "And try not to do any more damage before I ship you off the isle."

"Why, you cannot—"

"Try me, Macauley," Lachann said. "I would like nothing better than to finish you now."

Duncan put his hand on the hilt of his sword and stood fast behind Lachann, his feet slightly apart. He looked like an impenetrable wall, and Lachann knew would not let Macauley out of his sight.

Lachann turned to Catrìona. "Is your father conscious?"

"Aye," she said in a grudging tone. "But his head pains him terrib—"

"'Tis time we spoke with him of serious matters," Lachann said, taking Catrìona's arm. He looked at Anna. "Are you all right, lass?"

She nodded, though she was pale and obviously shaken. He could not yet tell her that all would be well. Not until he settled matters with the old laird.

"Duncan, send someone to the village for Father Herriot. Have him meet us in MacDuffie's bedchamber." He turned to Macauley. "In future, leave the servants alone, Macauley," he said before leading Catrìona to the keep. "And the same goes for you, Catrìona. Anna knows her duties. There is no need for you to browbeat her."

Lachann despised having to leave Anna that way, speaking of her in such terms. But he did not want to give Catrìona any more reason to cause her trouble. If Catrìona knew how he felt about Anna, there would be hell to pay, and Anna would be the one to pay it.

Chapter 30

Anna felt numb.

She stood frozen in place as Macauley stalked away with Duncan right behind him and Lachann escorted Catrìona from the close. 'Twas as though he'd completely forgotten she'd been present during the interchange with Macauley.

She might as well have been invisible.

Had she completely misunderstood his expression when he'd looked up at her from the practice field? Swallowing back the burning deep in her throat, she blinked away the tears that threatened to spill over onto her cheeks.

She heard Graeme calling to her, but she could not face anyone. Not now.

Lachann had sent for Father Herriot, and Anna knew that could only mean one thing.

Devastation.

She slipped away from the close, skirted 'round the courtyard, and went back to the chapel gate. She climbed down the rocky steps to the beach and ran up to the harbor. Then she backtracked up the lane that led to Kyla's cottage just down from the distillery. She needed a few sane moments with the one person she called family.

All was quiet when she approached, and Anna had a sudden fear that something horrible had happened. That Birk had finally done his worst and . . .

She knocked frantically at the door, instantly forgetting her own misery.

No one answered.

Herregud! Was Kyla lying injured inside and unable to come to the door?

"Kyla!" Anna called through her tears. "Where are you?"

She tried to see in the windows, but they were shuttered. Feeling close to panic now, she tried the door—

"Anna!"

Anna whirled 'round to see Kyla approaching the cottage from the lane.

"What is amiss, Anna? You look a fright!"

Anna leaned back against the door in relief, nearly too unnerved to speak. "I went into a panic when no one answered your door."

Kyla walked past her into the house. "I just went to sit with Sorcha Carnegie for a bit."

"I feared Birk—"

"My husband did naught when he returned home."

"Where is he now?"

Kyla looked away. "Out. I . . . I'm not sure where."

Anna forced herself to calm down. Her own problems were naught compared to Kyla's. No one was about to kill her. "He's t-treated you well since he's come back?"

Kyla nodded and narrowed her eyes at Anna. "What is it, Anna? What is wrong? Is it Lachann MacMillan?"

Ach, she should not have come. Kyla had her own worries, and 'twas thoughtless of Anna to bring more to her. "Come here, lad," she said, taking Douglas from Kyla's arms. She pressed a kiss to the bairn's head, but instead of feeling calmer, Anna felt just as unsettled as when she'd left the castle. Mayhap more.

"Something's happened," Kyla said. "Tell me."

"Naught. I—" Anna felt her chin begin to tremble, and she fought the tears that were sure to follow. "Ach, 'tis complicated."

"Aye?"

How could she tell Kyla what was wrong when she could hardly piece it all together herself? That for the first time in her life, she believed it might not be so very terrible to belong to a man. But only to a man like Lachann MacMillan. The very man who had just sent for the priest to marry him to Catrìona.

"Oh, Ky."

Her tears did fall then, and Kyla came and wrapped Anna in her arms with Douglas between them. "You fell in love with him, didn't you?"

Anna could only sniffle and nod. She felt as though her heart had been squeezed into a space that was too small.

"But he's promised to Catrìona," Kyla said. "And h-he's about to marry her."

"Will you not fight for him?"

"How can I, Kyla?" Anna whispered. "He will not give up Kilgorra. He cannot if he is to protect his homeland. And Catrìona is part of his agreement with Laird MacDuffie." How could she ask him to abandon his goal? Besides, 'twas too late. Father Herriot would soon be on his way to the castle.

"He cares for you."

He'd wanted her, aye. But so had Cullen Macauley. Was Lachann's seduction any different? Had *caring* been any part of it?

Herregud. She hoped so, but she just didn't know. . . . And in any event, what did it matter now?

"You've bedded him, *min kjære venn*?"

Anna nodded, and as she wept, Kyla remained quiet, just holding her.

"Anna . . . can you not trust Lachann?"

"Trust him?"

"Aye. To see what Catrìona is? To know what an exceedingly poor wife she will make him?"

"You do not understand, Ky," Anna said. "He has no choice. Even though he might know Catrìona's true nature—"

"Anna, the laird is ill. What happens if he dies and Catrìona is not married?"

The back of Anna's throat burned. She should have known better than to allow hope into her heart. Love was truly the most destructive force she could imagine, and she wanted no part of it. "Naught will change. Catrìona will choose Lachann for her husband—"

"You don't believe she'll choose Macauley?"

Anna shook her head. "No. Lachann will not allow it."

She stepped away. Ach, what was she doing here? She ought to have gone over to her isle. There she could have licked her wounds, and when she returned . . . "Kyla, what if I could find a way for us to leave Kilgorra?"

"What? No. 'Tis my home, and my husb—"

"Beats you bloody every time he has the urge."

"'Tis a wife's place to remain with her husband, Anna. And Birk is not all bad."

"No? What portion is good, do you think?" Anna retorted. "His feet? Or his ears? Because his hands and arms have taken great relish in hurting you. His mouth is where he puts the liquor that fuels his temper. And his head is where that beastly temper resides. If you cannot—"

"He is my husband, and I will not leave him," Kyla said, turning to face Anna.

The door burst open at that moment, and Birk strolled in. He took Douglas from Anna's arms and went to Kyla. He ran his beefy arm 'round her waist and pulled her to him. " 'Tis glad I am to hear it, wife."

Then he turned and cast a threatening glare at Anna, and she realized she did not have the knife Lachann had given her.

Lachann's mood skidded to black when he thought about Macauley putting his hands on Anna. He was very glad he'd taught her that little maneuver involving her knuckles and her attacker's nose. It had served her well.

He had tremendously enjoyed seeing the fool's face bloodied, and by a woman, at that. Certain that Duncan would keep track of Macauley until Lachann decided what to do with him, he took hold of Catrìona's arm and went into the keep.

He had hoped Duncan would think of some precedent for Lachann to become laird without marrying MacDuffie's daughter, but there was none. Lachann supposed he'd known it from the first. Now 'twas up to him to convince MacDuffie that he was the laird's most able replacement—without a wedding.

And as soon as he finished his business with Laird MacDuffie, he intended to find Anna and . . .

First he needed to settle things with MacDuffie. Lachann believed his argument would prevail, but however things turned out with the laird, Lachann would not marry Catrìona. He wanted Anna at his side, in his bed, in his life. He desired her above all else, including the lairdship of Kilgorra, and if he had to go to war with Macauley for the lairdship of the isle, he knew which side the Kilgorrans would choose. 'Twas perfectly clear they disliked Macauley.

"My father is not well this morn," Catrìona bleated.

"We'll see." He did not release her arm but led her through the great hall and up the stairs to her father's bedchamber. He hoped the man managed to stay alive long enough to make Lachann his heir with Father Herriot as his witness.

Chapter 31

Anna felt her backbone go as stiff as a birlinn's mast. She returned Birk's glare coldly. "Aye, Birk Ramsay. 'Tis glad you should be that your wife plans to stay. It makes you a fortunate man, though you cannot possibly understand how fortunate."

Birk turned to kiss Kyla's temple while keeping his calculating eyes upon Anna. His behavior toward his wife was a gesture of possession and control and naught more.

"No, 'tis you who does'na know how fortunate," he said, leveling a deadly gaze at Anna. "My wife and the bairn in her belly stay with me, ye meddlin' witch."

Anna's eyes darted toward Kyla's, and by her friend's expression she knew that what Birk had said was true. Kyla was with child again. She would certainly not leave him now.

Anna walked out of the cottage, torn over what to

do. At least Birk wasn't drunk. Anna could walk away knowing the man would not knock his wife about. At least not right now.

Feeling worse than ever, Anna retraced her steps, returning to the pier. She was relieved that everyone seemed to be occupied—likely at the granary—for she met no one on her way back. She did not have to try to act as though all was well.

She stopped at her curragh, and when she gazed out at the sea, she knew that Flora was right. The water was too rough for a crossing to Spirit Isle. Even the fishermen must have thought twice about venturing out in their birlinns.

She did not see any of them now, but she did notice a massive schooner tacking toward the harbor. Its flag was a bright red color with a blue cross etched over it, and a smaller design in one corner—exactly like the cloth she'd found in the trunk with her mother's things.

'Twas a Norwegian ship! *Herregud.* This was the ship that would take her to her Norse relations.

Away from Lachann and the woman he'd made his wife.

Lachann wanted to get back to Anna as soon as possible. But his prospects on the isle hinged on what transpired next—whether he would stay on Kilgorra as laird or return to Braemore and figure some other strategy for keeping his homeland safe from attack by sea.

He wanted to be able to tell Anna what their future would hold—whether they stayed here, or sailed down the lochs to make their home at Braemore.

He took Catrìona up to the laird's bedchamber, where the stench of illness permeated the room. Lachann girded himself against the unwholesome air inside.

"Father?" Catrìona touched MacDuffie's arm.

The man opened his eyes and gazed blankly into Catrìona's face. "I do'na like all this, lass."

"No, Father. I am sure you do not. You are ill, but you'll soon be better."

Lachann was not so sure. "Laird, I need a word with you."

The old man turned his head to face Lachann and looked at him from beneath his thick brow. "Aye?"

"Father Herriot is on his way."

The man looked at his daughter, then back at Lachann. "The last rites? Am I so very—"

"No, Laird," Lachann said. "The priest is coming to act as witness."

"Witness to what, sir?" Catrìona asked with more than a tinge of indignation to her voice.

"'Tis time to make me your heir," Lachann said. "Macauley is unfit—we suspect he set the granary on fire in order to sabotage my efforts at building an army."

"Why would he do such a thing?" MacDuffie demanded weakly.

"Because he wants me to fail in order to gain favor with you and take over."

"But—"

"Or prevent me from training our men to defend the isle if I become laird. Then his clan will swoop down like a flock of carrion birds and bleed Kilgorra dry."

"What proof . . . ," MacDuffie wheezed, "what proof . . . do you have of this?"

"Besides his past history," Lachann said, "he's been keeping you too drunk to notice that he's destroying your whiskey trade."

"He is not," Catrìona scoffed.

"Aye, he is." Lachann turned back to MacDuffie. "And I would bring Geordie Kincaid up here to speak of it were you not so ill."

MacDuffie began to cough, and Lachann gave him a moment. His suspicion that there was something more to the laird's illness took on a new significance as he observed the old man. Macauley was without scruples, and Lachann suspected he was capable of murdering MacDuffie to achieve his ends. Murdering him slowly, perhaps.

"Laird, you must not drink anything more that Macauley brings you."

"Why?" Catrìona demanded. "What are you suggesting?"

"Cullen Macauley and his clan have made a lifetime

habit of preying on those who have not the resources to fight them," Lachann replied.

MacDuffie's eyes drifted shut and his mouth went slack. Damn all. Lachann could not lose his attention now.

"Laird," Lachann said, and the man looked up. "Make me your heir. With Father Herriot as witness, give the word that I am to become laird in your place."

"But what about the marr—"

"No conditions," Lachann snapped. "I will train your men and arm the isle against invaders. I'll make improvements to the distillery. Those factors must be enough."

Catrìona made a sound of protest. "But—!"

"Silence," the old man rasped. "You believe that is all I demand, Lachann MacMillan?"

Catrìona jabbed Lachann in the chest. "Do you think you can just turn up in our harbor and depose my father from his lairdship?"

"I did not come to depose him, Catrìona," Lachann said.

"No, you came to marry me! Aye?" she demanded vehemently.

"That's a wedding that will never take place," Lachann retorted.

He felt his jaw clench tightly. He relaxed it forcibly, just as Graeme entered the room with Father Herriot. Laird MacDuffie gave a reluctant nod of resignation.

"Sit down, Catrìona," Lachann said. "'Tis time for you to follow an order or two."

Anna stood paralyzed, her hand at her breast. For years, she'd so desperately yearned to leave Catrìona and Laird MacDuffie. Now was her chance. This ship coming into the harbor was likely her only opportunity to escape the isle.

And yet the prospect of never seeing Lachann again did not seem quite so appealing now.

She closed her eyes tight and breathed deeply. She could not stay. *She just could not face the life she would have if she stayed.*

Resolved to do what she had to do, she returned to the castle, taking the overgrown path to Gudrun's cottage. Once inside, she lit the candles and located the crate where she'd found her mother's gown.

She undressed quickly, then took the deep blue gown out carefully. She slipped it over her head, telling herself she was doing the right thing—the *only* thing possible.

She managed to fasten the back of the gown, then tied the laces at the shoulders and neck. There were no shoes to go with it so Anna would go without, but she undid her usual braid, smoothed out her hair, and tied it in a simple knot at the crown of her head.

A few moments later, she left the cottage and started for the keep.

Lachann soon found that bringing Father Herriot to the castle to bear witness had not been necessary. Old MacDuffie bestowed the lairdship upon him without further argument, clearly shaken by Lachann's warnings of Macauley's treachery.

Even Catrìona had finally been taken aback.

"We make no formal transfer of power on Kilgorra, Laird," Herriot said as he and Lachann left MacDuffie's bedchamber and walked down to the main door of the keep. "The Kilgorran lairds have never performed any ceremony or signed any papers. You are MacDuffie's heir, Laird of Kilgorra now, whether Bruce MacDuffie survives or not. I will begin to spread the word. Everyone on the isle will hear of it within the hour."

"Thank you, Father, but I'm glad you witnessed his words."

"Aye. 'Tis my honor to serve you, Laird MacMillan," the man said.

Lachann walked with the priest to the door of the keep and saw him out. "I'll need your services again in another day or . . ."

He halted in front of the keep as a group of men dressed in fine, but foreign, garb came through the gates.

"*Hagl slottet!*" the leader called to him.

"Who are they?" he asked Herriot quietly.

The priest shrugged. "I do not know them, Laird."

Lachann waited for the men to come closer.

"Greetings to you, sir," said the first one in heavily accented speech.

"And to you," Lachann said. He wondered if all traders were so well-heeled, and whether they all came up to the castle to conduct their business.

Or if this was something else altogether.

"We have come from the Norse country," the man said. "I serve the Count of Leirvik, who has traveled to Scottish Kearvaig lands, and now Kilgorra, in hopes of finding here his sister and his niece."

An older, silver-bearded man came forward. He was dressed in as fine a suit as any Lachann had ever seen. Lachann extended his hand. "Count Leirvik?"

The man took Lachann's hand, nodding.

"Welcome. I am Lachann MacMillan, Laird of Kilgorra." To Lachann, it felt absolutely right to say the words. "Come inside."

Lachann took them into a comfortable sitting room near the great hall and found Alex MacRae already seeing to the fire.

"What can I do for you?" Lachann asked.

The guests settled themselves in chairs before the nobleman explained his business.

"Many years ago," he said, "*min søster*—my sister—displeased my father, and so was taken far from home to wed the Laird of Kearvaig. I was a mere lad . . . forbidden to go to her."

"I'm afraid I don't know your sister or niece, Count Leirvik," Lachann said. "I've not heard of any Norse-women here on the isle."

Count Leirvik frowned.

"But I've only recently come to Kilgorra," Lachann added as Catrìona came down the stairs and stood outside the room, listening.

"At Kearvaig, they told us Sigrid came to Kilgorra Island many years ago to marry MacDuffie. She brought with her the daughter, my niece, Annbjørg."

Catrìona made a rough sound of feminine dismay and quickly scuttled away as she dissolved into tears.

"I'm sorry, Count Leirvik, I know naught—"

"Laird . . ." Alex spoke respectfully, touching Lachann's sleeve. "I can explain this . . ."

"Please do, Alex."

"Sigrid was the widow of Laird Kearvaig when she came to Kilgorra and married Laird MacDuffie. Her daughter, Annbjørg, came with her."

"Ah. I understand," the count said. "Then you will kindly fetch her—"

"No. Sir, I'm . . ." Alex shook his head somberly. "Uh . . . I am truly very sorry to tell you that Lady Sigrid perished within a year of her arrival here, while birthin' Laird MacDuffie's firstborn son."

Count Leirvik swallowed heavily, and his face paled. He took a moment to absorb the information. "Ah, no."

A younger man put his hand on Leirvik's shoulder

and spoke to him in their language. Lachann did not understand the words, but he saw sympathy in the gesture and heard it in the young man's voice.

Alex interrupted the moment and looked at Lachann. "Laird . . . Lady Sigrid's daughter, Annbjørg—she is here."

The count took a moment to compose himself. He too looked up at Lachann, then at Alex. "May I see her? We would take her home . . . Betrothal plans have been made . . ."

"*What?* Annbjørg?" Lachann asked Alex, completely puzzled now. Though he'd not met every woman on the isle, it seemed he ought to know MacDuffie's stepdaughter. "She is here?"

"Aye," Alex replied. "We call her Anna."

Chapter 32

"*Anna . . . Anna MacIver?*" Lachann asked, astonished by Alex's words, though he should not have been. His Anna was as noble as any grand lady he'd ever heard of.

Alex nodded. "Aye, Laird."

Lachann stood. "Where is she now?"

"I'm not sure, Laird. I have not seen her in some time."

"Alex, will you see to supper for our guests?" Lachann looked at Leirvik. "Please, make yourselves comfortable here. I will find Anna and bring her to you."

Gesu. Betrothal plans? Lachann wondered if the bridegroom was to be the strapping young fellow who'd spoken those words of sympathy to Leirvik.

Well, Lachann was not about to give her up, even if she happened to be related to the noblest family in all of Norway. Anna belonged on Kilgorra. She belonged to him.

And yet Lachann knew he had to give her a choice. She had come to Kilgorra with her mother, and somehow the MacDuffies had seen to it that everything had been taken away from her, even her name.

He went down the steps to the kitchen and out the door, hoping he would find her at the small cottage behind the gardens, where he'd first known he would never love another.

Anna found that she was trembling.

All these years, she'd hoped for a way to leave the isle, and now that her escape was nigh, she felt anxious and worried, and more than a bit upset at the thought of leaving Lachann.

Maybe she should trust him, as Kyla suggested. He was nothing like Cullen Macauley, who would have seduced her—used her. No, Lachann had taken great care with her. He'd made gentle love to her, and Anna had felt cherished for the first time in her life, and by the man she loved.

She felt certain the Norse ship had come for her—or perhaps for her mother, for 'twas doubtful her mother's family had learned of her demise. What would they think of Anna? How would they react when they discovered she was naught but a servant here?

What would she do when she met them? Go? Or stay?

Wearing her mother's fine clothes, she left the cottage and started down the path toward the keep, only to be stopped by the shrill voice of her stepsister.

"Where do you think you're going, Anna MacIver?" Catrìona stood blocking the path, her face a mask of utter hatred. "And where did you get that gown?"

"'Twas my mother's, Catrìona," Anna said quietly. "Please let me pass."

"You think it looks well on you?" Catrìona said without moving. "'Tis an ugly rag. As ugly as your mother was."

Anna decided to ignore her. She continued on, moving to slip past Catrìona, but her stepsister grabbed her sleeve, tearing it a bit at the shoulder.

"Let go," Anna said. She would not allow Catrìona to ruin this moment.

"If you think I'm going to let you go off with those Norsemen, you are mistaken," Catrìona growled. "'Tis I who wish to leave, and I will!"

"Oh Catrìona, leave if you must, but please allow me—"

"Catrìona!" Lachann called out with the tone of command as he dashed toward them. "Leave her be!"

Anna tried to pull away, but Catrìona held tight. "He was mine!" she cried viciously and pushed Anna down into the flower bed next to the path. "You want her?" she shouted at Lachann. "Take her."

Lachann grabbed Catrìona's arm and pulled her away from Anna. Catrìona burst into tears and ran past them, toward the chapel.

Lachann reached down to Anna and pulled her to her feet. "Are you all right?"

Anna nodded, and a wee spark of hope took root in her heart. As Lachann looked her over, she felt mortified—for her own shaky demeanor as well as Catrìona's mean outburst. She wished she could just run back to the cottage and pretend she had not been so soundly humiliated.

"Anna . . . A ship has come . . . Norsemen," he said. His tone was suddenly formal, distant. So very different from when they'd lain together. "They are your kin."

"M-my . . ."

"Aye. You are Annbjørg, Lady Sigrid's daughter," he said, frowning. "You never said . . ."

Anna felt tears welling in her eyes, and she wiped them away. "'Tis been so long since anyone has called me Annbjørg, I . . . I hardly remembered my true name."

"So you know, then. The ship has come for you."

She looked into his eyes, but the expression in them was unreadable. He said naught about Catrìona, about Father Herriot, or anything that had happened since the incident with Cullen Macauley in the close.

He took her hand, and with some formality placed it in the crook of his arm, then escorted her in silence back to the keep. They entered through one of the main doors—not the servants' entrance near the kitchen.

Anna's heart was in her throat. She felt that at any moment, Catrìona would return and pull some evil trick on her, then force her back to the kitchen. Or shame her some other way in front of her Norse kin.

Lachann took her into the laird's sitting room, where four beautifully garbed men stood when she entered. The eldest, a man with a white beard, approached her, his expression stunned. He looked 'round at his companions. "She is . . . exactly Sigrid."

"I am Anna, sir," she said, containing her nervousness. "My mother was Sigrid."

"Ah, yes," the man said. He looked at Lachann, who released her. The Norseman took both her hands in his, then kissed her cheeks, one after the other. And when he spoke, his voice shook with emotion. "Annbjørg."

"Aye. 'Twas the name my mother gave me," she said shakily. "But I am Anna now."

"I am the Count of Leirvik, Sigrid's brother—your uncle. We came with the hope of finding my sister . . . And you," he said. "And of taking you home, to marry."

Anna felt the breath leave her lungs. "To . . . to marry?"

"Aye." He indicated the handsome young man who stood beside him. "Lars Frederickson is my wife's nephew—a prince—and he will make you a fine husband."

As young Lars bowed in Anna's direction, she glanced at Lachann, who stood immobile, looking at . . . well, at nothing, until Alex came in and announced that a meal had been laid on the table in the great hall.

Leirvik offered his arm, and Anna took it as they went into the hall. "You must tell me all you remember of your mother, my dear."

Anna presided over the meal with a quiet dignity suitable for the lady of Kilgorra. Lachann learned a few more details of her early life and surmised the details she left out.

And now everything would change for her. Catrìona and her father had turned Anna into a servant, obviously after the death of her mother. Lachann had seen the way Catrìona treated her, though he'd not been able to understand the animosity she felt toward Anna. What could the woman possibly complain of, when Anna went about her chores efficiently, and without the slightest objection?

Gesu. 'Twas no wonder Anna had said she would leave Kilgorra if given the chance. Why wouldn't she go with Leirvik now?

The Norseman spoke of his homeland, of the lavish house and all the amenities Anna would enjoy when she traveled to her mother's home with him. She would be treated as royalty, and her status would only improve when she wed Lars.

If she stayed on Kilgorra, her lot would change significantly, but there would be no horses and carriages, no society to speak of, and no culture beyond what she'd lived with all her life.

Aye, Lachann was a wealthy man, and he intended to make improvements on the island, but he could not compete with what Count Leirvik had to offer.

Chapter 33

They were calling Lachann "Laird." Anna did not know how that had come about—had he made his vows with Catrìona earlier? She thought again of the incident in the garden and was certain neither Catrìona nor Lachann had been pleased with the other. But that meant naught.

And yet, hadn't Catrìona said she intended to leave? Did she mean to leave with Count Leirvik?

A disturbance near the great hall interrupted Anna's troubled thoughts as Lachann left the table to see what was amiss. Anna excused herself and followed.

'Twas Graeme, leading a weeping and breathless Glenna down a back staircase.

Her face was cut and her lip was bleeding. "Glenna!" Anna stopped them, kneeling as she gently took her arm, which was also scraped. "What happened to you?"

"I was comin' up the stone steps behind the chapel with my basket of eggs from the village," Glenna cried. "I saw Laird Macauley."

"Aye?"

"He came runnin' down from behind the chapel to the beach, and he pushed me down."

"No!" Anna smoothed the child's hair back from her forehead. "Are you injured elsewhere, Glenna? Did you bump your head?"

Glenna sniffled as she nodded, and Anna felt the bump on the side of her head.

"Ach, what's happened?" Flora asked as she came up from the kitchen.

"Glenna's been hurt," Anna replied. "Let's take her downstairs."

"Come on, lass," Flora said, hovering like a mother hen over her injured chick. "Ye'll have a wee lie down now while Anna finds somethin' to sooth yer puir head. Where did ye fall?"

They went downstairs, and Anna turned to Lachann. Before she could ask him about Catrìona, he cupped her face. "See to your guests. I need to find Macauley before he can do any more damage."

Her guests?

"Lachann—"

"Later, Anna," he said. "We'll talk later."

Lachann rushed from the keep through the door Glenna had come in, and Anna stood watching as he hurried away, her heart and head a jangled mass of confusion. She was no hostess, and these men from Norway might have been her kin, but . . .

"I'm sorry," she said to Count Leirvik when she returned to the hall, "but we've had some difficulties here on the isle, and I . . ."

"May we help?" her uncle asked.

Anna shook her head. "No, sir. I'm sure Lachann will deal with it straightaway." She hoped.

"Then we will return to our ship for the night," Leirvik said, as he and his men stood and left the table. "We will see you in the morning. We can make our plans then."

He took Anna's hands and pulled her close to kiss her on both cheeks.

Anna felt no calmer when she saw them out to the castle gate. With Cullen Macauley free to do what he wished . . . he might start another fire. Or sabotage the fishing birlinns.

Her stomach was sinking fast as she hurried down to the servants' quarters, where Flora and the other serving maids hovered about Glenna.

"Glenna, was anyone with Macauley when he—"

"Nay, Anna. I saw no one else," the child cried, and Anna wondered where her stepsister had gone.

And where was Lachann now? He'd been so very quiet during the meal, listening intently to everything that had been said but offering naught. He'd voiced no opinions but had let her uncle go on about the wonders of Norway, as though Anna would choose her mother's homeland over Kilgorra—over *him*.

'Twas what she'd once wanted, and mayhap 'twould be a welcome escape if Lachann and Catrìona—

"Anna!" 'Twas Kyla, coming into the kitchen carrying Douglas. She looked as though she'd been weeping.

"What's wrong?" Anna asked. "What's happened?"

"Birk is drinking again," Kyla replied, holding back her tears. "He knocked me down, but I grabbed Douglas and ran before he could hurt me again. I . . . c-came here . . . I didn't know where else . . ."

"Aye, 'twas the right thing to do." Anna drew her friend down the hall to the servants' bedchambers. "Do you want to stay here? Or in Gudrun's cottage?"

Kyla wiped her tears. "I . . . I think the c-cottage. That way, if Douglas wakes in the night, he won't disturb anyone."

Anna nodded, feeling overwhelmed. "All right. Let's go now. I can come back later and get some food and a few things for Douglas."

"I saw strangers going down to the pier," Kyla said. "What's happening, Anna?"

"Oh, Ky," Anna replied, "I don't know where to begin."

They went out to the cottage together and Anna told her friend about the Norse uncle who'd come for her.

When she finished, Ky took her hand. "'Tis what you've always wanted—to leave Kilgorra."

And yet Anna's throat felt raw and thick at the thought of it.

"I will go with you," Kyla said. She shook her head and started to weep again. "This time, Birk tried to h-hurt Douglas."

"No."

"I will not allow him to injure my child," Ky said. "I will leave him first."

Anna hugged Kyla to her. "Oh, Ky. I am so sorry."

Kyla's tears finally dried, and she pulled back slightly. "They're saying Lachann is laird now."

Anna nodded. "He must have wed Catrìona . . ."

"No," Kyla said. "Father Herriot told Geordie Kincaid that Lachann insisted on being named laird now—without any conditions. No marriage."

Anna could barely take it in. Was that why Catrìona had been so angry? Because she'd lost Lachann? And Macauley was sure to be driven from the island now.

But it didn't make sense. "Why would MacDuffie agree to this without— "

"Because everyone knows Macauley set fire to the granary," Kyla explained. "Father Herriot said 'twas clear Laird MacDuffie understood he no longer had a choice in the matter."

Word had already reached Lachann's men that he'd been named laird. They wasted no time with congratulations but followed Lachann's orders without question and fanned out to search for Macauley. Lachann and Kieran found Duncan lying unconscious and bloody behind the blacksmith's shop.

Mungo Ramsay was nowhere near.

They roused Duncan, who said he'd been attacked from behind. He did not remember anything after that.

"What do you think Macauley will do next, Lachann?" Kieran asked.

Lachann thought a moment. "He wants me to fail. The granary fire did not accomplish that, but—"

"Aye. The munitions."

"Go on without me," Duncan said. "I'll be all right."

Kieran followed Lachann to the building where Lachann had ordered the weapons to be stored, but the lock had not been broken. Nor had anyone tampered with the stores of gunpowder.

"The cannons!" Lachann said as he hurried toward the castle wall. "He'll try to destroy the cannons."

They saw that the cannons on the castle walls were untouched. "He'll go for the one on Roscraig Peak," Lachann said.

"We'll have to move fast," Kieran said.

By the time they reached Roscraig Peak, Macauley was using a rock to pound a spike into the cannon's touchhole. The gun would be useless if he succeeded.

"*Gesu*, he's going to blow himself up!" Kieran said, for spiking a cannon was a dangerous task, especially if 'twas done with a spike that did not fit, and without a good hammer.

"Stop, Macauley!" Lachann shouted as he and Kieran took cover behind the trees. "Don't be a fool! You're finished here, no matter what you do to—"

"You've made yourself so bloody important here, MacMillan!" Macauley roared, hammering away. "But you cannot train an army when your weapons are gone!"

"I can replace the cannons!" Lachann called. "Don't be an idiot, Macauley! You can leave Kilgorra! Find some other laird whose daughter will have you—"

"Not after all my work here, MacMillan!" He pounded once again. "Kilgorra is—"

The cannon exploded, blasting the man ten feet into the air. He landed against the trunk of a stout oak tree.

"Bloody idiot," Kieran muttered. "He's killed himself."

"Make certain," Lachann said. "I'm going back to the castle."

He had to talk to Anna. Now.

Gesu. After the life she'd spent here on Kilgorra, 'twas no wonder she would want to leave if given the chance. But everything was about to change. Anna belonged here, belonged with him.

Catrìona paced nervously in front of the old chapel. She'd managed to exchange a few whispered words with Cullen and knew what her lover planned to do. 'Twas brilliant.

First, she'd had to entice Mungo a little bit in order to get him to attack Duncan MacMillan from behind and free Cullen from his surveillance. 'Twas not too difficult, for she'd been manipulating the big dolt for years with her body. Mungo would do anything she asked, just for one good look at her naked breasts, or sometimes a wee squeeze of her bum.

Cullen had left the castle a while ago, and Catrìona did not know where he would go when he came back to the castle after completing his task. She decided she should stay where she was, then she would surely see him when he returned. She wondered how difficult it could be to sabotage a few cannons.

And that wee accomplishment would be only the beginning. While the MacMillans were scrambling to deal with their ruined cannons, Cullen would dump their gunpowder into the sea, rendering their pistols and rifles useless. MacMillan would fail at what he'd come to do and would likely leave Kilgorra. Cullen would become laird.

But it was all taking too long. She muttered under her breath, "How dare you keep me waiting, Cullen Macauley . . ."

And how dare Anna take Lachann MacMillan from her, just as she'd done with everything else that mattered. Aye, Catrìona had seen the way MacMillan looked at Anna and knew her stepsister was the reason MacMillan had forced her father's hand—making him laird even as he reneged on his promise to wed Catrìona.

He meant to take Anna for his wife.

Catrìona made a low, guttural sound of disgust. There had never been anything to equal it. The most important plans she'd ever made—all shattered. She no longer had any choice in the matter.

Not that she really wanted MacMillan, anyway. She'd decided he was far too high-handed for her tastes. But it had been *her* choice to make, by God. And Anna had ruined it.

She knew now that Cullen had burned down the granary, and thought 'twas too bad he had not destroyed the distillery, too, and everything else MacMillan had come to value on the isle. Catrìona only wished Anna had been inside the granary when it had burned. 'Twould have served her right, and would have been Lachann's just deserts for the way he'd treated Catrìona—as less than a servant. Less than Anna MacIver.

At least she still had Cullen, and he would suffice. He'd been entirely malleable since his arrival on the isle, and she did not think that was only because he believed he might gain the lairdship through her.

Or was it?

She kicked a small rock out of her path to dispel that disturbing thought. Cullen would turn up at any minute. 'Twas only a matter of time. And they could decide together whether to stay on Kilgorra or leave for more sophisticated shores. An explosion suddenly shook the very walls of the castle, and Catrìona began to laugh.

Mayhap Cullen had figured a way to do more than just sabotage MacMillan's plans. Mayhap he'd destroyed the high-and-mighty laird from Braemore. She dearly hoped so, for she'd seen the way Anna looked at him, too. Losing him was going to destroy her.

'Twas almost full dark, and still Cullen did not return. Catrìona started back toward the keep to see if he was there, and when she heard the voices of Mac-Millan's men, she ducked behind the barracks. There was no point in confronting them now, when soon everyone would know. . . .

She stopped ruminating for a moment and listened to their words. " . . . blew himself up in front of Lachann and Kieran."

"What a fool," a second man said. "Well, Lachann is well rid of the bastard. Macauley and his clan have been naught but trouble since . . ."

No. It could not be. Catrìona wanted to scream. MacMillan could not have . . .

Catrìona slid down to the ground. Lord, Cullen was

dead? Her eyes welled with tears of anger and hatred. Everything she'd hoped for was gone, suddenly and irrevocably. Aye, Cullen had been a fool, but Catrìona intended to have the last laugh. She was going to get off this island, no matter what it took. And she was going to make sure her stepsister felt some of her pain.

Anna's manky cat wandered into view on its way toward the old storage cottage near the far wall of the castle.

The damnable thing was such a comfort to Anna . . .

Catrìona crouched down and called to it just as Mungo Ramsay came out of his shop.

"What is wrong, Catrìona?" he asked.

"Naught that you cannot remedy for me." She spoke sweetly to Anna's wee beast. "Come here, you filthy, horrid thing."

When she had the damned animal in her arms, she handed it to Mungo. "Drown it."

Chapter 34

Lachann returned to the pier, where Count Leirvik and his men had gathered near their ship, no doubt wondering what had caused the explosion. Some of the villagers came forward to question Lachann, with Geordie Kincaid taking the lead.

" 'Twas Cullen Macauley," Lachann told them, "attempting to sabotage the cannon."

"Did he set the fire, too, Lachann?" Kincaid asked.

Lachann nodded. "Aye. But this time, he managed to kill himself while spiking the cannon."

"I can'na say I am sorry," Kincaid said, and the rest of the people in the crowd muttered their agreement before heading back to their homes in the village.

"Who is Cullen Macauley?" Leirvik asked Lachann.

" 'Tis a long story, Count. But 'tis late for telling tales. Shall we meet in the morn? There is much to be settled."

The Norseman agreed.

Lachann knew Leirvik's business was unfinished, and he hoped to prevent him from achieving what he'd come to do. They decided to meet with Anna in the great hall of the keep after a good night's rest.

Lachann returned to the castle, intent upon finding Anna. Her uncle had made his intentions clear to her, but Lachann had said naught about his own. How could Anna make a choice when she did not know she had another option besides leaving? She could stay on Kilgorra.

As his wife.

He had only to determine whether her desire to leave the island was greater than what she might feel for him.

He stopped at the gate, thinking about the day he'd asked Fiona to go away with him. She'd shed a good many tears while telling him her duty was to her father, and that she could not go away with him. And she'd been steadfast in her decision.

The pit of his stomach began to burn.

He went down to the kitchen, and Flora told him Anna had gone out to the cottage with her friend, but that she would be back soon for their supper.

Lachann breathed a low curse. He'd hoped to have some time alone with Anna to make his proposal.

He wanted to talk to her before she saw Leirvik in the morn, so he hastened through the bailey and out toward the garden. But his blood ran cold when he heard her cries of distress.

Gesu. He was certain the cries were Anna's, and they were coming from the blacksmith's shop. "Stop, Mungo!" she screamed.

Lachann broke into a run. Neither the fire at the granary nor Macauley's attempted sabotage unnerved him as did Anna's cries. He arrived at the smithy shop in time to see Anna pounding on Ramsay's back and trying to pull him away from a trough full of water.

"Stop!" she screamed, but Ramsay kept his arms submerged.

Lachann did not waste time on Catrìona, who stood in the shadows, watching. He went immediately to the blacksmith and shoved him away from the trough.

Anna gave out a cry and pulled a bag from the water. She put it on the stone floor, but Lachann had to move quickly to duck away from Ramsay's massive fist. The man roared and struck again, missing Lachann's jaw by a hair.

With the next blow, Lachann caught Ramsay's fist in midair, then he slammed his body against Ramsay's as he kicked his leg behind him. The maneuver knocked the blacksmith off balance, and the man went down hard. The fall knocked the wind out of him, and Lachann took advantage of the moment to shove Ramsay onto his belly.

He slammed his knee down on the man's back and

reached for a cord that was hanging on the wall near his head. But as he bound Ramsay's wrists together, Catrìona screeched like a demon and fell upon him, scratching and biting, shrieking incoherently. Lachann quickly stood and faced her, grabbing her hands and pushing her against the wall of the shop.

"Catrìona!" He shook her to quiet her, then he turned to Anna, who was coaxing her cat from the bag. "Are you all right, Anna?"

Her face was covered with tears, but she nodded and spoke softly to the cat.

"Good God," Lachann said to Catrìona. "Are you responsible for this? What is wrong with you, woman?"

She tried to claw him. "You interfering bastard! Let me go!"

"Not on your life."

Anna had almost been too late, but she managed to revive Effie with some vigorous rubbing and no small amount of horror. Catrìona disgusted her, though it should not have surprised her that her stepsister would have had no qualms about harming an innocent creature.

She could almost excuse Mongo Ramsay, for he had never had a thought of his own and had always followed Catrìona's orders. But she'd always hoped he knew right from wrong.

'Twas clear she'd been mistaken.

"Can I help, Lachann?" she asked. "What should I do?"

But Catrìona answered the question with a raw screech. "You should go straight to hell, Anna MacIver! Or drown on your way to that cursed island of yours like you were supposed to do years ago!"

Her face became a mask of pure hatred, more twisted than Anna had ever seen it. And Catrìona did not stop her abuse even after Lachann asked Anna for another piece of twine. She shouted her insults without taking a breath while Lachann wrapped her wrists together and tied her securely to the end of Mungo's workbench.

When Catrìona and Mungo were both secured, Lachann crossed his arms over his chest and looked at them with distaste as well as disbelief. "Anna, go and find some of my men to help me here."

Anna was reluctant to leave him alone with such fiends, but as she ran to the courtyard, some of the castle servants and Lachann's men were already running toward Ramsay's smithy shop. They'd heard Catrìona's shrieks.

Cradling Effie to her chest, Anna watched as the men took Mungo to an empty building near his shop and locked him inside. Catrìona's evil glances unnerved her nearly as much as the invectives she screamed while Mungo was taken away.

"Do'na look at her, Anna," Flora said as she put her arm 'round Anna's shoulders. "She is naught but a wicked shell of a lass."

"Let's take this one to that chapel she's so fond of," Lachann said to Malcolm, his kinsman.

Catrìona continued her tirade, denouncing Lachann and cursing Anna. Her screeches did not let up until they faded away in the distance.

"Come along, my dear," Flora said, leading Anna to the keep. "We'll dry our Effie and give her some milk to soothe her nerves."

By the time Lachann returned from securing Catrìona in the little room at the back of the chapel, and Mungo Ramsay in a shed near the barracks, the keep was dark and quiet. Everyone had gone to bed. More than anything, Lachann wanted to find Anna, but he knew Flora had seen to her.

He did not know how Duncan fared.

He climbed the stairs to Duncan's bedchamber and found him lying quietly on his side. Lachann could see that the back of his head was caked with dried blood.

"Lachann?"

"I'm sorry," Lachann replied. "Did I wake you?"

"I'm not sure if I was dreaming, or just staring at the fire," Duncan replied. "I've got a hellish headache."

"What did he hit you with?"

"Damned if I know." Duncan winced when he moved. "So, Macauley is dead."

"Aye. Blew himself up."

"I heard," Duncan said. "All should be quiet now, eh? No more fires, no more sabotage attempts . . ."

"One can hope." Now that Catrìona and Mungo were locked up, the only threat Lachann needed to worry about was Birk Ramsay. And Lachann wasn't about to let *him* cause any trouble.

"I'm all right, Lachann. You needn't worry about me. Go on and get some sleep."

"Aye. I'll see you in the morning."

He looked in on MacDuffie before going downstairs and found Alex tending him. "How does he fare, Alex?"

"A little better, I think." Alex whispered his reply. "He just fell asleep. Laird . . ."

"Aye?"

Alex led Lachann from the room. "What will ye do with the old man? Let him stay here?"

Lachann shook his head. "I haven't thought that far ahead, Alex. I still have to figure out what to do with Catrìona and her lackey, Mungo Ramsay."

The servant shuddered. "We can'na be rid of them soon enough to suit us, Laird. In case you wondered . . ."

"Have you seen Anna?"

"She's gone to the wee cottage with Kyla. To keep her safe from Birk."

Lachann left the keep and went out to the cottage, though he doubted Anna would be awake. The small croft was quiet, and he saw very little light from the cracks in the shutters, so he let himself inside quietly.

Anna's friend and her bairn were asleep on the bed, and Anna slept soundly on a low pallet by the fire, with her cat curled at her feet. Lachann secured the door and lay down beside her, drawing her into his arms.

She made a sweet sound at the back of her throat and curled into him. Lachann did not want to think of all the cruelties Anna had to have suffered at the hands of her stepsister over the years.

And then trying to harm Anna's cat . . . 'twas indefensible. The wee animal had done naught to Catrìona. But it had nearly met its death because Anna had shown a fondness for it.

Lachann was glad the cat had survived, and not just for Anna's sake. 'Twas a gratifying failure on the part of Catrìona MacDuffie to inflict more harm on the stepsister she had wronged so grievously over the years.

It had been a long, drawn-out day, and at the end of it all, Lachann wanted only one thing. To ask Anna to stay.

But his question would wait until the morn.

Chapter 35

"**I** had the strangest dream," Anna said to Kyla when she awoke.

Kyla laughed. "You weren't dreaming."

"I . . ." Anna looked 'round the cottage. "You mean he was here?"

"Aye. You two were wrapped 'round each other so tight, if I didn't know better, I might have thought you'd been sleeping that way for years."

Knowing that Lachann had come to her and held her while she'd slept warmed and reassured her. She was anxious to find him before her Norse kin returned to the keep.

They gathered their things, but before they left for the keep, Kyla stopped her. "You're not going to go away with your uncle, are you?"

Anna shook her head. "Not if . . . I mean, I hope—"

"You must know your hopes are well founded,

Anna," Ky interjected. "A man doesn't spend the night on the floor, doing naught but holding a woman, unless . . ."

"Unless?"

"Unless she means more to him than one night in his bed. He cares for you, *min kjære venn*." Kyla handed Douglas to Anna and started looking through the crates. "Are there more of your mother's clothes in here?"

Anna pointed to the one where she'd found the gown she'd worn the day before, and Kyla opened it.

"Kyla, if we don't leave, Birk will—"

"We cannot think about Birk now," Kyla said. "We've a new laird, and things will be different."

Anna hoped so, but she knew Birk, and his temper had been getting steadily worse. What if—

"This one." Kyla drew out a brilliant scarlet gown with golden trim along the edges.

Kyla helped Anna dress, then they gathered their things and returned to the keep. Flora welcomed them into the kitchen and fussed over Anna's bonny gown, delighted that Anna's chance to leave Kilgorra had come. She wiped a tear from her eye. "I'll miss ye, lass."

"She's not going," Kyla said.

"What?" Flora pressed one hand to her breast. " 'Tis what ye've always wanted. You and Kyla—away."

Anna glanced uncertainly at Kyla and shook her

head. "Everything has changed." And her stomach felt as though 'twas turned upside down. After all these years, desperately wishing for a way to leave Kilgorra, the opportunity had arrived.

And yet she was going to risk everything and place her trust in one man. "Have you seen Lachann this morn?"

Flora shook her head. "No. I think he was up and gone early. So, ye're sayin' ye will'na leave Kilgorra and go with yer uncle?"

Anna shook her head. "I don't think so." She had been so very fearful of repeating her mother's failures, or Kyla's. There was no man on earth who could make her change her mind.

Except Lachann MacMillan.

"Well . . ." Flora said, "do ye think the Norseman would take Kyla instead?"

The *Glencoe Lass* had returned. Lachann and some of his men met with Rob and Stuart Cameron as soon as they came up to the keep.

"What news from Skye?" Lachann asked them then, though the question was practically moot now. Macauley was dead, and whatever reason he'd had for leaving Skye could not possibly matter now.

"Lachann, what we have to say is not—"

"Tell me now. What did Macauley do to her?"

Stuart looked him in the eye. "You know?"

"I suspect."

Stuart nodded. "Her father believes he poisoned her, but he could prove naught."

"Aye," Rob added. "Macauley had fallen out of favor with the old laird and his brothers. They said they'd erred and should have taken you as Fiona's . . ."

Rob stopped to clear his throat and Stuart continued. "After it became clear Macauley would never be named laird, Fiona sickened strangely. She started to have headaches. Confusion. Soon she was unable to eat—"

"Her hair started to come out," Rob said. "And she could'na keep anything down. Or in."

"Was there fever?"

"No, Lachann."

"He's been poisoning MacDuffie's whiskey," Lachann said.

"*Gesu,*" Rob muttered.

"The bloody bastard is dead now," Kieran said. "He was blown to bits by his own scheme."

The Cameron brothers appeared stunned, and Kieran said he would explain what had happened later.

"I have a new mission for the *Glencoe Lass,*" Lachann said. "I want you to take Catrìona MacDuffie to Glasgow."

"Aye, Lachann. Today?"

"As soon as possible."

He gave the Camerons the name of a good contact in the town, a man who would assist them in finding a house for Catrìona and setting up a system for her to draw an allowance Lachann intended to provide.

"Give her a bed on the *Glencoe Lass*," he said, "but keep her locked up for the duration of the voyage. And be wary. She—along with the blacksmith—are exceedingly treacherous. Do not trust either one."

"The blacksmith?" Stuart asked.

"Aye. I'm sending Mungo Ramsay, too. He can stay with Catrìona in Glasgow if he wishes. If not . . . Well, 'tis not my concern. He can find some gainful employment that does not include bullying children and drowning cats."

"Beg your pardon, Lachann?"

Lachann shrugged. "Just be exceedingly careful with both of them. I'll have some of the men bring them to you, and I want you to get underway as soon as you take on the supplies you need for the voyage."

"Of course." Rob and Stuart gave a respectful bow of their heads. "And . . . congratulations, Lachann. You gained the lairdship without a troublesome wife to ruin the distinction."

Ah, but he did intend to have a wife, just not the one he'd planned on.

He returned to the keep, went to his bedchamber and dressed in his finest clothes, then met up with some of his men to greet Count Leirvik and his entourage when they arrived at the castle.

Anna was already there. She welcomed the Norwegian guests as graciously as would the lady of the keep. But Lachann took note of the tension in her neck and shoulders. Ah, how he wished he could ease it for her.

As Lachann's men and the Norsemen gathered in the great hall for the breakfast Flora had prepared, Anna stood at her stepfather's table, at Catrìona's chair. She seemed hesitant, as though she believed she did not belong there.

Lachann pulled out the chair and indicated that she should sit. *Gesu*, but she was beautiful in her scarlet gown, and when he breathed deeply of her scent, he wanted nothing more than to take her up to his bedchamber and demand the answer from her that he craved.

But he had to give her the chance to make her choice. The Norsemen and Braemore men remained standing until Anna took her seat.

The servants brought the meal, and in heavily accented speech, Count Leirvik told tales of the mother Anna had barely known. He spoke of his homeland in Norway, and the exceptional home she would have when she traveled there to take her place as Sigrid's daughter—and Lars Frederickson's wife.

"Your travel plans are premature, Count," Lachann said.

Anna looked up at Lachann then, and he thought of the risk he was about to take.

Aye, 'tis well worth it.

"I do not understand, Laird MacMillan," Leirvik said.

Lachann placed his hand upon Anna's and looked into her bonny eyes. "Anna. You said once that you wanted nothing more than to leave Kilgorra." He swallowed thickly. "I would ask you to stay."

Leirvik stood and spoke firmly. "I am afraid that is impossible. My niece is a princess. She belongs in Norway with her family—with her own people."

"Uncle—"

"We've learned of your situation here, my dear Annbjørg, and Sigrid would have been proud of your . . . er, tenacity all these years," Leirvik continued. "She would have been pleased by your beautiful nobility, which was never subdued by the conditions under which you were raised."

"Please, Uncle," Anna said, embarrassed by the compliments. "I only did what—"

"My dear . . . ," Leirvik interjected. "We would have you sail with us upon the morrow. Come home to Norway, where you belong. Marry Lars Frederickson. Return to your family."

Anna looked at her uncle, and when she turned to look at Lachann, he felt his heart pounding like a hammer in his chest. *Gesu,* but he loved this woman. He did not want to lose her.

Anna's breath felt tight in her chest. She could barely hear her uncle's words, not when Lachann's request resonated so deeply within her.

The room went silent when she looked into his eyes and spoke the words that had lodged in her heart on that very first day when he'd stepped onto the pier and rescued Kyla. "I will stay with you, Lachann MacMillan, wherever you go—be it Kilgorra or Braemore, or anywhere else. Because I love you as I never expected to love anyone."

Lachann got up from his chair and pulled her into his arms, kissing her as though she was more precious than the lairdship of Kilgorra, more valuable to him than the farms and the distillery and army he was working so hard to establish.

"I love you, Anna MacIver," he said between kisses. "Marry me."

Anna's heart swelled in her chest. "Aye. I will marry you."

His men cheered and Lachann kissed her again, then turned them both to face her uncle. "Count Leirvik, with your permission, I would wed Anna on the morrow, and ask that you stay to witness our nuptials. Take happy tidings of your niece back to your home—"

"Laird MacMillan—"

"Norway is not my home," Anna interjected. "It

never was." She placed her hand over Lachann's heart. "I would stay, Uncle."

Count Leirvik hesitated for only a moment, then gave a curt nod of his head. "After all your years of neglect and abuse here . . . it seems fitting that you should become mistress of Kilgorra."

Lachann's men came to kiss Anna's hand and congratulate her, and Anna wondered if she would ever have a moment alone with Lachann.

It finally came when her Norse relations returned to their ship, with the promise to return to the keep later, for a betrothal celebration.

When all was quiet in the hall, Lachann took Anna in his arms, and she forgot about all the worries of the day when Lachann fitted his brawny length against hers. He was warm and hard, and the tender stroke of his strong hand on her back was incredibly arousing. As were his scent and the rasp of his unshaven jaw against her skin. She burrowed her face into the indentation at the base of his throat and felt a flood of sensation surging all through her body.

She could have wept with the sheer pleasure of it, the wonder of belonging. . . .

"Anna."

His deep voice shuddered through her, and as she tipped her head back, he lowered his and captured her lips with his own.

Anna heard a low growl as he deepened their kiss,

sliding his hand down and pressing her hips into his groin. She could not help but move against him, eliciting yet another low growl.

This time from her.

He broke their kiss, taking her hand and leading her up the stairs to his bedchamber. There, he pushed open the window and let the sound of the surf roll over them.

"The sweet sound of home," he said. "But know this, my sweet Anna. There is naught that I need but you."

Anna felt her eyes fill with tears. "I've never belonged anywhere . . ."

"Until now."

"Lachann."

He took her in his arms again and kissed her deeply, easing her mouth open for his tongue. Her muscles all seemed to melt as he shifted again, moving her to the bed, easing her onto it and sliding over her. One of his legs slipped between hers, and the exquisite tension she'd felt when he'd taken her to his bed returned.

She arched her back as his mouth nipped and tasted her. He pulled her lower lip into his mouth and sucked, and Anna slid her fingers into the hair at Lachann's nape and held him tighter.

He slipped one hand to the ties at her shoulders and opened her gown, easing it down to give him access to her breast. He fondled it gently, bringing the tip to a hard, sensitive peak that sent an intense spear of sensation directly to Anna's womb.

Her breath caught when he left her mouth and began to press nibbling kisses down her throat. Anna nearly came off the bed when he sucked her nipple deep into his mouth.

"Lachann . . ."

He did not stop but slid one hand down to her waist, then slid her gown up, and up . . .

"*Herregud*," she whispered. Or mayhap the word remained unsaid.

He touched her at the crook of her legs, creating a quivering tautness that was enough to make her mad with need. Anna grasped his shoulders tightly while he fondled and teased, creating a maelstrom of sensation. She bucked against his hand, wanting more, needing—

"Lachann!"

"Aye, lass. Come for me."

His intimate touch made her feel as though her body would ignite like the powder in the guns he'd brought to the isle. And suddenly, she did explode, and sparks of intense sensation shuddered through her blood and into her bones. Her muscles quivered and she pulled Lachann to her, desperate to be one with him.

She pressed her lips to his chest and he groaned, moving slightly, spreading her legs with his own. "Give me your hand."

"Lachann, I need . . ."

"Aye. So do I." His breathing seemed labored, but he

guided her hand to his shaft, that hard, pulsing, utterly male part of him that strained for her attention.

She encircled him, weighing the length and breadth of his arousal, knowing she wanted nothing more than to join with him. In the flickering light, she saw the muscles of his jaws clench, but he took her mouth in another searing kiss, at the same time spreading her legs with his thighs.

She felt him then, positioning his hard male flesh against her welcoming softness.

"Aye, Lachann," she gasped, needing him *now*. Needing that perfect union she'd never believed in before he'd come to her.

His next movements were slow and tentative, as though taking care of the most fragile, most precious treasure in all of Kilgorra. But Anna wanted more, she needed him now.

"Please . . ."

"Aye, lass."

He lifted her hips and surged into her all at once. Then he held perfectly still. "Anna?"

"Aye." She nearly wept the word. And then she moved against him.

Chapter 36

As Anna enveloped Lachann with her entire body, sheathing him so tightly, he felt as though his heart would burst. Such intimacy was entirely foreign to him, and he knew that what he felt was only possible with his Anna.

He had hoped she would defy her uncle to stay with him, and Lachann's love for her swelled at the thought of her unflagging loyalty. It meant as much to him as her love.

He moved within her, setting a rhythm that she followed, and they flowed together as naturally as the waves of the sea on the shore. He kissed her deeply as they moved, wanting to savor every part of her body, wanting her soul.

He looked into her eyes, so beautiful, so passionate. "I love you, lass."

All his muscles clenched, his world narrowing to include only her, and him, and the space they shared at that moment.

His blood roared in his ears. Bursts of flame shot through him, making him feverish. He plunged deeply, catching Anna's open, intimate gaze. She arched against him, drawing him in ever deeper, and Lachann felt himself losing control. Raw pleasure shot through him, and as she ground her hips against him, he found his release. Her own shuddering pleasure magnified his a hundredfold.

He remained inside her, holding her close, their breaths coming in short, labored pants. He never wanted to leave.

Gently, he brushed a few tendrils of her silken hair from her forehead. Then he kissed her softly, repeatedly—her forehead, her eyes . . . her lips. And *Gesu*, but he wanted her again.

"Are you all right?"

She made a small sound of contentment and nodded, shuddering again with the aftereffects of her climax.

Lachann withdrew and rolled to his side, pulling her with him. She fit him so incredibly perfectly, and when she pressed a kiss to his chest, he thought he might just incinerate like the embers in the fireplace.

A long while later, Lachann lay beside Anna with his elbow bent and his head propped up on his hand. He caressed her arm and shoulder while Anna rubbed her fingers across his prickly jaw.

"What's this?" he asked, when his fingers traced the raised scar on her forearm.

"From a burn when I was small."

"How did you get it?"

She shrugged. "'Twas naught."

"'Twas Catrìona."

Anna hesitated before she spoke. "Aye. She has always enjoyed hurting me. But getting Mungo Ramsay to drown Effie was the worst thing . . ." She hesitated, and her breath caught as a forgotten memory returned to her.

"What? What is it?"

Anna blinked back tears. "Gudrun brought me a bonny orange kitten once. And it . . . it just disappeared. We searched everywhere—"

"*Gesu.* The woman is a menace."

"My stepsister resented me from the day I arrived with my mother on Kilgorra."

"But I doubt you were her only victim," Lachann said. "That kind of meanness never confines itself."

Anna supposed he was right. She was just glad to see Effie curled on the fur rug in front of the fire, sleeping lightly, as cats were wont to do. She was none the worse for her brush with death.

"You did not know your mother was Norse royalty?"

Anna shook her head. Unable to get enough of him, she traced the outline of his lips. "I was barely more than a bairn when my father died and we left Kearvaig. Gudrun said we came here because my mother had met Laird MacDuffie and liked him very much. She knew he was widowed, too."

"But MacDuffie abandoned you when she died?"

"He seemed to . . . to just forget about me," she said. "But my mother's maid, Gudrun—and Flora, of course—saw that I was cared for."

He remained silent, frowning fiercely.

"What I know of my mother's life—it seemed to be one misfortune after the other," Anna said. "And her marriages did not improve matters for her."

Lachann tipped his head down and kissed her lightly. "You will not follow her path, love."

Anna felt a surge of emotion building in her chest. "I believe you."

Aye, she believed him, with all her heart. With Lachann as her husband, her life would be whole, no matter what the challenges on the isle might be.

"Oh!" Anna sat up suddenly. "So much has happened—did you find Macauley? Is Duncan all right?"

"Aye, Duncan has a nasty bump on his head, but he'll survive."

"And Macauley?"

"He tried to sabotage one of the cannons." Lachann's countenance darkened as he spoke. "But it exploded while he was at it."

"Explo—" Anna swallowed. "Then he's . . . dead?"

Lachann didn't know how long they slept, but he took his time with Anna, waking her gently with light kisses and feathering caresses. He made love to her slowly and with care, cherishing every moment with this woman who had defied her kin to marry him.

She could have gone with Count Leirvik and become a princess in his country. And yet she chose to stay with him.

"What will you do about Catrìona?" Anna asked when they were sated and she lay contented in his arms.

"I've decided to send her to Glasgow," Lachann replied. "Do you remember last night when she pushed you in the garden . . . she said she was the one who wanted to leave."

Anna nodded. "Do you think she meant Kilgorra? Meant to leave the isle?"

"I don't know what she meant. But I think 'twould be best if she did go. I won't tolerate her petty cruelties or . . ."

"Or what?"

"Her use of the chapel," Lachann said. The night Catrìona had taken him out there, he'd begun to suspect another facet of her true nature. "'Tis one thing to meet a lover. But Catrìona . . ."

Anna nodded against him. "She had many. The islanders hoped you would not find out, because then you would leave . . ." She put her hand on his chest, and he covered it with his own. "And we so desperately needed a good, strong laird."

"And what do you need, Anna, love?"

He heard her swallow thickly. "I need only you, Lachann," she replied. "For most of my life, I thought of little else but finding a way to leave Kilgorra, to get away from Catrìona and this keep."

He felt her warm breath on his naked chest, and he encircled her with his arms, rolling her to her back.

She lay beneath him, looking up. "But I never knew I would love someone as I love you."

It occurred to Lachann then that if Fiona had truly loved him, she would have disregarded her father's command that she stay and marry Macauley. Her feelings for him could not have run quite so deep.

'Twas late in the afternoon when they went down to the village. Some of Lachann's men were up on Roscraig Peak, replacing the cannon Macauley had destroyed. They heard the echoes of hammers working beneath the Peak at the granary.

Lachann took Anna to the edge of the village and kissed her. "I'm going back to the granary and see how the work goes," he said.

"I want to look in on Davy MacDonall, then I feel I should visit my uncle on his ship," she replied.

"Would you like me to accompany you?" he asked.

Anna shook her head. "You have other matters to attend to."

He cupped her chin in his hand. "I love you, lass."

Anna closed her eyes for a moment and basked in wonder at the depth of his affections. Even now, 'twas difficult to believe the reversal of fortunes—of Catrìona being caught in her viciousness, of Anna's family coming for her.

Of Lachann's love.

She walked up to the MacDonall cottage, feeling rested and happy. Janet soon joined her, and they continued together toward the MacDonall cottage.

"Ah, ye look as bright and happy as a bride should be," Janet said. She gave Anna's cheek a slight pinch. "The laird looks like a well-pleasured man—"

"Janet!"

The healer laughed. "Ach, my lass—keepin' yer man satisfied is no cause fer embarrassment. Everyone is pleased to have Lachann MacMillan as laird, and you as his wife."

Mayhap, but not half as pleased as Anna.

"'Tis said Lachann locked Catrìona in the old chapel last night. His man Kieran said he's plannin' on sendin' her away to Glasgow. And Mungo Ramsay with her."

"Aye?"

"Ye did'na know, lass?"

"I knew of his plan for Catrìona, but we did not speak of Mungo."

"I can well imagine you had other things to do," Janet said with a sly wink. "It seems a good solution," she added. "Kilgorra needs no more of Catrìona's poison. And Mungo . . ."

Anna agreed with Janet. The sooner Catrìona was gone, the better.

They reached Davy's home and went inside. While Janet gave the lad some medicine to drink, Anna spoke to Meg and assured her that Lachann intended to help the family in any way he could.

She stayed a short while, then left the cottage to head down to the pier. She'd gone only a few steps when she heard footsteps behind her and someone shoved her hard, knocking her down.

"Catrìona!"

Her stepsister laughed, and Anna scrambled up to her feet. "Aye. You thought I was locked away, did you?"

"I-I—"

"Well, I was. For a time. But a clever woman has her ways . . ."

Catrìona advanced on Anna and Anna backed up, unsure what her stepsister was about but assuming she would try to do her worst.

"Drowning that horrid creature of yours was not enough to destroy you, Anna MacIver," Catrìona said. "'Twas a measly cat. And besides . . . your damnable *champion* rescued it."

Anna looked 'round, hoping someone was near and would see them. But they were alone, and as Catrìona stood glaring at Anna, her words began to sink in.

"My cat? What do you mean she was not enough to . . ." Catrìona's meaning became clear. "No, Catrìona! You cannot!" Anna shoved back at Catrìona and ran past her, frantic to get to Kyla. For that was all Catrìona could possibly have meant—that she'd put Kyla in danger, for Ky had always been more important to Anna than anyone . . .

"Ach, aye, dear sister!" Catrìona shouted with a vicious grin. "You finally understand. But you're too late!"

Anna had to get to Kyla, but she did not know if her friend had gone home or if she was still at the castle. As Meg MacDonall and Janet and the other neighbors came out of their cottages to see what was amiss, Anna called to them to start searching for Kyla and Birk.

Ach, 'twould be so easy for Catrìona to incite a drunken Birk to kill Kyla.

In a panic, Anna ran toward Kyla's home, but she heard roars of anger and cries of terror coming from the direction of the pier.

It took only seconds for Anna to get down there. Wee Douglas was crawling across the wooden planks toward his mother, but Birk had Kyla by the hair. He whipped her 'round and slapped her hard, knocking her to the ground, splitting her lip.

"Birk!" Anna screamed. "Get away from her!"

But Birk went after Kyla again, and Anna assailed Birk, frustrated that she was not strong enough to effect much damage on the enraged man. Still, she pummeled his back with her fists, and weak as her blows might have been, at least he turned from Kyla to ward off her attack.

Anna ducked away, and he somehow missed striking her.

Birk roared with frustration and drew his flaying knife from his belt.

And Anna realized she had no weapon to use.

"Birk!" Kyla cried, and he turned toward her with murderous intent in his eyes.

Panic rose in Anna's chest. She glanced 'round for something—anything—she could use to thwart Birk, but she found naught. The man was going to kill Kyla, and there was naught she could do.

Chapter 37

Lachann was on his way down to the pier when he heard the commotion. When he saw Birk Ramsay take a swing at Anna, he drew his pistol from his belt. "Anna! Move away!"

But like a vicious animal with the taste of blood on his chops, Birk roared and went for Kyla with his knife.

"Ramsay! Halt!"

The bastard stopped for half a second to look back at Lachann, at the pistol he held, primed and ready for shooting, but he roared Kyla's name and raised the knife.

Lachann pulled the trigger.

The explosion was deafening, and the sharp smell of gunpowder dispersed in the air. Birk fell and did not move again. Kyla lay under him, reaching for her bairn.

As Anna screamed for Kyla, Lachann rushed to Anna and saw that she was unhurt. He wanted naught but to pull her into his arms, but he pushed Birk off Kyla and helped Anna's friend to her feet. "Are you all right?"

Kyla was pale and shaken, and did not answer him. She was hurt, her face fresh with bruises and a few small cuts. And Lachann did not regret at all what he'd had to do.

It had all happened so fast that men from the *Glencoe Lass,* as well as those from the Norse ship, were still climbing down to the pier to see what was amiss.

Anna seemed not to notice the crowd that had gathered 'round them. She picked up Kyla's bairn and put her arm 'round her friend. " 'Twas Catrìona that did this, Lachann," she said, brushing away her tears. "She got out of the chapel and somehow . . ."

Lachann turned to the men who'd followed him down from the granary. "Start searching. Find Catrìona and bring her to me! Someone go up to the chapel and see what happened to the guard I posted."

Roy Ramsay pushed through the crowd to Lachann. "*Gesu,*" he said under his breath, then he went to Kyla. "Lass . . . I should have done more to stop Birk. Can ye forgive me?"

Anna and Lachann took Kyla home and put her to bed. Janet came in to tend to the cuts on her face, then gave her something to help her sleep. When Kyla was settled into her bed, Anna came out of the small bedroom and spoke to Janet and Lachann. "She is with child."

Janet nodded. "I know. But she is far better off without a husband than with the one she had."

Anna silently agreed. But she felt shaken by all that had happened, and more than a bit worried about Ky. Her friend had said naught since the shooting on the pier. She just lay shaking in her bed.

Janet put her hand on Anna's shoulder. "I heard what Catrìona said outside Meg MacDonall's cottage, lass."

Anna looked up at Lachann and wiped her tears. "'Twas Catrìona who put Birk up to this last beating. She intended for him to kill Kyla . . . t-to hurt me."

"Well, she nearly succeeded," Janet said. "If not for yer sharp shot, Laird . . ."

"We'll find her, Anna," Lachann said. "I won't allow her to hurt anyone else." He was pacing restlessly, waiting for word that his men had found the witch and had confined her. But it was Roy Ramsay who turned up.

Birk's father stepped inside. "I'll sit with Kyla, if ye do'na mind."

Anna nodded and handed Douglas to him. She knew Lachann was anxious to join his men in the search for Catrìona. Anna felt the same.

"Bar the door," Lachann said as he and Anna went to leave. "Catrìona will be a threat to Kyla's well-being until she is confined on my ship and far out to sea."

They met Duncan and another of Lachann's men on their way down to the pier. "We've seen no sign of Catrìona, Lachann. She's vanished."

"No," Anna said. "I know where she might be."

They started down the beach, but Lachann stopped while his men walked ahead. "I don't want you any-where near Catrìona," he said. Thinking of the woman who was still at large and capable of doing Anna some harm made his blood run cold.

"I have something to tell her," Anna said. Lachann had never seen such solid resolve in her expression.

"Tell her later," he said, "when she's in chains in the cargo hold of my ship."

Anna shook her head and started walking. As she took the path to the beach, Lachann reloaded his pistol. He was glad Anna had such confidence in him, but he did not like her taking this risk. Still, he understood her desire for satisfaction. Catrìona had done some terrible things, not the least of which had been her attempt to get Kyla killed.

Gesu, the woman's blatant callousness chilled him. She was the coldest human being he'd ever encoun-tered.

Except, perhaps, Cullen Macauley.

Lachann had received word that Mungo Ramsay was still locked in the shed up at the castle, but who knew whether Catrìona had other allies on the island. One of her men, perhaps.

He and the others went with Anna down the beach, farther than Lachann had yet explored. The terrain was rocky and rough, and only passable on foot.

"Do you see the castle wall just there?" Anna pointed to the high wall above the caves on the left.

"Aye. And the gate . . . behind the chapel?"

"Look closely, and you can see a way to climb up. Or down."

Lachann noticed the ledges that formed a natural staircase up and over the caves in the wall. "Catrìona got out that way?"

Anna nodded. "'Tis the only way out of the castle besides the main gate."

"'Twould have been good to know this sooner."

"I'm sorry, Lachann. I should have thought to tell you. This is where Cullen pushed Glenna down."

Lachann took Anna's hand and kissed it. "You can show me the entire island . . . after we get Catrìona away."

They walked in silence, in hopes of taking Catrìona by surprise. They followed the curve of the beach, and Anna stopped them suddenly, just before the land took a sharp turn to a deep inlet. She whispered to Lachann, "This is one of her places. There is a cave just past that thicket."

"Wait here, Anna. Wait until I can make sure she is no threat to you."

She gave a reluctant nod, and Lachann gave her a quick kiss. He motioned for his men to spread out as they approached the cave. As they moved closer, they heard voices from within, both male and female. It sounded like an argument.

"I will'na kill for ye, Catrìona," the man said, his voice raised in frustration.

"Then what good are you to me, Eòsaph Drummond?" 'Twas Catrìona, her voice shrill.

Lachann did not wait but signaled for his men to storm the cave. He held his pistol in his hand, and when the three of them stood blocking the entrance, the man Catrìona had called Eòsaph tried to make a run for it.

The sight of Lachann's pistol stopped him, but Catrìona was not so wise. She ran at Lachann, but Kieran was too quick for her. He knocked her feet out from under her, grabbed her, and wrestled her to the ground as she kicked and screamed for Eòsaph to do something.

"Restrain her, Kieran," Lachann said as Anna came to stand alongside him.

"With pleasure," Kieran replied.

"Laird . . . ," Eòsaph murmured. "I . . ."

"Stand still, Drummond, until I know what part you have in all this."

"Naught! I've done naught! She told me to wait for her here, and that's all I've done."

Catrìona caught sight of Anna then. She screamed

and spit out her fury, but Anna stood quietly, waiting for her stepsister to take a breath.

Then she spoke. "You failed, Catrìona. You tried to make my life a misery, tried to take away all that I love . . . but you failed, in every way. I will not miss you when you are gone."

Chapter 38

The wedding was to be delayed for two weeks, out of deference to Kyla. Anna wanted her friend's body healed, if not yet her soul when she witnessed the nuptials. Anna knew Ky's feelings about losing Birk were mixed, and her friend had to deal with the changes brought on by her pregnancy as well.

But Anna took her up to the castle to be cared for, and to live as a sister in a far different way than her own sister had behaved toward her.

On the afternoon they watched the *Glencoe Lass* sail away with both Catriona and Mungo locked away inside, Anna took Lachann to her small curragh. "I want to take you to Spirit Isle."

"Aye?"

"Would you like to see it?" she asked.

Lachann smiled. "Only if the *sluagh dubh* does not render me mad for setting foot on its territory."

Anna jabbed him in the ribs and looked 'round. "You know there is no *sluagh dubh*."

"No?" He pressed a hand to his chest in an exaggerated gesture. "Do not tell me that you—"

"Kiss me, Lachann. Just kiss me."

He did so, pulling her tight against his body. "What brought this on?"

"'Tis a wondrous placc and . . . I want to share it with you."

"But . . . ?"

"But you can tell my secret to no one," she admonished.

"Of course." He realized that for Anna to take him to her isle was a show of deep trust. "No one will learn anything about Spirit Isle from me."

"Let's go then. Now."

They climbed into her curragh, and Lachann took the oars. He watched Anna as he rowed, her head tilted back, her face toward the sun.

"You are so very fine, my Anna," he said.

"You will spoil me with your compliments, Laird MacMillan," she said, smiling.

It was surprising how much pleasure Lachann took just from pleasing her. He'd come to Kilgorra expecting to marry a woman who only just sufficed. And yet he'd found Anna MacIver, who was so much more than merely tolerable.

It amazed him how quickly she'd become his heart

and soul, and he finally understood his brother Dugan's reticence in agreeing to Lachann's marriage to Catrìona—a woman he had not even met.

They reached the isle and he saw that it, too, was surrounded by a network of underwater rocks. "How do you navigate all this?"

"I'm used to it." She showed him where to go, and together they pulled the curragh onto the shore and tied it to the stake that protruded from the rocks. "This won't come loose. Even if the weather turns savage when I'm here, the curragh will still be here when it clears."

"Savage weather?" His heart felt as though 'twould stop. "Anna, promise me you will not come when the weather is bad."

"No, I never plan it that way," she replied with a laugh. "But weather has been known to change. Come on."

She took his hand and led him to a narrow cave. He stepped inside and followed her as she made a turn or two, then he found himself crawling on hands and knees behind her. There was light at the opposite side, and when they came out, and he was able to stand to his full height, he was astonished by the magnificence of the place. Her isle.

'Twas ringed by a jagged wall of black, just like the outside. But here, the ground was covered by the brilliant mossy green of his beloved highlands. In the center of it all was a loch as clear and blue as his beloved's eyes.

He let out a low whistle. "'Tis no wonder you keep the place secret."

"This way."

She led him to a cave with furnishings that appeared to have been accumulated over some time. Years. 'Twas a warm day, but there was a pit ready for a fire that would keep the chill out of the cave. 'Twas made to be comfortable, and he could see how Anna would want to come here to escape the demands of the castle—of Catrìona.

There were two pallets—Anna's and Kyla's, he assumed—ready to be unrolled for their use, and dried meat and some berries stored securely in tightly covered boxes.

"You are completely at home here," he said. He slid his arm 'round her waist and pulled her close.

"Aye. But just wait," she said, slipping away from him. "Take off your clothes, Laird."

"Are you trying to seduce me, Lady Anna?"

Anna unfastened the laces at her shoulders and turned to him for assistance with the fastenings down her back. Then she slipped out of the gown and walked perfectly naked to the water.

He watched with his heart pounding in his ears as she turned to face him, backing into the water. And Lachann knew that his life here, with Anna, was all that he would ever desire.

Lachann wasted no more time. He pulled off his

clothes faster than any man had ever disrobed and joined her in the water. She swam ahead of him, but he caught her easily and took her in his arms. "You are so much more than I ever hoped for, Anna love. You are all I will ever want."

He began to make love to her in the cool water of the loch, but she took his hand and drew him toward the shallows, where hot springs bubbled up from the rocky bottom. It felt like heaven, and he lay back against the rocks, pulling his woman over him.

He started with a gentle kiss, but then his hunger for her became raw and fierce, and swept through him. He savaged her with his tongue, nipping lightly with his teeth. He wanted her so badly he felt he was in a fog of pure desire.

Ach, she was so very beautiful. Her lush breasts and narrow waist, the fleeting fragrance of her desire, the warm center of her . . . everything about her drew him, but he forced himself to go slowly, to delight in every moment.

He nipped her neck just below her ear and slid his hands up from her waist to the soft undersides of her breasts. She arched in response, pushing the tips of her breasts closer to his chest.

She touched his own pebbled nipples, and he stifled a groan while he savored the sensations wrought by her light caress. Never before had a woman's touch wreaked such havoc with his senses. He could hardly believe it when fire shot directly to his groin.

Closing his eyes tightly, Lachann enjoyed the burn and determined to return it tenfold. "Ah, my Anna . . ."

He floated just above a rocky ledge and pulled her onto him, prolonging his endurance. He felt her open for him as she straddled his hips, and he knew 'twould take only one smooth movement to slip into her hot sheath.

He held back, and as she lowered herself over him, he drew one of her peaked nipples into his mouth. He circled the lush tip with his tongue and smiled at her sharp gasp.

"Lachann!"

He reached down, seeking her most sensitive part. Dipping his fingers inside her, he found her ready for him.

Still he held back. He teased her nipples while he touched her intimately, rubbing that wee nub softly at first, but increasing the pressure as her hips bucked against his hand.

"Aye, bonny Anna," he said. "Take your pleasure."

She shuddered, then seemed to melt bonelessly against him, her breasts against his chest, her face just above the water.

Lachann kept his eyes on hers, stirred by the intensity of emotion he saw in her gaze.

"I love you, my Anna . . ."

She slid against him, and Lachann thrust deeply into her.

She sheathed him so tightly that Lachann knew naught would ever feel so incredible, so intensely right.

They began to move together, Anna meeting every thrust of his hips, welcoming him inside. She smiled down at him when he spilled into her, and when his muscles clenched in a glorious spasm of delight, the love that surged through his body and soul was immeasurable.

Anna tightened 'round him once again and shuddered her own pleasure, and it seemed there was nothing more in this life that Lachann could possibly desire.

Epilogue

Every Kilgorran who could travel from home came to the village to celebrate the marriage of their new laird to his lady—Anna MacIver—or Annbjørg of Kearvaig. Only Bruce MacDuffie stayed home in the wee cottage where his father had lived long ago at Langabhat Point, overlooking the southern tip of the island.

He'd chosen to retreat there . . . to die, once it had become clear that his health would not return. Alex MacRae went with him, to care for him until the end.

Catrìona and Mungo Ramsay were gone, and some of Lachann's men thought he had gone too easy on her. He'd given the Camerons a purse with adequate funds to set up a trust that would keep Catrìona in modest circumstances. Comfortable, but she was never to have enough to pay for travel expenses back to Kilgorra. He trusted they'd seen the last of her.

After the marriage ceremony, while the Kilgorrans

danced and drank and celebrated, Lachann rowed Anna to Spirit Isle, where they intended to stay for a few days.

They wasted little time putting away the provisions they'd brought, before Lachann took his wife into his arms. He kissed her deeply and thoroughly, loving her as he would love no other.

"You know that my heart is yours, my sweet Anna."

"And mine is yours." She slid her hands up his chest and back to his nape, releasing his hair from the queue that held it.

He felt humbled as he looked at her. She was so very bonny, and she'd endured a world of hurt at the hands of her own family. He would see to it that she never suffered again. Kilgorra was their home, and they would watch it grow and prosper.

Standing in her cozy cave, Anna pushed away Lachann's plaid and shoved his shirt down his arms, quickly baring his chest while he worked the laces of her gown. She licked his pebbled nipples, making him a desperate man. A man who could barely wait to take possession of his wife.

He laid her down on one of the beds in her cave and kissed her deeply, passionately, showing her his heart and soul. For she was everything to him.

He made love to her slowly, relishing every kiss, every taste, every caress they shared. He held her close, adoring her with every fiber of his being as they moved together.

And when it was over, he pulled her against him and brushed kisses across her lips, touching his lips to her cheeks and chin.

They lay quietly together while their breath slowed and their hearts' rhythm returned to normal.

"Did I tell you that the *sluagh dubh* of Spirit Isle makes men go mad?"

"Aye." He smiled against her forehead.

"But you are not afraid of losing your mind, Lachann?"

"I've already lost it, Anna love."

"Oh?"

He nodded. "I lost it the first day I saw you, and the madness I feel for you will never end."

She laughed softly, and Lachann knew that truer words had never been spoken.

At Avon Books, we know your passion for romance—once you finish one of our novels, you find yourself wanting more.

May we tempt you with . . .

- **Excerpts** from our upcoming releases.

- Entertaining **extras,** including authors' personal photo albums and book lists.

- Behind-the-scenes **scoop** on your favorite characters and series.

- **Sweepstakes** for the chance to win free books, romantic getaways, and other fun prizes.

- Writing **tips** from our authors and editors.

- **Blog** with our authors and find out why they love to write romance.

- **Exclusive content** that's not contained within the pages of our novels.

Join us at
www.avonbooks.com

AVON

An Imprint of HarperCollins*Publishers*
www.avonromance.com

Available wherever books are sold or please call 1-800-331-3761 to order.

FTH 1111

*G*ive in to your Impulses!

These unforgettable stories only take a second to buy and give you hours of reading pleasure!

Go to *www.AvonImpulse.com* and see what we have to offer.

Available wherever e-books are sold.

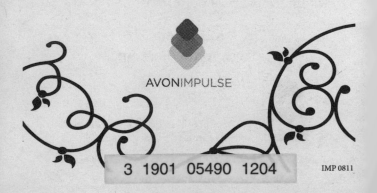

AVONIMPULSE

IMP 0811